THE
ONES
WHO ARE
HIDDEN

BOOKS BY KERRY WILKINSON

OTHER

Down Among the Dead Men

No Place Like Home

Watched

Kerry Wilkinson

THE ONES WHO ARE HIDDEN

bookouture

Published by Bookouture in 2023

An imprint of Storyfire Ltd.
Carmelite House
50 Victoria Embankment
London EC4Y 0DZ

www.bookouture.com

ISBN: 978-1-83790-355-9
eBook ISBN: 978-1-83790-349-8

ONE

DAY ONE

'You're into weird things, aren't you?' Oliver asked.

Millie Westlake took a moment to consider the question. It wasn't so much that she was *into* weird things, it was that weird things happened around her.

'Can I show you something?' Oliver continued, not waiting for his first question to be answered. Something must have passed Millie's face because he instantly added: 'Not like that. I didn't mean— I'm not— I have a girlfriend—'

Oliver was stumbling as Millie assured him she knew what he meant. They were standing in the door frame of his flat and he half turned, before pushing his hair away from his ear and angling the helix, so she could see the back.

Millie wasn't entirely sure what was going on. She was trying to pick up her son from the guitar lesson he'd been having with Oliver. Weird things really *did* happen to her, though men showing her the backs of their ears was definitely a new one.

There was some sort of mark on Oliver's ear, more of a charcoal smudge than anything else. Some sort of circular... *thing*.

'I'm not sure what you're showing me,' she said.

'Look closer,' Oliver said, as he hunched lower.

Millie tried to think whether she'd ever looked at the back of someone's ear before. It was the final frontier of body parts.

As she squinted, Millie could see interlinking rounded triangles, with a circle in the middle. The sort of thing a child might draw.

'I still don't know what it is,' Millie said.

'My girlfriend reckons it's a flower.'

Millie could see it now he'd said.

Oliver stood taller and allowed his hair to fall back into place.

'It *might* be a flower...' Millie acknowledged, wondering why he was asking. Every other time she'd met him had involved a normal interaction.

Oliver nodded in agreement.

From behind him, a toilet flushed and then Eric appeared in the hall, guitar in hand. Millie's son was going to turn nine in coming weeks. His dad had custody and had been trying to push Eric into various after-school activities. He said it was to help their son discover what he was passionate about, though Millie suspected he was tired of having him around.

'How's my little Jimi Hendrix getting on?' Millie asked.

'Who?' Eric replied.

'A famous guitarist.'

That got a shrug. Jimi Hendrix didn't have an Xbox Live account, and he didn't live-stream his Minecraft building sessions on YouTube, so the chances of her son being impressed was small.

'Do you want to wait in the car?' Millie said.

Eric shrugged and chirped a 'bye' to Oliver and then headed around the fence, off towards Millie's vehicle.

'How's he getting on?' Millie asked, turning back to Oliver, assuming the ear weirdness was done.

The bitten bottom lip said more than words: 'He's... *enthusiastic...*'

That got a laugh. Millie had suspected as much. Eric never talked about guitar practice. He didn't seem to hate it but he definitely wasn't excited about going.

'Eric's mainly interested in Xbox, stickers, and his friends,' Millie said. 'His dad reckons he needs to branch out and try other things. He wants Eric to get what he calls "a real hobby".'

'Isn't a hobby whatever you're interested in?'

'Alex's parents signed him up for everything when he was a kid. Mine, too, I suppose. If Eric's not into this, he'll end up doing drama, or singing, or who knows what else.'

Oliver winced a little. He was mid- to late-thirties, a year or three younger than Millie – and the first time she'd met him was a few weeks before when she'd picked up Eric from his first guitar lesson. These were the most words they'd ever shared, although he clearly knew who she was away from being Eric's mum. That wasn't uncommon in Whitecliff. Her father had been a local TV newsreader, and then her parents had died suddenly and unexpectedly. With Millie inheriting everything, some still thought she knew more than she had ever let on.

'Your husband—'

'Ex-husband.'

'He paid for twelve sessions up front but I wouldn't want to force anyone to come. I can refund if—'

'If Eric didn't want to be here, he's not the sort of kid who'd stay quiet. I think it's probably best to get through the twelve and see how it's going then.' Millie almost turned to go before remembering the oddness of moments before. 'What's with the flower thing?' she asked.

Oliver was touching his ear through his hair. 'My girlfriend spotted it last night. She took a photo and showed me.'

'Why did she do that?'

'It doesn't come off. We both tried rubbing it and I gave it a wash. Nothing moved it.'

Millie was unsure what to say. She had no idea what he was talking about.

'She said she thinks it's a tattoo,' Oliver added. 'But she went off on a hen do this morning. I didn't have anyone else to show and ask a second opinion. Then I remembered you were picking up Eric and that you were into weird stuff...'

Millie didn't bother to correct him a second time to say she wasn't *into* weird stuff.

'I'm not sure what you're saying is weird,' Millie commented.

'Because I've never had a tattoo. I don't know what it is.'

Millie really was confused now. She asked for a second look and then Oliver showed her the mark again. Now she knew what she was looking for, it seemed clear that it was a small tattoo of something that looked like a flower on the back of Oliver's ear. The stencilling was smudged and faded.

'It looks like a daisy,' Millie said.

Oliver twisted to face her properly once more. 'I've never had a tattoo,' he repeated.

'Could it be a birthmark?'

'I don't know. The first time I saw it was last night when my girlfriend took a picture. Who looks behind their own ears?'

Millie realised she was absent-mindedly rubbing her own ear. Oliver had a point. She doubted she'd ever looked behind her own ear. Why would she? *How* would she?

'It doesn't look like a birthmark,' Millie added, even though she'd been the one to suggest it. 'How long's it been there?' she asked.

'That's the point. I have no idea. Plus how can you get a tattoo and not know? I've been drunk but never *that* drunk.'

Millie thought on that for a moment. She had no tattoos,

either. 'I'm not sure what you're saying. That someone tattooed you without you knowing?'

'I guess so. And I have no idea when. It could've been there for years. I tried searching online for things like "tattoo on back of ear" – and stuff like that. I couldn't find much but there's a Twitter post from this woman in Steeple's End from a few months back. Look.'

Oliver had his phone in his hands. He tapped something on the screen and handed it across for Millie. It took her a few moments to realise she was looking at a photo similar to what she'd just seen. It was slightly blurry but there was a smudged tattoo of a flower on the back of someone's ear. It had been posted by someone named Georgia a little after new year, with the caption: 'Anyone know what this is?'

'I messaged her this morning,' Oliver said, as Millie passed back his phone. 'I sent her the photo of mine.'

'Did she find out what it was?' Millie asked.

'She says she's never had a tattoo. Her husband found it and thought it had been drawn on. We're going to meet up tomorrow and see if we can figure out what it might be, or where it came from.'

'You've never met her before?'

A shake of the head. 'As far as we can tell, we don't know each other. We have nothing in common, other than living in towns along the coast from each other. That's why we're meeting up.' He was rubbing his ear again. 'Have you ever heard of anything like this?'

'Two people with identical tattoos, who say they've never had a tattoo...' Millie almost laughed. 'I've definitely never heard of anything like that.'

Before she could add anything else, they were distracted by the toot of a car horn. Millie turned to see Eric leaning across to the driver's seat of her car. He had the type of grin that he had when he knew he was misbehaving.

'I've got to go,' Millie said. 'But there's someone I can ask. He knows more about this sort of thing than me.'

She still wasn't sure what 'thing' this was, and then the car horn beeped a second time.

'You'll have to excuse me,' Millie said. 'I have a son that needs telling off.'

TWO

Eric's telling off had been about as firm as it ever was from Millie – which meant there wasn't a lot to it. She knew she should be harder except, with her ex having custody, her time with her son was limited. She gave him a longer leash that she knew she should. He knew it, too.

They were on their way across town as Eric hummed to himself from the passenger seat. Millie had already passed the Big Tesco when she remembered what she was supposed to be doing. As she pulled over in front of a corner shop, Eric looked across, confused.

'I told Guy I'd pick up some ketchup,' Millie said. 'I figured that's what you'd want on your hot dogs?'

Eric turned to take in the shop. 'Can you get me some stickers?'

'After your stunt with the car horn...?'

'My hand slipped.'

He grinned and it was hard for Millie not to copy. She wasn't quite sure from where his cheek had come. She'd never had that confidence as a child and she doubted Alex was any different. Perhaps it was a generational thing? Her father had been a newsreader and had no issue with standing up and talking in front of others.

'Your hand slipped *twice?*' she asked.

That got a shrug. 'Can I come in?' he replied.

'If you sit still while I'm in the shop, then I'll think about getting you stickers,' Millie said.

Eric wriggled deeper into his car seat and agreed that he could definitely sit still while she was gone.

Millie locked him in the car and then headed into the shop. It was the typical place that sold a random selection of seemingly everything. If someone wanted to pick up a morning newspaper, some gravy granules, a can of WD40 and a reduced-price chocolate advent calendar five months after Christmas, this was the place. The type of shop that carried a smell like no other: a mix of decades-old dirt in the carpets, blended with spilled bottles of Irn-Bru. Borderline chemical warfare.

The door jangled as Millie headed inside. There was a pile of out-of-date crisps in a basket to the side, with '10p' scrawled on a flap of cardboard above. Millie grabbed a pair of those and then headed into the nearest aisle, searching for ketchup as the door clinked behind. She was busy wondering why USB cables were on a shelf next to vinegar when someone brushed past her.

Millie's British instincts kicked in and she was about to apologise when she realised she hadn't done anything wrong. She half expected the man to say sorry to her, except he kept moving quickly towards the counter at the back of the shop. Millie almost looked away, putting it down as one of those things... except he was wearing a balaclava.

Everything happened so quickly and yet it felt as if Millie was watching in slow motion.

'Empty the till.'

There was a bloke behind the counter, who was staring

wide-eyed at Balaclava Man. He had thinning, receding dark hair, even though he was probably mid-twenties.

'You deaf?'

'No, uh...'

Balaclava Man had his left hand jammed tight in his hoody pocket and a brown paper bag in the other. He pushed the bag onto the counter and the cashier took it. The register opened with a ding and then the man scooped a handful of notes from the drawer into the bag.

'Quicker.'

Millie was frozen with the two packets of reduced-price crisps in her hand. Balaclava Man wasn't that much taller than her, though he had a chunkiness across his middle. His back was largely to her, although she had the sense he would know if she moved. She was focused on the hand that hadn't moved from Balaclava Man's pocket. Instinct told her there was probably only a hand in there – but she didn't want to find out for sure.

'There,' said the man behind the counter. He pushed the bag of money back across and Balaclava Man snatched it before taking a step away. He spun quickly and jogged along the aisle next to the one in which Millie was standing. His face was angled away from Millie and he didn't stop as he banged open the door and disappeared outside.

Millie stared after him as the door slammed back into place. There was a momentary gust of wind, which sent the pile of cheap crisps tumbling to the ground with a gentle *tick-tick-tick*.

And then... silence.

'Are you... OK?'

It took Millie a moment to realise it was the man behind the counter who was talking. She turned to see he was staring at her. She blinked and looked between the cashier and the door, wondering if it had really happened.

'I think so,' Millie managed. 'You?'

'I think so.'

Neither of them sounded sure.

'My son's in the car outside,' Millie said. 'He wanted to come in but I told him no. He's only eight...'

She wasn't sure why she'd said it, other than it was at the front of her mind. She wondered how things might have gone if Eric had been at her side. Would he have tried to talk to the robber? Would he have asked what was going on? Would he have been scared? Millie crossed to the window and peeped through the gap to where Eric was sitting obliviously in the car, where she'd left him.

Back at the counter, the boxes of stickers were sitting next to the till. There was every chance Eric would have headed directly for them after entering the shop. He could have been *right there* if Millie hadn't told him to sit still.

The man behind the counter was blinking as if staring into the sun. Millie wondered if she was doing the same.

'What's your name?' Millie asked.

'Uh... Chris.'

'You should probably call the police. Or I can?'

'Right, yeah, um, the police. Yeah. What's the number?'

Millie coughed a humourless laugh. 'Nine-nine-nine,' she told him.

'Do you think it's an emergency?'

'You've just been robbed...'

'Right, yeah. Of course...'

He stammered something that Millie didn't catch and then pulled out a phone from underneath the counter.

'I'm going to check on my son,' Millie told him. 'I'll come back. The police will want to talk to us both.'

Chris was busy staring at his phone, as if he'd forgotten how it worked. Millie left him to it and headed towards the door. She placed the two packets of crisps back in the basket, even though half the pile was now on the ground.

As she considered picking them up, Millie spotted a key

sitting next to the fallen bags. The key was attached to some sort of rectangular plasticky fob, like the ones used to swipe into office buildings.

Millie picked it up and turned it over in her hands, before calling to the back of the shop.

'Is this yours?' she asked.

Chris still seemed confused by his phone and barely looked up. 'What is it?' he shouted back.

'A key.'

That got a blank shrug and a shake of the head.

Millie stared at the key, realising she should have probably left it where it was. She was certain she hadn't stepped over it on the way in. If it didn't belong to her, and it didn't belong to Chris, there was only one other person who could have dropped it.

THREE

The smell of crisping onions was on the breeze as Millie pressed back into the deckchair. Guy stood over the barbecue, tongs click-clacking in his hand, like a lobster ready to kick off at a chef. The onions were on a metal pan over the grill, and he flipped them around, before rotating the sausages.

On the other side of his garden, Eric tore from side to side, chasing an energised labradoodle. Barry was getting on a bit but the dog had a turn of speed when he wanted. Millie watched her son play with Guy's pup and, for a moment, the robbery was out of her mind.

She and her ex-husband were probably in agreement that the Xbox had been doing too much parenting of their son in the last couple of years. Alex's solution was lots of classes; hers was the outdoors. Guy lived on the outskirts of Whitecliff, on top of a hill, along a track that nobody else bothered to drive up. The woods were steps from his garden – and Millie had been bringing Eric to his house more often now the weather was on the turn into spring. He always appeared to enjoy it.

Guy was her godfather and an old, old friend of her father. She was nearing forty, while he'd recently turned seventy. Eric had actual grandparents on her ex-husband's side – but Millie knew he wouldn't have as much fun with them as he did at Guy's house.

Barry was sitting tall as Eric held a ball in his hand. He arced back and feigned to throw – not that Barry realised it was fake. He tore off in chase, as Eric held the ball high over his head.

'He falls for it every time!'

He was calling to Millie, who was aware that Guy's dog would spend hours chasing phantom balls. It was very much the taking part that mattered and all about the participation trophy, as long as that trophy involved a scavenged sausage.

Barry was already at the opposite fence when he stopped, turned in a circle, and looked back to see Eric still clutching the ball. With no hint of resentment, he bolted back across the patchy lawn towards the boy.

'You shouldn't tease him,' Millie said.

'He likes it.'

'He likes it more when you actually throw the ball.'

This time Eric did hurl the ball, with the same result that the dog hurtled off after it. Eric chased as well, trying to get to it before Barry. Four legs thrashed two and then led Eric on a chase as he leapt the low fence and darted into the trees.

Millie might have been alarmed at such a thing, if it wasn't for the fact that Guy's place was so remote. It had only been a couple of weeks before that Eric had invited a few of his school friends and they'd ended up playing capture the flag in the woods. Eric only knew it was a game because he'd played the virtual version on his Xbox. He had been amazed that they could play for real.

'There's a *real flag*?' he'd said, as if Guy had suggested walking on the surface of Mars.

Sun was dappling through the trees, sending slits of light across the moss and dirt. After a long winter, Millie was

enjoying the shift into spring. Being a coastal town, Whitecliff
never felt more than a day or two away from something close to
a hurricane. In the moment, on evenings like this, it was as good
as anywhere.

Then she remembered the shop.

'You OK?'

Millie realised she'd been staring into the trees as Guy
brought her back to the present. Eric and Barry were back in the
garden, sitting in the corner, both panting breathlessly. Millie
hadn't seen them cross the fence.

'I'm just glad I didn't let Eric in that shop,' Millie replied. It
felt as if she'd already told him that at least once. Maybe more
than once.

'He seems happy...' Guy replied.

'I didn't tell him exactly what happened. Just that there'd
been an accident and I was waiting to tell the police what I saw.
I didn't want to scare him.'

Barry was nudging Eric with his snout, trying to get the boy
to play with him again. He'd been re-energised since Millie
started bringing Eric around regularly. Guy loved his dog – but
he couldn't play in the same way an eight-year-old could.

'How were the police?' Guy asked.

'They asked a lot of questions but I couldn't remember very
well. They wanted to know what the robber was wearing – and
I knew it was a hoody but not what colour. It feels like a badly
remembered dream.'

Millie turned to look at Guy, as he lifted a pair of sausages
from the barbecue and put them on a plate. He called to Eric,
who leapt up and raced Barry to the cottage. Guy pressed the
sausages into a pair of buns and told Eric he was out of tomato
sauce. It was only then that Millie remembered she was
supposed to have bought ketchup on the way. Eric grumbled
about that but accepted a dollop of Branston Pickle instead –

and then he was off to the other side of the garden, with a very attentive dog in tow.

'Are you sure you don't want anything?' Guy asked. He plonked himself in the deckchair at her side and was cradling a hot dog covered in blackened onions that was making Millie's mouth water.

'Luke's cooking later,' Millie replied. 'I said I'd eat with him.'

That got a hint of a smile from Guy as he bit into his food. Millie was wishing she'd told her boyfriend that she already had plans for tea.

Guy had already moved on: 'It's normal not to remember everything clearly,' he said. 'I once covered a car crash and there were two women involved who couldn't even agree on the colour of the car. One was certain the vehicle that hit them was red, the other was sure it was black.'

Guy had spent decades working as a journalist in White-cliff. After being made redundant, he'd set up his own news website. Millie had met him when she had been trying to find out if a woman really had been pushed from a roof. Her real job was supposed to be her dog-grooming business, though she often found herself looking into oddities alongside Guy.

The older man bit into his hot dog as the onions dribbled off and slopped into his lap. Millie sniggered as the older man picked them up with his fingers, gasped about them being hot, and then sat staring at the damp patch on his crotch.

'It's a good job you live in the middle of nowhere,' Millie said.

'Gonna have to do a wash now,' he mumbled to himself.

Millie watched as he patted himself with kitchen roll, before drying his fingers and having a second go.

'There was a camera in the shop,' Millie said. 'I didn't see it when I was there – but the police did. They were fiddling with that when I left. I guess it doesn't matter if I remember what colour his hoody was. They'll be able to find out for themselves.'

Guy nodded along as he ate.

On the other side of the garden, Eric was biting off pieces of sausage and feeding them to a grateful Barry. Guy was watching as well. The boy and the dog were good for each other.

'Odd place to rob,' he said, almost absent-mindedly. As if talking to himself.

'What do you mean?'

'How much could he have got? Hundred quid? Bit more? You can get up to twelve years in prison for robbery from a shop. Admittedly, that's top-end but even low-level stuff will get you tagged and some strict community service. Doesn't seem worth it for such a small amount.'

Guy had done a fair bit of court reporting over the years and knew a lot more about things like sentencing than Millie. Now he'd mentioned it, it felt like he had a point. Those sorts of shops dealt in small amounts, especially now that a lot of people tapped their card, or phone, to pay for things. Apart from maybe pubs, what other places were handling vast quantities of cash?

'Could it be someone after drug money?'

Millie almost winced as she finished the sentence. It was something like her mother might've said while watching the breakfast news.

'Maybe,' Guy replied, although it sounded as if he was being polite.

It felt as if he was right. It really *was* a lot of risk for not that much reward. The robber hadn't even bothered to ask for the cashier's phone. Or Millie's, for that matter. Wouldn't they be worth at least as much as whatever was in the till? Or were phones not worth stealing now they had tracking, and all that sort of thing?

The pangs of age had crept up on Millie and she shivered

them away. There didn't seem much point in dwelling on what had happened. The police had her statement and presumably the footage, so they could hopefully figure it out from that.

'I've got something else to ask you about,' Millie said, before telling Guy about the mystery tattoo on the back of Oliver's ear. 'He doesn't know where it came from,' she added. 'He says he's never got a tattoo and that he has no idea how long it might have been there.'

Guy had finished eating his hot dog, though, in doing so, had added two more grease stains to his clothes.

'That's a new one for me,' he said. 'I've never heard of anyone finding a tattoo they didn't know about. Are you sure it wasn't a birthmark?'

'It didn't *look* like a birthmark – and there's a woman in Steeple's End who has something that looks really similar. They're meeting up tomorrow to see if they might have anything in common.'

That got a thoughtful-sounding *hrm*.

On the other side of the garden, Eric and Barry were lying side by side in a sliver of sunshine, having seemingly run each other into the ground.

'They'll both sleep well tonight,' Millie found herself saying – and she sounded like her mum again. When she was young, Millie had been signed up for a series of after-school activities, much like Eric. She'd sometimes get picked up after eight, having left for school twelve hours before. Her mum would say she'd sleep well – and here was Millie doing the same thing. She'd sometimes find herself telling Eric to sit up straight, and later wondering why it mattered. It didn't, other than that her mother used to tell her the same thing. If the worst issues a child had were slouching a bit, and sometimes putting their elbows on the table while they ate, then those things really weren't worth complaining about. Millie wondered if turning into their parents was something that came to everyone eventually.

'Did you say it was a daisy?' Guy asked.

Millie needed a moment to realise he was talking about the tattoo. 'Something like that,' she replied. 'Some sort of flower.'

'That *does* ring a bell. I remember something from years back about a daisy symbol.'

Millie hadn't been expecting anything. Even with Guy's local knowledge and vast archives, it felt very niche and unlikely.

'I'd have to check the archives.' Guy wafted a hand towards the cottage – and the piles of newspapers and notebooks within. There were tens of thousands of documents that, if Millie was being kind, was organised in a way only Guy understood. To someone less charitable, it was a mess that nobody understood. 'Daisy...' Guy repeated the word to himself in the way he did when he was trying to shuffle the memories from his decades of news reporting. His recollection could swing from recalling precise conversations of forty years before, to having no idea where he'd left his phone – even though it was in his hand. 'There's definitely something,' he added.

The peace was broken by a grumbling engine making its way up the track. There was no through road and, aside from Guy, Millie, and Royal Mail, there was no reason for anyone to drive to Guy's house – particularly in the early evening.

Millie and Guy both sat up taller as a battered navy van chuntered into place behind Millie's car. It was a somewhat familiar face who got out of the driver's seat.

It was Christmas Day the year before that Craig had knocked on Millie's door and introduced himself as Guy's son. In the time Millie had known Guy, he'd never mentioned having children. Craig was a few years older than Millie and it felt like the sort of thing he should have probably told her.

Except Guy insisted Craig *wasn't* his son. He said Craig was the nephew of his dead wife and, technically, not related to Guy in any way.

Millie hadn't been sure what to make of any of it. One of them was lying – and she chose to believe it was Craig.

Craig was wearing sunglasses and a bucket hat as he stepped around Guy's open gate and strolled towards them. He was tall and skinny, which was the opposite of Guy. He lifted his glasses onto his forehead, peering under the rims to take in Millie. He stood over them and glanced across to Eric and Barry, before settling on Guy.

'Can we have a word?' he asked.

Guy hadn't shifted to acknowledge the other man's presence. 'OK.'

Nobody spoke for a moment until Craig added: 'In private.'

Guy offered a hand to indicate the space around them. 'How private do you want? Nobody comes up here.'

Millie felt Craig's gaze shift back to her. 'I meant—'

'I know what you meant,' Guy interrupted. 'And, if you have something to say, then you can say it here.'

Millie squirmed a little, caught in the middle. She watched as Eric propped himself up on his elbow and stared across the garden towards them, wondering who the newcomer was. Since meeting him properly at Christmas, Millie had only run into Craig a couple of times since – and never in any way other than passing. Eric would have no idea who he was.

Craig cleared his throat loudly and then: 'Have you thought about... what we, uh... talked about?'

Millie was watching Guy but felt Craig's eyes flit across her.

'I gave you my answer,' Guy replied. He was using another square of kitchen paper to dab the various grease stains on his clothes. The scorched onions had definitely been a bad idea.

'I know what you said – but I explained about... you know...'

'And I *gave you my answer*.'

Guy stood and moved around Craig, heading for the barbecue. He disconnected the fuel tank and then started on the grill with a wire brush. Craig hovered awkwardly over Millie. She sensed him grasping for some sort of reply but, when nothing came, he huffed an unhappy 'Fine!' and then stormed back to his van. It took him seven back and forths to turn around – and then he roared off in the direction of wherever he'd come from.

As soon as he was out of sight, Guy stopped the scrubbing. He put down the large brush on a side table and re-joined Millie. He was drumming his fingers on the arm of the chair, chuntering under his breath, until: 'He wanted money.'

'How much?'

'Enough. A lot. Same as usual.'

'Why would he ask you for money if you're not really family?'

It sounded as if Millie doubted Guy's version that Craig wasn't related to him. She thought about clarifying but then wondered if that's how she meant it anyway.

'It's complicated...'

Guy sighed and glanced up to the sky. Millie wondered whether she'd get a proper reply.

Across the garden, Eric and Barry were walking along the edge of the fence. Eric was talking to the dog, though Millie couldn't hear what he was saying.

'I know I told you some of this,' Guy added – and there was a definite reluctance in his tone.

Perhaps like most men of his generation, Guy didn't do a lot of talking about things like feelings. He never lingered on the loss of his wife to cancer, certainly not around Millie. He could talk for fifteen minutes straight about a council meeting on which he'd reported when he was in his twenties, and yet the sudden passing of his wife, to whom he had been married forty or so years, was off-limits.

'Carol and I couldn't have children,' Guy continued. 'Craig was Carol's weak spot – and he knew it. He stayed with us a few times when he was younger and his parents weren't getting on. We never adopted him, or fostered, or anything like that. He was Carol's nephew but she treated him like a son when he was with us... and she wanted me to as well.'

'It sounds as if that wasn't what you wanted...?'

Guy paused, probably considering the right choice of words. 'He stole some things. There was a necklace Carol had inherited and it disappeared. He always denied it – but things don't just walk out of drawers and go missing. But *he* went missing. A lot. We'd wake up in the morning and he was nowhere to be seen. The bedcovers would be untouched but his stuff would be gone. We'd see and hear nothing from him for a couple of years, and then he'd be back asking Carol for money.'

'How old was he?'

A shrug: 'Every age. This happened on and off from when he was a teenager all the way through to a few years ago. Every time he had a break-up, or some business idea that fell apart, he'd show up. He might spend a night or two, maybe a week, until Carol gave him some money, and then he'd be gone again.' Guy paused for breath. He was talking to his feet. 'He didn't come to her funeral.' There had been a hint of anger before but now his voice was quieter. 'It wasn't the money. She invested all that time into him, all her thought and love – and then, when it mattered...' A long pause. 'When it mattered, he couldn't be bothered to show up.'

Millie had no idea how to reply. She had never met Carol as an adult and barely knew Craig. She could understand why Guy was angry about him failing to attend the funeral, although she wondered if that had clouded his judgement about everything that had gone before.

'Why's he still hanging around?' Millie asked. 'He's been in the area since Christmas.'

'Money,' Guy replied. 'As soon as he gets what he wants, he'll be gone again.'

FOUR

After leaving Guy's, Millie dropped off Eric at his dad's house. It was a measured exchange, watching him and waving from the car, and then getting out of there before the loss felt too encompassing. She headed back to her place, where Luke's large white work van was parked on her drive. She found him in her kitchen, bubbling down a pan of risotto rice.

They didn't live together – but had a key for each other's places. They'd been seeing each other for a few months and had reached the stage of sleeping over a couple of a times a week. That, and eating food off their laps, while half-watching something off the iPlayer.

'Just in time,' he said, as Millie dumped her bag on the table. He scraped a fillet of salmon from the griddle and laid it on a plate – before repeating the procedure for a second.

'I could get used to this,' Millie said. She had gone from eating Pot Noodles by herself to having someone prepare a meal that was almost ready as she arrived home. As well as being a kitchen fitter by trade, Luke had turned out to be an adventurous cook. The sort who'd see a photo above a recipe, figure it was a starting point, and then throw a bunch of stuff in a pot and see what came out. Most of the time, *most*, it worked.

Millie eyed the rice, and the orange specks within.

'Finely chopped butternut squash,' Luke said. 'With a hint of chilli.'

'We have different ideas about the meaning of the word "hint",' Millie replied.

That got a laugh. 'I promised there wouldn't be a repeat of the enchilada debacle.'

'Debacle' was one word for it. Luke had not only figured a tablespoon was as good as a teaspoon – but he'd also used hot chilli powder. That was a night Millie wouldn't forget any time soon. There was some degree of payback in that, because he'd done the cooking, Luke had insisted it 'wasn't that hot'. He had finished every last bite as if to prove the point, repeating three or four times that 'it isn't that bad'. It had been a different story when his rumbling intestines woke him up in the early hours of the morning.

Millie sat at the kitchen table as Luke finished serving the food. What he lacked in presentation, he more than made up for in portion size. As well as the salmon and rice, there were green beans, carrots and toast.

Luke wasted no time in scooping rice onto a triangle of toast and then munching. Millie hadn't started when he grinned wickedly. 'What?'

'You know what.'

'If you're not having toast on the side of every meal, you're doing it wrong.'

They'd been seeing each other for close to six weeks when they'd revisited the all-day breakfast place where they'd first had a proper conversation. Luke had ordered toast with a side of toast and, since then, there had been no going back. He really did eat toast with everything.

Millie had a forkful of rice and was grateful to discover that, on this occasion, their definitions of 'hint' appeared to match.

'Have you heard much from Nicola?' he asked.

'Her flight to Magaluf got cancelled, so she spent last night in a Premier Inn by the airport. They bumped her onto a plane at half-four this morning – and I've not heard from her since.'

'Oof. Half-four. I bet she loved that.'

Millie's friend was less than a year out of a divorce and the trip to Majorca was her first-ever solo holiday. She'd tried to persuade Millie to go with her but the idea of two almost forty-year-olds prowling a resort known for its youthful overindulgence made Millie feel physically ill. Even if it hadn't, the cheap and copious alcohol would definitely have done the job.

Luke sliced his fish and then, predictably, wrapped it within the rest of his toast slice. Millie couldn't decide if he was some sort of culinary genius, or a monster. She was about to try her own when the doorbell sounded. The two of them looked to one another as couples did when an evening of suburban peace was interrupted. The unspoken *I don't know who it is* rippled between them, before Millie remembered it was her house.

She headed into the hall, where the shape of someone short was silhouetted through the dimpled glass of the front door. A woman wearing a Whitecliff FC shirt jumped away when Millie opened the door, as if she'd not expected it to be answered.

'Oh,' she said, 'I did wonder if you'd be in. I'm Heather.'

She said her name as if she expected Millie to know who she was. As well as the football top, she was clasping a basket that was covered with a tea towel.

'Do we know each other?' Millie asked. It was a gamble because there was every chance Heather lived a couple of doors down and Millie had somehow forgotten the other woman's face.

'I run the corner shop,' Heather said. 'Well, *co*-run. Co-own, really. Me and my husband. After the police had been, my son said there was a witness. I recognised your name, obviously. Because of your dad and all that...'

Millie wasn't sure what to say. After her parents' death, she'd inherited and moved into their house. She not only had a degree of notoriety in Whitecliff but people knew where she lived. This sort of visit wasn't common – but it also wasn't *uncommon*.

'Oh...' Millie found herself saying. 'Right... the shop.'

'We're just glad everyone's all right,' Heather said. 'Chris went straight to the pub after work. Probably not healthy but it's hard to blame him after being held up at gunpoint.'

Millie wondered what she'd missed as she realised she'd repeated 'gunpoint'. Was there a gun?

'He said it *could* have been gunpoint,' Heather added.

It wasn't strictly untrue. It *could* have been gunpoint in the same way it could have been a finger in a pocket.

'He's only been back at the shop three weeks,' Heather continued, seemingly unaware Millie was temporarily lost. 'He was working at the tip but got laid off. He's been doing shifts in the shop ever since he was thirteen. Didn't expect him to still be doing it when he's about to turn thirty – but that's what you do when you have kids, isn't it? We told him there's always a job with us if he wants.'

It had been a fair amount of oversharing – and Heather seemed to realise as much when she stopped for breath. She gasped and then hoisted up the basket, before thrusting it towards Millie.

'This is for you.'

Millie took it and, as Heather looked on expectantly, she lifted the tea towel to see a mound of cakes, muffins, biscuits, and a loaf of bread. A business card was tucked into the side.

'I got into baking a couple of years back,' Heather said. 'Tried to get on *Bake-Off* but I couldn't even get a reply. I do the car booter every Sunday and have a bit of a following there. Anyway, I figured I'd drop something round as a thank you for hanging around and talking to the police. I think I got a bit carried away...'

Millie checked the basket's contents again, where there were enough treats to feed a family of eight for a week. Aside from the cakes, the bread might last Luke's toast addiction two days. It seemed incredibly generous.

'This is very kind of you,' Millie said. 'But you didn't have to. I didn't really—'

'I wanted to. We were so worried when Chris told us everything that happened. He said it was your idea to call the police.'

Millie tried to remember whether she'd done that. Everything about the robbery felt like a blur.

'I think we were both in a bit of shock,' Millie managed.

Heather was nodding away. 'Do you have a son?' she asked.

It was blunt, though Millie answered without thinking. 'Eric,' she said. 'He's eight.'

More nodding. 'I remember my Chris at that age. Used to sit under the counter in the shop and play on his Gameboy. If not that, he was out playing football all the time. That's all it was with him. Football, football, football.' Heather patted the badge on her top. 'Now we follow the team everywhere, while he got bored of it. You'll know what it's like when your lad discovers girls.' She paused. 'Or boys. You never know nowadays, do you? Each to their own and all that.'

Heather was about to add something more when headlights flashed from the road. She glanced towards them and then back to Millie.

'That's my husband,' she added quickly. 'I told him I'd only be a minute. He's always saying how I talk too much. Reckons I could talk for England. I just wanted to say thanks and make sure you were all right.'

Millie said she was fine but it felt like more of a reflex than anything more. Someone asks 'How are you?' and 'All right, you?' is out before a single synapse has passed through the brain.

'I wondered if we could swap numbers?' Heather added. 'Nothing weird, just to check in, what with the police and all that. I'll let you know if anything comes back.'

Most sentences beginning with 'Nothing weird' ended with something on the furthest edges of bizarre – but Millie didn't feel as if she could say no. The numbers 'oh-one' got a curious glance from Heather, though she continued typing until Millie had finished.

'Is that a landline?' Heather asked, knowing the answer.

'I don't really use a mobile,' Millie replied. It was a lie but she had said it a few times in recent months. It was such an outlier in the modern day that strangers were too shocked to question it. She'd get a frown as a reply.

Heather said she'd call if she heard anything – and then turned and headed towards the road and the headlights.

Millie watched her disappear around the corner and then returned into the house. In the kitchen, she placed the basket on the counter and then sat back at the table. She'd called Luke earlier to tell him she was running late, because she'd had to give a statement to the police.

'I didn't know if you wanted to talk about it,' he said. 'I wasn't listening in but...'

Voices travelled in Millie's house. When she'd been with Alex, he'd have been on her as soon as she got through the door, wanting every last detail of what she'd witnessed. She and Luke always had some sort of understanding over what they each wanted to talk about.

When Millie didn't reply properly, Luke changed the subject: 'I didn't know you had a landline,' he said.

It took Millie a moment to realise he was talking about the number she'd given Heather.

'I don't,' Millie replied. 'When I started working with Guy, he told me to give out his number if I didn't want to use my own. Reckoned it was safer if I was unsure about someone.'

Luke nodded towards the basket. 'Are you unsure about her?'

Millie thought for a second. 'Probably not. I suppose I don't really like people having my number.' In the aftermath of her parents' deaths, Millie had faced outright hostility from many in the community. She didn't have much privacy, but she valued what she had.

Luke had shifted his attention to the basket: 'Mind if I...?'

He already had the tea towel lifted when Millie said 'Go for it' and then made a series of appreciative noises as he sifted through the goods.

When he was done, he passed Millie a small notecard that read: 'Heather Speed. Entrepreneur. Baker. Thinker' above a phone number.

Millie almost laughed. Nobody could simply say what they did nowadays. Binmen were refuse consultants. Cashiers were guest service agents.

That flicker of Millie becoming her mother skipped through her once more.

She put down the card and then managed a bit of fish, before poking some of the rice around the plate. Luke was back in his seat and almost finished with his.

The yawn was out before Millie could stop it. 'Long day,' she said, as she realised she *did* want to talk about the robbery. 'I didn't tell Eric what happened,' she added. 'I said there was an accident in the shop and implied someone had fallen. I'm glad he wasn't there.'

And, like that, Luke knew she'd changed her mind. 'Was there anything to identify the robber?' he asked.

Millie started to say something about a hoody and then realised she wasn't quite sure if he *had* been wearing a hoody.

Perhaps it was a sweatshirt? Except there were pockets, so maybe it was a jacket?

Considering how recently it had happened, Millie was worried that so much had fallen from her mind. Maybe none of her memories were real? Was it definitely a man?

As if to convince herself it had happened, Millie picked up the mobile she'd told Heather she didn't use. She loaded the most recent photo and then passed it across for Luke to see.

'I found that in the shop door,' she said. 'I probably shouldn't have picked it up because of fingerprints and all that – but I didn't think of that at the time. The police have it now but I took a picture.'

It was a photo of the key and the fob. Luke looked at it and was about to pass back the device when he stopped, frowned, and then pinched in to get a close-up.

'Do you know what this is from?' he asked.

'Some sort of office, I assume. The police officer didn't seem to know. She reckoned they'd look into it.'

'It's from a storage company,' Luke said, as he turned the screen for Millie to see. 'I had a unit for a few months when I was moving house. You get a fob like this that lets you into the building, and then you have your own padlock.'

Millie took back her phone and had a proper look at the photo. As far as she could tell, there were no distinguishing features on the fob. It was a plain, cream, rectangle.

'The officer left me her details,' Millie said, as she went through her bag. She found the card and then laid it on the table, next to the one Heather had left. 'Do you reckon I should call her? Or text? She said it was her *actual* number, not just her desk.'

Luke suddenly seemed reluctant. 'Other places might use the same fobs...'

That was true – but Millie figured it couldn't do any harm

to pass on the information. She sent the text and then put the phone back in her bag.

Millie had another forkful of fish and then prodded a bit more of the rice. They both knew what was coming.

'Sorry...' she said. 'I'm not that hungry.'

Luke didn't mind, mainly because he was already scooping what was left of her fish onto a slice of toast.

'How was your day?' Millie asked. She was trying to teach herself to ask such things. After being single for a while, and married before that, the simple things had been forgotten.

Luke finished his mouthful of fishy toast. 'I finished ripping out the rest of that horrible green kitchen I was telling you about. There's a lot of mould that needs to be sorted – but I half expected that. Same as usual, really.'

It really did sound like more of the same. Luke worked by himself and had a steady stream of work that, to Millie's untrained ear, sounded more or less identical every day. She was starting to worry that her days were also beginning to sound a bit repetitive. When Oliver said she was into weird things, it was all too true.

'What are you up to this weekend?' Luke asked.

'I'm seeing Jack and Rish.'

A clouded look passed Luke's face. He'd done his best to hide it in the past but his thoughts were clear. 'I can't believe you still hang around with that guy after what he did.'

'It's not as simple as that,' Millie replied – even though it probably was. She wasn't adverse to pretending problems weren't in front of her if it made life easier.

Before she could say anything more, her phone buzzed. The text from Oliver was a welcome distraction from the awkward territory.

Do u want to visit Georgia with me 2moro?

It wasn't clear why he'd asked – and he offered no further explanation. But Millie had no hesitation in asking where and when. If there was one thing that was going to get her to forget about the robbery, it was finding out why two strangers had the same tattoo they each claimed they'd never got.

FIVE

DAY TWO

Steeple's End was the closest town to Whitecliff, which meant – predictably – that they were two places perpetually at war with one another. Steeple's End built a new stand for their football stadium, so Whitecliff built a bigger one. Whitecliff had a welcome sign that claimed the town was 'world-famous', so Steeple's End tagged a note onto theirs insisting they were 'known across the galaxy'. At a charity event the year before, a Steeple's End councillor had put his back out trying to hit a punching machine. He'd only done so because a councillor from Whitecliff had been pictured doing the same two weeks before.

It was petty – and yet the towns had united with the fire of a million suns when someone from *The Observer* had written a throwaway line in an article, that described the entire area as 'run-down'. He'd ended up closing his Twitter account after what could only be described as a torrent of regional-based abuse.

Millie had grown up in Whitecliff and, by default, felt slightly disloyal simply by being in Steeple's End. When she'd been at school, the goal was always to get better test results as a whole than the rival school in Steeple's End. Whenever there had been football, rugby, netball, or hockey matches between schools, she and her friends had always shown up to support Whitecliff, despite not being too bothered about sport. It was the done thing.

Despite that, it was hard to ignore the appeal of the beach at Steeple's End. The one in Whitecliff swept for miles along the bay and would be packed with tourists through the summer. Along the coast, it was smaller and sandier. Like some sort of Mediterranean cove. Dinky fishing boats were docked around the marina, with a low sun shimmering across the water. While Whitecliff had three of every shop, Steeple's End had one. Whitecliff was the summer blockbuster, compared to the indie darling of Steeple's End.

Oliver nodded towards the shop behind them as they waited next to a bus stop. 'Have you ever seen shops like this anywhere other than Britain?' he asked.

The awning was lined with rows of inflatables, including bananas, pineapples, traditional rings, and orcas – an animal which had never been seen in the waters of Steeple's End. In front of the windows were stacks of multicoloured plastic buckets, next to a large basket of matching spades. There were handwritten signs, promising six sticks of rock for a pound – plus postcards, some weird sort of sea-salt gum, and then the usual assortment of mugs, plates and every other sort of ornament that could fit the name of the town. The type of stuff that lined every grandmother's house in a forty-mile radius.

'There must be another country that sells rock,' Millie said, although she couldn't name one. It felt likely that other places wouldn't pretend such an appalling creation was edible.

'I used to spend all my pocket money in places like this when I was a kid,' Oliver said. 'Used to be twelve sticks of rock for a pound back then. It's a surprise I have any teeth left.' He eyed Millie for a moment and then: 'Are you all right?'

She wasn't sure why but Millie ended up telling him about

the robbery the day before. There was an urge to talk about it, yet she didn't know too many people.

He covered his mouth with his hand and gave an 'Oh my God!'

Before Millie could add anything more, a woman appeared in front of them. She was wearing a black skirt and white top, with an enormous bag over her shoulder. It was so big, she was leaning slightly to the side.

'Are you Oliver?' she asked.

He was touching his ear as he replied. 'Georgia? I recognised you from your photo.'

Perhaps purposefully, she scratched her own ear.

They stared at one another for a moment before Oliver turned to Millie. 'This is my friend,' he said. 'She's been helping me try to find out what's going on.

The 'friend' part was overplaying it, though Millie didn't mind too much. She half expected Georgia to offer some sort of objection: it was, after all, none of her business what might or might not be tattooed behind Georgia's ear. Instead, Georgia said it was 'great' that they had someone to help, before turning back to Oliver.

'I guess this is where I show you mine if you show me yours...?'

The two strangers grinned at one another, before Oliver hunched and turned, before shifting his hair to the side. Georgia craned in and then told him to hold still while she took a photo. When it was Georgia's turn, she angled herself so Millie could see the mark behind her ear. Oliver took a photo and, from what Millie could see, the looped circles in the shape of a daisy were identical to his.

They looked at each other curiously for a moment and then, as a family weaved their way around them on the pavement, Georgia led them across to one of the benches that overlooked the cove. Off to the side of the beach, a young couple had come out to take advantage of the morning sun. A woman in a bikini was lying on a towel, eyes covered by sunglasses. A few metres away, a man was digging a hole in the sand with a pink plastic spade that was surely meant for children.

'When you messaged me, I wondered if we might be related,' Georgia said. 'But it doesn't seem like we know the same people. I was looking at the photo you sent but we've got different colour eyes, different hair colour, different everything.'

Oliver *hrmed*, as if he'd been thinking the same. 'You found yours months ago,' he said. 'Did you ask your parents about it?'

'I would've – but they both died years ago.'

'I'm sorry.'

That got a hint of a shrug: 'They had me when they were already in their fifties.'

Millie must have shifted, or perhaps even flinched, because Georgia nodded past Oliver towards her.

'D'you have kids?'

'A boy. He's eight and runs me ragged. I can't imagine doing all that while being fifteen, twenty years older.'

That got a gentle laugh. 'I've got a daughter. Isla. She's four – and she's exhausting. Didn't start sleeping through the night until three or four months back. I'm like you, can't imagine doing all this while being that much older. I don't know how Mum and Dad managed it.' She looked to Oliver. 'Have you got kids?'

'Never got round to it...'

'What about your parents? Have you asked them about your ear?'

Something happened with Oliver's features that Millie didn't quite catch. Perhaps a gulp, or a twitch of the eyebrow?

'There's only Mum. Dad had a heart attack a few years back.' He rubbed his ear. 'I only found this a couple of days back and Mum's at Center Parcs with one of her friends.'

Georgia let out a low whistle. 'I've never been.'

'She saves up every year,' Oliver replied. 'She and her friend go for five or six days. It was her treat to herself after Dad died.'

'Oh... I didn't mean...'

Oliver brushed it away – and the two of them continued comparing notes, trying to find something in common that could explain what was going on. They talked about their schools and clubs of which they'd been a part. Georgia had played a bit of hockey as a teenager, alongside a few girls that Oliver knew. Oliver had once worked in a pub, where one of Georgia's friends did a few shifts. The links were indirect and vague; the sort of thing any two people of roughly the same age would have if they lived in neighbouring towns. Though Georgia said they had lived in Whitecliff at some point, her entire life had been spent in Steeple's End.

The two of them threw names of people and places at one another for a good half-hour until conversation dwindled. Millie chipped in – but, after all that, the best they could come up with was that they were both only children.

'That's not really a link,' Georgia said, pointing towards the beach in front of them. 'There'll be a bunch of people over there who don't have brothers or sisters.'

It was hard to argue with that. If anything, Georgia and Millie had more in common, considering their parents had died and that they were both only children, with their own only child.

The man digging the hole was still going. He was waist-deep, sweat steaming as he puffed away. His girlfriend remained unimpressed, sunbathing on her front.

'I really figured there'd be something,' Oliver said. He was holding his phone, looking at the photo of the tattoo behind Georgia's ear that matched his own. 'There *has* to be something we're missing?'

Georgia hefted her massive bag onto her shoulder. 'I have work soon,' she said. 'I was going to get a sandwich first.'

'What do you do?' Oliver asked, alert again at a topic they had somehow not got to.

'I'm a waitress in the Nemesis Café by the outdoor market.'

'Is that the one that does those rainbow cupcakes?' Millie asked. 'My friend, Jack, keeps saying he's seen them on Instagram.'

'That's us! You should come by. Everything's baked on-site.'

There was a basket of muffins sitting in the boot of Millie's car – but she didn't want to be rude. 'Sounds good.'

'Come now. I'll sort you out with something.'

Oliver didn't need asking twice. It didn't matter if someone was a billionaire, or living under a bridge: a promise of free and/or cheap food was irresistible.

The three of them stood and headed across the road towards the small village centre. They passed the tat shop and an ice cream place, then headed through an alley until emerging in a cobbled square.

'Are you smuggling bricks?' Millie asked, nodding at Georgia's bag.

That got a laugh. 'I need to cut down,' Georgia replied. 'Mum was the same. She'd say she never knew when she might need something. I used to think it was ridiculous when I was younger – and now I'm the same. My husband reckons I must be training as a weightlifter.'

'What do you keep in there?' Oliver asked. He patted his pockets. 'Keys, phone, wallet. What more do you need?'

Millie and Georgia exchanged a glance.

'Girls don't get pockets,' Millie told him.

'What do you mean?'

A roll of the eyes. 'Ask your girlfriend.'

Georgia hooked her bag higher on her shoulder and grunted involuntarily. 'I could probably lose some of the receipts,' she said. 'I've got various business cards, contact details for Isla's nursery, all sorts. Most of it's on my phone anyway. I really do need a clear-out...'

She hefted up the bag once more and led them across the square, past a café, and towards a second alley. Millie and Georgia were already a few paces ahead when Oliver called after them. He'd stopped next to a sandwich board and nodded towards some steps leading down to a basement.

'What d'you reckon?' he asked. 'We could ask if they know anything...'

The board at his side read 'On The Edge Tattoos', alongside a series of elaborate squiggles.

Georgia checked her phone and shrugged. 'I've got a bit of time...'

Oliver led the way this time, almost stumbling down the narrow steps and ducking under a beam before heading through a door.

The tattoo studio was hot, cramped – and surprisingly quiet. The clipped BBC tones of a newsreader sounded in the background as a woman in a denim vest sat with a sandwich in one hand and her phone in the other. She blinked up as the three of them stumbled in.

'Are you Thomas?' she asked, looking to Oliver. ''Cos you'll have to give me ten minutes.'

'I'm not a customer,' Oliver replied. 'But I did wonder if you could answer something weird for me.'

That got a frown. 'Depends how weird.'

Oliver crossed towards the woman and then hunched in front of her, before shifting his hair away from his ear. It happened so quickly that the tattoo artist didn't get a chance to object.

'Is this a tattoo?' Oliver asked, pointing a finger to the back of his ear.

The woman looked over Oliver's shoulder towards Millie

and Georgia, silently asking if this was some sort of prank. When she got nothing back, she squinted towards Oliver's ear.

'What else would it be?' she asked.

'Maybe a birthmark?'

The woman leaned in closer, narrowing her eyes further. 'Get that while you were drunk, did you? I don't do removals here, if that's what you're asking.'

Oliver stood. 'I'm not after a removal.' A pause. 'Well, maybe I am. I've not thought that far ahead.'

There was another bemused glance from the tattooist towards Millie and Georgia, as if asking whether they were Oliver's carers, and wondering if an intervention was due.

'We both have one,' Georgia said decisively. She approached and then twisted to show the tattooist her identical mark. 'But neither of us asked for it. We don't know how long we've had them and we'd not even met until today. We found them recently and we're trying to figure out what they are – and why we have them. I guess we were wondering if you'd seen anything like them before?'

The woman looked between them, probably still wondering what sort of prank was being played. 'They look like daisies,' she said. 'And they're definitely tattoos. I don't know what to tell you other than that.'

SIX

In many ways, the tattoo artist was telling them what they already knew – but there was a degree of certainty in that an expert was confirming it. The remote possibility that they could be birthmarks, or anything else, was gone.

The tattooist took a bite of her sandwich and then put it down on a plate. She chewed thoughtfully, looking between Oliver and Georgia. 'What do you mean neither of you asked for it?'

'Exactly that,' Georgia replied. 'I've never been tattooed – and neither has he. My husband found mine months ago and I didn't know what to tell him. We might have had these for years. Nobody checks behind their own ears, do they?'

That got a *hmmm*, and then she asked for a second look. This time, Georgia and Oliver crouched next to each other as the tattooist examined both their ears.

'They're not quite the same,' she said after a few seconds, talking to Georgia. 'Yours has four petals that are more or less equal but his are all over the shop.'

Georgia and Oliver turned and stood once more.

'How old do you reckon they are?' Oliver asked.

'Years. They're faded, blurred, and stretched. Ears are one of the body parts that never stop growing, so that's not a surprise. Minimum ten years but probably longer. They would have both been done within a year or two of each other. Maybe at the same time.'

She had the final bite of his sandwich and chewed some more.

'I still don't get it. How can you not notice?'

That got a joint shrug. 'I've always had long hair,' Georgia said. 'My husband mentioned it a few months back. He said he'd seen it a few times before but assumed it was a freckle. If anyone else had ever spotted it, they hadn't said.'

The tattooist didn't appear completely convinced – but it sounded possible.

'I've never had short hair,' Oliver said. 'And I was single for ages until recently. It's not like there's a queue of strangers lining up to look at each other's ears.'

'I've never heard of anything like this,' the tattooist said.

She asked a few questions about whether Georgia and Oliver knew each other, and how they'd met. Each reply was met with a longer *hmmm*.

'There have been a few cases of branding I've heard about,' she said. 'Something in Scotland, where a dad put crosses on the chests of his daughters. I think he ended up being sectioned. I don't know what yours might be about, though...'

The four of them stood apart and it was as if they were all silently rubbing their chins, not knowing what to make of it.

'There's someone you can ask,' the woman said. 'The guy who used to own this place lives in the flat above the art gallery. He's been doing tattoos in Steeple's End since the seventies. He's called Keith.' She glanced up to a clock above the door. 'It's early, so he should be sober enough. Tell him Catriona sent you but... be polite. He's a grumpy sod. Tell him I said he was the expert. He'll like that.'

Oliver thanked the woman for her time and then the three of them bundled their way back up the stone steps into the sunshine.

'Kinda fun, this,' Georgia said, and there was almost a skip to her step. 'Bit of a treasure hunt.'

She seemed more light-hearted than Oliver but then, to her, it probably was a distraction. She had a husband and son away from whatever this was. Plus, she'd found her tattoo a while before. For Oliver, with his girlfriend away, and part-time teaching-from-home gig, perhaps it meant a bit more?

Georgia knew where she was going, leading them back the way they'd come across the square, through the alley, and onto the front. They followed the row of shops until she stopped outside a window with a series of paintings on display.

'Looks like that's the place,' she said, nodding at the door to the side of the gallery.

Oliver looked between the two women, slowly realising he'd been assigned the task of ringing the doorbell. 'How grumpy do you reckon he is?' Oliver asked.

'On a scale of one to ten,' Millie explained, 'I wouldn't bring up someone's grumpiness unless it was a minimum seven.'

'Definite eight or above,' Georgia added.

Oliver turned to the door and reluctantly pressed the doorbell. Nothing happened for a good minute, except for him shuffling awkwardly from foot to foot. When the door eventually opened, the man on the other side wasn't what Millie would have expected. She'd pictured some sort of biker type: all leathers, tattoo sleeves and beard. Instead, there was a spindly man, with rimless glasses, and shorts that were borderline obscene. His skin was orangey-brown and laced with thick, hardened wrinkles, like a sodden old paper bag that had been thrown in a hedge just before a heatwave.

Keith peered over his glasses towards Oliver. 'You better not have brought me all the way down the stairs to try to sell me something. Last person who did that is tied to an anchor some-where at the bottom of the bay.'

He spoke with such determined tones that Millie was only ninety per cent sure he was joking.

'Catriona sent us,' Oliver replied quickly. 'We had a ques-tion and she said you were the expert.'

The man rocked on his heels, eyes narrow with suspicion. 'Did she now. What were her *exact* words?'

Millie tried to remember, not that it mattered because Oliver was going deeper with the brown-nosing.

'"Ask Keith. He's the expert."'

Keith thought on that a moment. 'That doesn't *sound* like something she'd say.' He started to close the door – but Millie got in just before he could.

'She called you a grumpy sod.'

The door reopened, first by a crack – and then all the way. Keith clapped his hands. 'That's more like it. And she's right: I *am* a grumpy sod. So what do you want?'

It was Georgia's turn – and she explained quickly about the matching tattoos neither of them had wanted, or got. Keith listened with barely a blink, as if this was the sort of thing he heard every day. It was only when Oliver showed him the daisy behind his ear that Keith's expression changed.

'You know what?' he said. 'I *have* seen one of those before...'

SEVEN

Oliver and Georgia exchanged a look that was part confusion, part relief.

'You've seen someone with a daisy on their ear?' Oliver asked.

That got a nod. 'Years ago. Probably twenty or more. Bloke had something like that on one ear – like yours – and he wanted a matching one on the other. He kept saying how it had to be exactly the same. I was trying to explain that the one he had was older and had faded. That the new one would be brighter and bolder but he wanted me to try to match the colour so they looked the same.'

'Did you do it?' Oliver asked.

That got a side eye. 'I'm a professional. What do you think?'

Oliver didn't risk a reply.

'Something about a relative,' Keith added. 'I figured he had a ma or grandma called Daisy. Something like that.'

Oliver had cowered into submission – and it was Georgia who risked Keith's grumpiness. 'I know it's a long shot, and that it was a long time ago,' she said, 'but do you have any idea who it might have been?'

Keith weighed her up with narrowing eyes and then started to nod. 'You don't forget a name like that. Was odd for anyone, especially a white guy.' A pause. 'Am I allowed to say that now? You can't get away with anything nowadays. You're not one of those woke snowflakes, are you?' He nodded at Georgia as Millie held back a roll of the eyes.

'I think you can say "white",' she replied.

'Dashrian,' Keith said, tapping his temple. 'Always stuck up here. I used to see him in the market. Dunno if he's still there. I've not been inside since they wrecked it all. Used to be a good place to buy records. Then the council got involved and took a bunch of money off the lottery. Tarted the place up. All bright lights and places selling coffee with stupid names. Can't stand it now. Dashrian used to work on the Stereophonics stall.'

There was a moment of confusion that even Keith recognised.

'The place that sells all the smoking gear.' He waved his hand up and down, like he was massaging a long cylinder, or, er... 'All that Stereophonics stuff.'

'H*ydro*ponics...?' Oliver asked.

That got another withering look. 'Same difference. Anyway, I haven't got time for this. You tell Catriona she's got some cheek.'

Keith slotted back behind the door and slammed it, leaving the three of them staring at where he had stood moments before.

'I think he's what you call "a character",' Millie said.

'I can think of another word,' Oliver added.

Georgia was checking her phone again. 'I've got to get to work,' she said. 'But I'm on the other side of the market, so we can walk through on the way.'

With that, she was off at a pace, her bag of bricks weighing her down on one side. Millie was almost at a jog to keep up as they retraced their steps again, before passing the tattoo shop, heading along two cobbled alleys, and then emerging in a court-yard, with a curved sign across the top of the entrance.

Millie felt a tingling sense of déjà vu as they passed under-neath. The sign was fresh and new, saying the market had been established in the 1930s. It was next to a plaque adding that a little under a million pounds had been donated by the National Lottery to fund a renovation.

Millie had a vague recollection of visiting with her parents when she was young. The sign had been crumbling then, with chipped, faded letters – and it had felt so tall. Millie remem-bered dim lights, the smell of fish, and feeling so small among the crush of people.

Now, as they continued into the covered area, the aisles were wide and the lights bright. There was an artisan coffee cart off to the side, with rows of syrups next to a menu board that, with the Italian names, was presumably what had enraged Keith so much.

Another stall was selling American candy, while the one next to it had hundreds of dreamcatchers pinned to various poles. Dinky wind-chimes were jangling into each other, creating an orchestra of annoyance.

It was a long way from the stinking fish market that Millie remembered – not that there was time to stop and look at any of it. Georgia bounded around a stall selling old video game consoles and cartridges, and continued along the aisle until she arrived breathlessly at the hydroponics stall. There were rows of bongs and various pipes, plus books and a handful of posters with slogans like, 'Yes Weed Can!'

A man was on a stool behind the counter, reading some-thing on his phone. Greying hair hung to his shoulders and there were a pair of piercings through his left eyebrow. His vest was tie-dye, with 'eat the rich' stencilled on the front. He looked up as Millie, Oliver and Georgia arrived, taking them in momentarily, before looking back to his phone.

Millie felt something prickle the back of her neck. She felt the man with the balaclava brushing past her, but, when she turned, he wasn't there. Nobody was. In the distance, the wind-chimes continued to tinkle.

'You just browsing?' the man asked, with the merest glance away from his phone. He had already made up his mind.

It was Georgia who replied: 'Are you Dashrian?' she asked.

The man didn't move at first but, when he looked up again, there was a lackadaisical sigh, as if he knew they were about to waste his time. 'Who?'

Georgia suddenly sounded unsure of herself, possibly because she was still trying to get her breath. 'Dashrian,' she repeated, somewhat unsteadily. 'I think that's what he's called...?' She turned to Millie and Oliver for reassurance and, as far as Millie could remember, Georgia had repeated the same name Keith had told them. The first part of the name sounded like hair dye, then shin, as in a part of the leg.

The man on the stool lowered his phone and sat up a little straighter. He was a good twenty years older than them, in his late fifties, and looked Georgia up and down in a way that made Millie shiver.

'I guess you mean Dash,' the man said. 'He died years ago. Why are you after him?'

His indifference had switched to what felt like an unhealthy interest in Georgia as he gazed across at her. Millie felt the hairs on her arms rise, as if something had tickled its way across her skin.

It was Oliver who answered.

'We're trying to find out something about a tattoo,' he said.

Before the man could object, Oliver was pushing aside his hair to show off the mark behind his ear. The stallholder dragged his gaze away from Georgia for long enough to take in Oliver's tattoo, which made him raise his eyebrows.

He pouted his bottom lip and made a popping noise. 'That's a strange one,' he said.

'Georgia's got one, too,' Oliver said.

'Georgia, huh...' The man switched his attention back to Georgia, who had slotted in at Millie's side. Millie could feel Georgia's hesitancy. 'Is yours in the same place?' he asked.

Oliver was mithering on obliviously. 'We heard Dashrian... Dash might have had a similar one,' he said.

'Who told you that?'

'The bloke who used to run the tattoo shop.'

That got a thoughtful-sounding *hrm*. 'I dunno what to tell you. Like I said, he died a while back. Years ago.'

His stare flickered to Georgia once more. It was time to leave but only the two women seemed to realise. Millie took a step away, guiding Georgia by her arm – but they'd barely moved when the man's attention returned.

'Don't you work at the caff out back?' he asked, talking to Georgia. 'I've seen you around, haven't I?'

Georgia was cornered and she knew it. 'Sometimes,' she said, hesitantly. 'Not always.'

'I'm Daniel,' the man said. 'Do you have a card, or something? A phone number? I can ask around about Dash and see if anyone knows anything? Most of the stallholders have been around for years...'

Before Georgia could give her number, or Oliver could jump in with anything stupid – like listing their full names, addresses, and inside leg measurements – Millie got in first. She asked if Daniel had a pen and then told him Guy's landline number.

'You can leave a message if nobody answers,' she added.

Daniel obviously knew it was a landline and pulled a face, much like Heather had the night before. Not that he could complain. He muttered something about letting them know if he heard anything – and then Georgia guided them through the warren of stalls until they emerged on the other side of the market. They were in a courtyard, with a series of tables and chairs littered around the edges. Like something from Rome or Madrid, but with an overflowing bin at the side.

'Thanks for that,' Georgia said, talking to Millie.

'It's my friend's landline,' Millie explained. 'He told me to give it anyone if I'm not comfortable giving my actual number.'

Oliver had a curious, confused, look about him but didn't say anything about Daniel. 'What do we do next?' he asked. It did feel like something of a dead end.

'I'm still waiting to hear back from my friend,' Millie said. 'He reckons something about the daisy rings a bell. He worked on the paper in Whitecliff for thirty-odd years. Forty. He knows a bit of everything and everyone.'

This time it was Georgia and Oliver who exchanged a look. Millie understood it. This was their dilemma, their bodies.

Georgia nodded towards the café a few paces away, that had rows of rainbow cupcakes in the window, ready to move on. 'Maybe it's better to let it go?' she said.

Oliver sighed. 'I was so sure we'd come up with something. Like we shared a cousin, or something. That we'd be related.'

It felt as if Georgia had already moved on. 'I'm already late,' she said, before looking to Millie. 'It was nice meeting you.'

EIGHT

The smoking shelter at the back of the nursing home had become more of a gossip corner in the years that Millie had been volunteering. Her friend, Jack, who worked full-time at the home, had first given up smoking, and then vaping. The covered area was still an escape, where Millie and Jack could sit and chat. Sometimes the subject was the home and its residents; every once in a while, it was something fundamental about their lives. More often than not, it was whatever they'd watched the night before. Occasionally, they even talked about their children.

'Guess where I was this morning?' Millie asked.

Jack was staring across the valley beneath the home, doing a poor job of disguising his tiredness. His blinks were long and the yawns were regular: 'Legoland?'

'Why would I be at Legoland?'

A shrug: 'You said to guess and I panicked.'

Millie snorted. 'I was at the Nemesis Café in Steeple's End. The one that does the rainbow cupcakes. I know someone that works there now.'

That got a low, appreciative '*Ooooh*' and then: 'Is that where all the muffins came from?' Jack poked a thumb towards the home behind them. 'I've never seen anyone with a hip replacement move as quickly as Elsie when she spotted that basket you brought in.'

'She did get a bit of a sprint on. I thought I was the only one who noticed.'

'You can't go bringing a basket of muffins into a place like this unannounced. You'll start a riot. These people hold grudges for the most trivial of reasons. People will blank the person who lives in the room next door because they sit in the wrong chair. Eating the last piece of shortbread is a declaration of war.'

Millie would have laughed, if Jack wasn't being serious. Because they were on the subject, she told him that she had witnessed a robbery the day before and that the muffins had been offered as some sort of thanks for sticking around.

Jack seemed part-bemused, part-concerned. He asked if she was all right and Millie was back to reflex answering that she was fine.

They sat together, staring silently across the valley for a minute or so. Maybe longer. Millie didn't mean to dwell, didn't want to. In the moments of silence, she felt the man in the balaclava brushing past her in slow motion.

'I saw a robbery when I was about fourteen or fifteen,' Jack said.

'You've never told me that.'

A shrug: 'I guess it never came up. I was in a petrol station, trying to buy ciggies, 'cos they'd serve you underage there. Then this bloke with a motorcycle helmet came in.'

'What did he do?'

Jack bit his lip. 'I can't really remember. I know he was tall and had all the leather gear on. I think there was a badge on the back of his jacket. He went to the counter and told the guy to empty the till. The bloke serving was only a few years older than me. Eighteen, or nineteen? He was blinking loads and went "sorry?" as if he hadn't heard what the guy said.'

'What happened then?'

Jack rubbed his eyes: 'That's where it's all fuzzy. I think he opened the till and handed over some notes. It would have been loads back then but I wonder if I really saw that part. There's a blank. On the way out, the guy in the helmet knocked over this display of books and maps. There was this really loud bang, which made me jump. I was over by the ice cream freezer with my friend, Alice. We both just sort of... stood there. Like it was happening to other people.'

They sat quietly for a while longer. Across the valley, past the houses, the sea was calm. A lone sailboat was drifting away from the shore. There were no clouds and, on days like these, it felt as if the water went on forever.

'I'm already forgetting parts of what happened,' Millie said. 'It was only yesterday but I can't remember if the guy with the balaclava was already in the shop, or if he came in after me. I know he *must* have come in after but it didn't stick. I keep thinking he might have been in the corner all along.' She paused and then added: 'Do you still think about it when you go into petrol stations?'

'I used to. It's all pay at the pump now, so I haven't been in one for years.' He tapped her knee. 'Are you sure you're OK?'

Millie didn't answer so quickly second time around: 'It's all very... *recent*. I had a moment this morning, at a market stall, where I felt something tingle the back of my neck. I thought... I thought there was someone there but there wasn't.'

Jack nodded with understanding. 'I used to nick things from shops,' he said, more quietly. 'Nothing big. I'd put CDs in my waistbelt, or magazines, or chocolate. That sort of stuff.'

'There's a bit of a difference between that and robbing a place with a knife.'

'You didn't mention a knife...'

Millie knew that was true and wondered why she'd mentioned one this time. Had the robber been carrying a knife? Had she *seen* a knife? Hadn't Heather said something about gunpoint?

'Someone told me phantom memories are common with this sort of thing,' Jack said. 'After Isaac had that allergic reaction at the Winter Wonderland, I couldn't quite remember how it all happened. I was trying to tell the nurses at the time – and then Rishi later – but it was all messy in my head.' He scratched his temple, as if to emphasise the point.

Millie had been at the Wonderland with Jack when his son, Isaac, had a reaction to a nut. He could have choked if not for a nurse with an EpiPen being in the area. Jack had later told her that he was struggling with being a father to his adopted son, and that he missed his old life, and the lack of responsibilities. He'd brought it up once and then never again. As if pretending it hadn't happened would mean it wasn't real.

Millie had never pushed. They didn't have that sort of friendship. They could confide anything, yet they didn't challenge each other. Perhaps that was why they were still friends?

More time passed. The ocean remained still.

Jack leant forward and sniggered to himself: 'How's your toast monster?'

Millie laughed. 'Working hard. There was a loaf of bread in the gift basket and he took that with him this morning. It's probably gone by now. He takes a toaster with him to work.'

'Are you joking?'

'Benefit of working by yourself, I guess.'

They sat watching the ocean for a while longer. The boat was further out to sea, more of a speck than anything identifiable.

'Can I say something?' Jack asked and, before waiting for a reply, he went for it anyway. 'It's just, whenever I ask about him, you always talk about something you watched together, or ate together. Or his work. You never talk about, well... you as a couple. Or whether you actually like him. It sounds like you're talking about a friend, or a brother, or...' He tailed off and then added a quiet: 'Sorry...'

Millie took a breath and continued staring at the boat, not that she could tell it was a boat any longer. It was a dot of black among a literal sea of blue.

He was right and she knew it. She'd known for a while, except nobody – including Luke – had ever bothered to say it out loud.

'Perhaps that's a good thing?' Millie said. 'Maybe a new relationship doesn't need to be explosive and instinctive?'

Perhaps there wasn't a proper answer? Millie didn't know whether she believed what she was saying. Whatever was going on with her and Luke felt like the right thing for the moment. Something she needed and, if Luke wasn't objecting, then what was the issue? Perhaps it was something he needed as well?

Either way, Jack didn't reply.

'Are you still coming out with Rish and me this weekend?' he asked. It was a welcome change of subject.

'Of course. Let's go to Steeple's End. We can visit the Nemesis Café. We've been talking about it for long enough.'

'That is a good idea. It's only up the coast but I can't remember the last time I went.'

'*Down* the coast,' Millie corrected.

'Up. Down. Whatever. Who decides these things?'

'Maps. Gravity.'

'You know north and south are human constructions.'

Millie snorted. 'Here we go...'

Jack laughed this time. 'I think Isaac got in my head the other night. He started asking about how we knew what was real and what was a dream – and then he wanted to know how this wasn't all one long dream.'

'Kids will do that to you. When Eric was younger, someone

told him about sharks and he was convinced he'd get eaten by one if he went anywhere near the beach. I kept saying we didn't get sharks here and he'd say: "But they can swim!"'

Jack was only half-listening as he swiped at his phone. When he looked up, there was something on his face.

'What?' Millie asked.

'Someone's been arrested for a robbery,' he said. 'It's on Facebook. Was yours at a corner shop?'

'Yes.'

'It says that police raided a unit at a storage place. Reckons they found the stolen cash...'

Millie had forgotten that'd she messaged the police officer with the details Luke had told her the night before. It felt odd that the robbery had happened barely twenty-four hours ago and now, suddenly, it was solved. She wondered who was under the balaclava.

'They got him,' Jack added enthusiastically. 'That's good, isn't it?'

Millie remembered the way the hairs had risen on the back of her neck earlier in the day. That flittering thought of the man in the balaclava brushing past. It felt too easy that it was all over.

'Yes,' she agreed. 'It's good.'

NINE

Millie knocked on Guy's front door and, when nobody answered, she tried the handle. She had a key, not that she particularly needed it. Guy never seemed to lock the cottage.

She found him in his office, which was more of a bomb site than usual. Newspapers were scattered across what appeared to be every surface – including Barry. The dog was laid on his side, with a paper over the top of him, like a tent. Not that he seemed remotely concerned.

Guy was typing, while squinting at the monitor. He glanced sideways to Millie and then focused back on the screen. 'I heard they arrested someone,' he said.

'When did you hear that?'

'This morning. One of my contacts sent me a tip. I was going to call you but was waiting until I heard about an actual charge. He's still being questioned at the moment.'

Millie was only partially surprised Guy didn't know the name, address and full criminal history of the person who'd been arrested. Then she figured he probably did.

She didn't want to think about the robbery too much.

'Have you heard the name Dashrian?' Millie asked.

Guy stopped what he was doing and turned towards her. 'That's a name I've not heard in a long time.'

'But you have heard it?'

That got a nod and a head scratch. 'Going back decades. I suppose you don't forget a name like that.'

Millie pictured Keith the tattooist telling them the same thing.

'You'd have been small,' Guy said. 'Maybe four or five. A really long time ago.' He gave her a smirk as Millie cleared a couple of papers so she could sit on the second chair. Barry twisted to glance at her and then went back to snoozing under his newspaper duvet. 'There was a commune just outside Steeple's End,' Guy added. 'This group living in the woods. I think they built a shack or two – plus there were tents. The locals were suspicious, obviously. You know what it's like. Anything out of the ordinary and the rumours start.'

Millie knew more than most about the speed at which innuendo flew around small towns. She'd lived it herself. She'd been the subject of it.

'We used to hear all sorts on the paper,' Guy continued. 'People would phone up and say it was a coven of witches, or that they were devil worshippers. Some would claim they heard chanting at night, or that their pet cats had gone missing. This was all very nineteen-eighties. Before your time – but there was a lot of talk about video nasties, satanic panic, and all that. Politicians would jump on it and the big tabloids would feed it.'

'What was really going on in the woods?'

A shake of the head: 'I don't know. Not for sure. There was never any proof anyone had done anything wrong. If they'd been sacrificing pets or worshipping the devil, you'd have thought someone might have got a picture or two. Anyway, Dashrian was the son of the man in charge of the commune.' A pause. 'Maybe that's the wrong phrase. The whole point of a commune is that nobody's in charge. His dad

was the one who set it up. The leader, I suppose. Whatever
you want to call it.'

'Do you remember his name?'

'Jaelryn. I doubt that was his original name but it was what
we knew him as. There were stories of young people running
away from Whitecliff and other towns, then ending up at the
commune. That's how I heard about them. A woman came to
our office and said her daughter had run off to live with the
devil-worshippers. The police wouldn't help her as her
daughter was eighteen and had gone by choice. She wanted us
to write a story anyway but there wasn't a lot to write.'

Millie thought about Eric and how she'd take it if he
suddenly disappeared to live with a mysterious group somewhere. She hadn't taken the current situation well – and that
was with him living across town with his dad. She could understand why a mother might go to a newspaper office as a last
resort, back when that *was* the last resort. Now, it would be
posts on social media.

'I talked to one of my colleagues in Steeple's End,' Guy
continued. 'This was at a time when every town had at least one
reporter. He'd had a couple of reports of young people heading
off to live in the woods with Jaelryn and the commune.'

'Did they have a name?' Millie asked.

'It was very self-important,' Guy replied. He clicked his
fingers, trying to spark the memory. 'Children of... Something. I
never met Jaelryn as the commune wasn't on my patch – but
that other journalist went to visit. He told me everyone there
insisted they were there of their accord. This was during the
Thatcher years, probably just after the Falklands. Jaelryn told
him they had checked out of society because they were against
consumerism and capitalism. Against nuclear weapons and war.
I wouldn't say it was a popular sentiment at the time – but it
wasn't *un*popular. There were always people handing out flyers
and arranging protests.'

Millie had the vaguest of memories about watching some cartoon at primary school about hiding under a desk if they got the call that a nuclear bomb was on the way. She can't have been older than five or six, and had been terrified that the Soviets would attack. Then another early memory was watching on television as people climbed on top of a graffiti-covered wall and started pulling out chunks of cement. Her dad had said it was a historic day as the Berlin Wall was coming down. She could stop having those nightmares about nuclear bombs because this meant it wouldn't happen.

For a moment, Millie was that little girl, looking for reassurance from her father. And then she was back in the present, remembering what had happened to him, and why.

Guy hadn't noticed her checking out and was still talking: '...talked to a couple of families and he spoke to Jaelryn. We ended up running the story with a joint byline in both papers. I'll have a copy of it somewhere.'

He angled around Millie to glance towards the hallway and the rest of the cottage. Stacks of newspapers lined every wall, in places all the way to the ceiling. That paper could be anywhere. Not a needle in a haystack but a needle in a needle shop, on a street made entirely of needles.

'You seem to remember it well...' Millie said.

Guy took a breath and for a second, a faraway look passed across him. She'd spent a moment drifting in the past and, now, so was he.

'Carol's brother joined,' he said quietly. Almost reluctantly.

Millie needed a few seconds to think it through. Guy's former wife's brother... which meant... 'Craig's dad?' Millie said. She thought of the other man who'd stood over her the day before. This time in Guy's garden, when he's been asking about money.

Guy nodded.

'Is Craig's dad still alive?' Millie asked.

'He was when I saw him last week.'

Millie paused a moment. Sometimes it felt as if she knew everything about Guy, other times nothing at all. 'Do you think he'll talk to me?' Millie paused and then corrected herself. 'To *us*?'

Guy glanced up to the clock above the giant map on the wall. 'Not at this time of day.'

'Why?'

'Nigel will be eight pints down and onto the whisky by now.'

Millie's 'it's not even four o'clock' got a raise of the eyebrows before Guy added: 'We'll try tomorrow, before the pubs open.'

'I can't do first thing,' Millie said. 'I got a call while I was on my way here. I have to go to the police station...'

TEN

DAY THREE

Millie was in a side room of the police station. There were a couple of battered chairs that had foam spilling from the sides, plus a table with a ripped copy of a farming magazine on top. It was like the waiting room of a dentist's office, if that nuclear bomb really had fallen.

A uniformed officer had led her inside and asked if she wanted anything to drink. 'The coffee from the machine's awful,' he said. 'But I can pop to the Costa if you don't mind waiting.'

'Am I going to be here long?' Millie asked.

That got a sideways glance to the door and what looked like a momentary panic that something had been said out of place.

'I'll get you something from the machine,' he said quickly, before hurrying from the room.

It was a different officer who returned with a milky coffee in a small plastic cup. She passed Millie the drink and then said it 'shouldn't be long' before disappearing.

It was another five minutes until the door went again. This time, Millie recognised the constable who entered. Lucy had been the one who'd interviewed her at the shop after the robbery.

'Sorry for the delay,' Lucy said, as she slotted onto the second of the chairs. 'I was in a meeting with my boss and couldn't get away.' She glanced to the coffee cup. 'Didn't someone offer to get you a proper one?'

'I didn't think I'd be here very long...'

'No, well...' There was a moment of ominous silence and then: 'First, I wanted to say thanks for your text about the key fob and the storage unit.'

'My boyfriend recognised it,' Millie replied.

'Someone on our team had already identified it as a fob for a storage unit but we were still searching for the right one when I got your tip. You saved us a few hours, and we appreciate it.'

The sentiment was welcome, although Millie didn't know why she'd had to drive out to the station to hear it.

'I heard there'd been an arrest...?' she said.

A nod. 'I can't confirm anything but I've seen the Facebook posts. There have been developments.'

It sounded particularly vague.

Something tickled the back of Millie's neck as she remembered the moment in the market when it felt as if someone was behind her. She wondered if it would happen again. Whether she'd ever be able to walk into a shop, or shopping area, and feel safe.

'Do people get released after this sort of thing?' she asked. 'Before court, I mean.'

'That depends on the situation,' Lucy replied. 'For something like this... probably.'

The details from the shop were already beginning to drift. Millie remembered that frozen sense of fear and confusion more than she did the actual incident. The robber had worn a balaclava and she wondered if she'd know who he was, even if she was standing next to him.

And then it was as if Lucy had read her mind.

'I know this is going to sound strange,' she said, 'but the reason I asked you here is that we'd like you to take part in an identity parade.'

Millie stumbled over a reply and then reached for her coffee as a distraction. It tasted like some sort of cross between bleach and gravy.

'But I didn't *see* him,' she said. 'Not properly. He was wearing a balaclava.'

Suddenly, Millie wondered whether the robber *had* covered his face after all. Had she seen him? Was it definitely a 'he'? She had never felt such uncertainty in the past.

'I realise the robber was covering *most* of his face,' Lucy said. 'But there might be something else that stuck. The eyes, for instance. The mouth. Sometimes it's surprising the things that people remember.'

Millie was clutching the coffee cup to her lips, even though she wasn't drinking. 'Do I have to be in a room with a group of people and then pick someone out?'

'No – that's all for TV. It's not been like that for years. Everything's done on a laptop. We show you a series of short videos. It's someone turning their head to the camera, which gives you a side view and then front-on. If anyone jumps out, you say – and that's that. You don't have to be in a room with anyone other than the officer who's setting up the software.' A pause. 'That's if it's working. The laptops round here are a million years old. I'm surprised they don't have us doing stuff on Etch-A-Sketches.'

She laughed, though Millie didn't join in. It still felt as if there wouldn't be a lot she could do to help. Almost two days on and she'd forgotten everything important about the robbery.

'Don't you have camera footage?' she asked.

'We do – but it's not enough to identify a suspect, except for a close estimate on height and weight.' Lucy glanced towards the door, leaving Millie to wonder if there was someone on the other side. Perhaps the 'boss', she had mentioned.

There was a sense that things had already been decided because, as Millie agreed, she was asked to wait a while longer – and then, after only a couple of minutes, another officer arrived, along with a laptop and a series of wires. Although technically a laptop, the keyboard was as thick as a bike tyre and the officer grunted like a weightlifter as he hefted the device onto a desk.

He introduced himself, although Millie immediately forgot his name, and then he started connecting cables from the computer to the wall. He chatted amiably as he worked, mainly about the weather and some new roundabout that had been installed at the end of his road. There might have been something about his council tax going up to pay for it.

Millie listened but took in none of it. Instead, she tried to focus on the man who'd brushed past her in the shop. He'd definitely been in the same aisle as her, hadn't he?

'... Are you OK?'

Millie realised the officer was talking to her as he gently touched her arm. She jumped and he apologised.

'You were miles away,' he added quickly.

The room felt brighter than it had and Millie wondered whether someone had been playing with a dimmer switch. Not that the officer noticed anything was wrong. He directed her towards the screen and said there would be ten short videos, with people turning to face the camera.

'If you recognise anyone, remember the number,' he instructed. 'You're supposed to watch all ten.'

With that, he stepped away and left her in front of the screen. It was as he'd said: a series of short videos which involved white men, with dark hair, starting sideways to the camera. After remaining in position for two or three seconds, they would turn to look directly down the lens.

Millie tried to pay attention, to look for the details. Some had brown eyes, others green. A couple had a day or two of stubble, while others were clean-shaven. Nobody jumped out – they were all the sort of bloke she'd pass in the street on any day, at any time. Unremarkable and normal.

The ninth face turned to look at her and it was as unrecognisable as the others. Millie felt something squeezing her insides as the screen went black, ready for the final face. She would surely recognise something in this person's eyes, or mouth, or...

He appeared side on, with short, slightly greying hair around his ears. There was the hint of a freckle or two on his pale cheeks – and then he turned to look at her and...

Nothing.

Millie had no idea who he was. If anything, he looked a little like the man who'd set up the equipment – but not really.

The screen went blank again and then the man began packing away the laptop as the door went. Lucy was back, face full of optimism and hope.

'How was it?' she asked, which wasn't what she was *really* asking.

'I didn't recognise anyone,' Millie replied.

Lucy's features didn't twitch. 'That's not a problem,' she said, breezily.

'Sorry,' Millie replied. 'Does this mean you'll have to let him go? That he might do it again...?'

The man with the cables was rattling around them and Lucy gave him a stare that seemed to get across her message better than any words. He mumbled something Millie didn't catch, and then disappeared, leaving them alone on the chairs.

'Have you talked to anyone about what happened?' Lucy asked.

'I told my boyfriend and my friend. I said not to pass it on and that—'

Lucy gently touched Millie's knee. 'I can get you a number for victim support, if you like...?'

The room was suddenly cold, as if a fan had been switched on that was pointing directly at Millie. She felt dimples rise on her arms.

'I'm all right,' Millie said, too quickly.

Lucy removed her hand and smiled kindly. 'It was a shocking thing to experience,' she said. 'Nobody should have to be in the middle of something like that.'

It was colder still. The fan had been turned up and Millie's clothes were no protection against the icy wind. She stood abruptly. 'I need to be somewhere else,' she said.

Lucy stood too but made no effort to stop Millie. 'You have my number,' she said. 'Call if you think of anything else.'

ELEVEN

The wind whipped along Whitecliff promenade, sending flurries of sand and dust *tick-tick-ticking* into the curved wall that protected the front from storm waves.

Millie pulled her jacket tighter and blinked away the thoughts of how she'd shivered in the police station. She had something else that needed to be done.

Guy was standing next to a lamp post, scanning a newspaper as he somehow held onto it, despite the hurricane. He must be one of the last people who still bought an *actual* paper each day, let alone read it.

As Millie reached his side, he lowered the page and turned to her. 'How were the police?' he asked.

'They wanted me to do a line-up.'

'How did that go?'

'I didn't recognise anyone – probably because the robber was wearing a balaclava.'

She thought Guy might share her thought that the entire thing was ridiculous, but, if he did, he kept it to himself. Instead, he nodded across the road towards The Bucket And Spade. Whitecliff's biggest pub had been named many things across the years. Millie had first been served underage in there when it was The Black Swan. Since then it had gone through at least six names, before reaching its current title. She doubted this new title would last too long.

It was a few minutes until eleven, just short of opening time, and there were already a handful of people milling around outside the doors. Millie had done a little bar work when she'd been younger – and they'd had their regulars, too. It was the same faces, more or less every day. It was easy to be derisive – but they were the ones who gave little, if any, trouble. That was a lot more than could be said for those who only came in for a few pints on the weekend.

Guy tucked the paper into his satchel and then mumbled something Millie didn't catch. A moment later and she was hurrying after him as he bounded across the road. They slotted in alongside the man at the back of the queue. His face was blotchy and red; his once-dark hair had departed to leave a balding crown.

'I thought I might find you here, Nigel,' Guy said.

The man turned to take him in, before glancing to Millie. 'What do you want?' he asked, talking to Guy.

Before anyone could respond, there was a clunk as the doors opened. The line began to edge forward – and Nigel wasn't waiting for anyone. He dragged his left leg as he shuffled after the man in front of him. There was no hesitation in his attempt to escape the wind.

Nigel slotted around a pair of booths and headed for a table close to the fruit machines. For someone with what looked like a dodgy leg, he moved quickly enough that Millie had to rush to keep up.

He plonked himself down and then turned to take in Guy. 'You getting 'em in?' he asked.

Guy patted his pockets. 'What you having?'

'The usual.'

'What's that?'

'They'll know. Tell 'em it's for Nige.'

Guy turned to Millie. 'Do you want a coffee, or...?'

'Whatever you're having.'

Guy headed off towards the bar as Millie took the seat across from Craig's father. He paid her no attention and was instead staring across towards the bar as his hand trembled. There was little to no resemblance between Nigel and Craig. Father was short, balding and overweight. Son was tall with feathery ginger hair.

Millie wondered whether she should say something, perhaps explain who she was – except even that would sound awkward. She was Guy's god-daughter but also his friend and colleague. Except she also had her own business and he was twice her age, which made it difficult to explain.

In any case, Nigel remained silent, except for the way his fingers stuttered a beat on the tabletop. He didn't speak until Guy arrived back with a tray.

'You took your time,' he said.

Guy didn't respond. He placed a pint of bitter in front of Nigel, next to a whisky shot. Then he laid down a teapot and cup for himself, before offering Millie a mug of coffee.

'I know tea isn't your thing,' he said.

Millie didn't tell him that the coffee at the police station still had her stomach grumbling. She whispered a thanks instead and, by the time she looked up, Nigel had already downed the whisky. He let out a loud, satisfied gasp, before reaching for the pint.

'What do you want?' he asked, talking to Guy.

'Craig's been round a few times recently.'

'Still asking for money?'

Nigel gulped a large mouthful of the brown liquid as Guy waited.

'What do you think? Guy replied.

'He came to me, too,' Nigel said, with a laugh. 'I dunno why he thinks I have anything.'

Another mouthful was gulped and the pint was already a third gone.

'Did he tell you why he and Hayley split up?' Nigel asked.

'No.'

'He was at it behind her back with some girl who works at the Londis. Hayley kicked him out – and then it turned out the girl had a boyfriend, so she didn't want to know. Ended up back in Whitecliff, didn't he?'

Millie almost laughed. It was such a small-town story that she felt as if she'd heard the same thing a dozen times before.

'I don't know where he's sleeping nowadays,' Nigel added, in between having another sup of his pint. 'Probably stringing along some other girl. Only turns up when he wants something, that one.' He cradled his drink and then squinted towards Guy. 'Speaking of someone who only turns up when they want something...'

Guy didn't take the bait. He removed the teabag from the pot and put it on the saucer, before pouring himself a cup. There was a delicacy about it, especially compared to the guarded pint across the table.

'You've got me there,' he said eventually. 'Millie and I were wondering if you could tell us about your time in Steeple's End...'

He left that hanging, with no introduction of who Millie was, or why she was there. It was the first time he'd mentioned her name.

Nigel stiffened at the mention of Steeple's End. He sat up straighter and downed another large mouthful of his pint. There was only a third left.

'Who's asking?' Nigel replied.

'Me,' Guy said. 'And Millie. She's my god-daughter.'

Nigel eyed her for the first time properly. 'You're that news-reader's girl, aintcha?'

Millie reached for her own drink and used the mug as a shield, for the second time in a little over an hour. 'Right.'

'I heard you bumped him off for the money. And your mum.'

The comment used to sting but it barely registered now. 'Lots of people have heard that.'

'It true?'

The coffee was still hot but Millie drank anyway, taking her time. She wasn't used to being asked so directly – but she'd learned how to deal with strangers.

'If it *is* true, do you think I'd tell a stranger in a pub?'

She looked Nigel dead in the eye and he cracked immediately into a laugh.

'Fair enough.' He winked at Guy. 'She's a live one.'

Millie wasn't sure what he meant by that.

Nigel downed the rest of his drink and then nodded to the bar. 'Same again,' he said, talking to Millie this time.

It felt like a challenge, not that Millie flinched.

Guy said he was fine, so Millie headed to the empty bar, where she ordered another usual 'for Nige'. By the time she was carrying the pair of drinks back to the table, Guy and Nigel were at the quiz machine. Guy slipped a two-pound coin into the slot as Nigel pressed the buttons with the familiarity of someone who'd done the same thing many times. He accepted the drinks without a word, downed the shot, and then plonked the bitter into the holder at the side of the machine.

'What do you wanna know?' he asked, talking to Guy.

'Whatever you have to say. What was it like, for one?'

Nigel gave no indication he'd heard anything Guy had said, despite them standing next to each other. The general knowledge questions on the machine began and Nigel started pressing buttons. Despite what seemed like a clear case of alcoholism,

Nigel's knowledge was wide and deep. He answered questions almost immediately about horse racing, a Eurovision winner, the Latvian President, Dickens, the third person to walk on the moon, and the writer of *All The Young Dudes*. As he hovered over a pop question, Millie chipped in to say that Girlstar was the answer and, though Nigel pressed the button, he didn't acknowledge her help.

He'd already won back the two pounds, plus more, when he reached a question about a Maori translation. Millie had no idea and, for the first time, Nigel glanced towards Guy. 'Any idea?'

'Sorry.'

With no help coming from Millie, Nigel stabbed one of the buttons and then waited as the machine paused and then flashed red, to say he was wrong.

He sighed and slumped. 'Knew I should've cashed out earlier,' he said, talking to himself. 'This machine cheats, everyone in here knows it.'

That went without reply as he dragged his leg back to the table. Somehow, his pint was half gone. Millie and Guy slotted back into their spots as Nigel continued as if none of the previous ten minutes had happened.

'There was a girl,' he said. 'Craig would've been four or five and at that pain-in-the-arse stage. His mum and I never got on at the best of times and then I met this bird at the bookies. She said it was her last day and that she was off to live in the woods. Somehow, I got talked into it and, next thing I know, I'm a Child Of Enlightenment.'

It had been a whirlwind few sentences and Millie needed a moment to take it all in. It was hard to miss the similarities between Nigel and his son. The cheating and moving on to the next woman.

Guy was seemingly used to this sort of disjointedness. 'I knew there was a name,' he said. 'The Children of Enlightenment. That's it.'

'What do you want to know?' Nigel asked.

'As much as you remember,' Guy replied. 'We're interested.'

'Why? It was years ago.' A pause and then a cloud darkened Nigel's features. 'They've not started up again, have they?'

'Not as far as I know...'

For a moment, and for the first time since Millie had met him, Nigel was flustered. He reached for his pint, downed a third in one go, and then plonked it back on the table. 'Right. Of course. It all burned down.'

Millie looked between the men. 'There was a fire?'

Guy was studiously failing to acknowledge her, which meant he'd wanted her to find out from Nigel instead of him.

'At the commune,' Guy said. 'This was two or three years after my colleague visited Jaelryn. It had been up and running for a while by then, to the point that locals had sort of forgotten about it. All those complaints had stopped coming in. It was one of those things that existed – and then there was a fire that burned down the cabins and the tents and...' He tailed off, as if he expected Nigel to pick up the story. When he didn't, Guy added: 'Nigel had left by then. From what I gather, quite a few had. It was a much smaller group by the time of the fire...'

Nigel finished his drink and then hunched forward, the glass clasped tight in his hands. 'I know it was in all the papers and on the news. I saw the pictures of the smoke and the scorched ground. I guess, at the back of my mind, I wondered if he survived it...'

'Jaelryn?' Guy asked.

'Who else?' Nigel turned to Millie. 'Do you know who that is?'

'Not really.'

'Lucky. I was twenty-four, twenty-five when I went out there. I can't even remember the girl's name. The one from the bookies. It was this place where we were supposed to grow our own food and raise our own animals. There'd be no stress and we wouldn't need money. A way out of regular life. I was so sick of Craig and the missus that I was well up for it all. I didn't realise it would be so much work.' He sat up straighter and made a point of cricking his back as he gazed longingly at the empty glass. 'I still can't sit up all the way,' he said.

'What did you do?' Guy asked.

'Everyone had a job. It was all divided, so the women would cook, clean, and look after the kids; while the men would do the lifting and building. Then we'd clear the stones and the bushes. We'd plant the fruits and the vegetables. Same thing, day after day. It was knackering.'

Nigel's hand was trembling again as he let out a long sigh.

'Why did you stay?' Millie asked.

Nigel stretched for his empty glass and then pressed back into his chair. The hint was as obvious as it got and this time Guy was on his feet, promising to be right back.

There was a general hum of the pub and the faint dinging of someone on a fruit machine. Something clinked from the kitchen beyond but Millie felt alone with Nigel as he sucked in his cheeks and licked his lips.

'I was just joking about your parents,' he said.

Millie didn't know how to reply. She told him it was fine, even though she wasn't sure it was.

'Do you know we're brothers-in-law?' Nigel asked, nodding towards the bar.

'That's what he told me.'

'Carol was my older sister,' he said. 'She was the black sheep of the family... or the white one, I suppose. She settled down properly. All the rest of us...' Nigel tailed off, and it felt as if the thought itself had drifted and gone.

Before he could add anything else, Guy reappeared – this time with two pints of bitter and no shots. If there was an issue, Nigel didn't let it show as he supped the foam from both drinks. It acted like some sort of reset, as if wiping out the previous couple of minutes. They were instantly back to Millie's question.

'I sometimes wondered myself why I stayed,' Nigel said. 'Everything felt normal at the time. An escape from the missus, and Craig. The work felt like it had a purpose. I was never into the church, or God, or anything like that – but there was this sort of... *spiritual* thing.' He waved a hand in a circle, trying to conjure the word that didn't come. 'Jaelryn was in charge, not that he'd have ever said that. We were all supposed to be equal. He'd give a talk each night about being at one with the earth, or something like that. We had a community and it felt... *real.*'

Millie could almost feel it, too. There were times when she craved that sense of family. Where she missed what she once had with Alex and Eric – not because she wanted Alex back, not because they hadn't had problems, but because there was a connection.

'What happened to the girl from the bookies?' Millie asked.

That got a small shrug. 'That was the other thing about being there...'

He hadn't said it, yet Millie knew what Nigel meant. Every time mysterious cults or communes appeared, there always seemed to be younger women, with an older man in charge – and that meant one thing in the end.

'She was with Jaelryn for a bit,' Nigel said. 'Like all the women. It was supposed to be an honour. When he moved onto the next person, the women were sort of... passed back to the rest of us.' He glanced up, catching Millie's eye for what felt like the first time. 'I know that sounds bad but I don't know how else to put it.'

'Does that mean you and her got back together...?'

A shake of the head. 'I hurt my back and couldn't work. The rule was that if you couldn't work, you couldn't stay – so I left. Went back to a normal life, I guess. Then I heard about the fire a while later. They found bodies but I don't think many were identified. They didn't know if it was some sort of pact, or an accident. There was always an open fire in camp at night, so I think it might've spread to one of the cabins, or the bases where we had tents. Everything was wooden.'

Millie wondered if this was why Guy had kept back the information about the fire. It wasn't his story to tell but, perhaps, it was Nigel's.

'If Jaelryn told people to burn down the cabins, what would they have done?' Millie asked.

'Probably what he said.'

'What if there were people inside?'

He thought for a little longer on that. 'Probably still what he said. Maybe.'

'What if *he* was inside?'

A shrug. 'We did what he told us to.'

Nigel was holding on to one of the two pint glasses, though he hadn't had a drink in a while.

They had talked around the issue a lot, with Guy taking a back seat – but Millie finally remembered they were there because Oliver and Georgia had matching tattoos. And because Keith the tattooist had told them he'd seen one other person with the same.

'Who's Dashrian?' Millie asked.

Nigel's eyes narrowed. 'How do you know that name?'

'It came up.'

There was a long pause, in which Nigel huffed noisily through his nostrils. 'Jaelryn's son. Would've been twenty or twenty-one when I was there, so a bit younger than me. He was trouble. I grew up in a rough school, so I knew the type. He could get away with anything – so he did.'

From somewhere behind, there was the sound of a glass hitting the ground and then a cheer. Nobody at the table moved.

'What did he get away with?' Millie asked.

'The only violence I ever saw at that place was from him. He'd slap the women if he thought they weren't working hard enough. Some of the men, too. Usually the larger ones because he wanted them to know he was in charge, even if they were bigger and stronger than him.' A pause. 'It's because of him I did my back. There was this big stone we were moving and he was supposed to be helping. He let it drop but I was still holding one end, so it fell and something went pop.'

Millie still couldn't understand why people stayed if that's how it was like – and then he answered that for her.

'Dashrian wasn't around that much. I don't know where he went but there'd be days at a time when he wasn't there. Those were the days it felt as if we were building something. You'd sleep under the stars, you'd eat food you'd grown yourself, you'd talk and you'd listen. It was so... peaceful.'

Millie guessed it wasn't quite so peaceful for the woman Nigel had left behind in the outside world to look after a young, tearaway Craig.

'Dashrian was about control and fear. With his dad, with Jaelryn, he liked the women. But he could never run a place like that with only women, because he needed the men to do the manual work. I didn't realise that until I'd left. It was all about community and spirituality while I was there. Dashrian would show up when he was hungry, or horny. He'd never cross his dad but he didn't mind messing with the rest of us.'

'I heard he was dead,' Millie said.

Nigel examined her for a moment, before gulping down the rest of his third pint. 'He wasn't in the fire and I heard he was in Steeple's End for a while. Then I heard he'd died and thought it was good riddance.'

Guy had been quiet for a long time. When he spoke, there was a croak to his voice. 'I remember the thing about the daisy now,' he said. 'That was your symbol, wasn't it? The Children of Enlightenment.'

And then, suddenly, it all felt inevitable. Nigel half turned and bent his ear, so that Millie and Guy had a view of the smudged, faded, daisy that was tattooed on the back.

'That's what Jaelryn always said,' Nigel replied. 'He reckoned the daisy was a symbol of purity.'

TWELVE

It was Eric who answered the door as Millie leant on the frame, waiting for Oliver. Her son had his guitar in his hand, ready to go, and was already out the door when Millie stopped him.

'How was practice?' she asked.

She got a mumbled 'good', before he started to ask what was for tea.

'Can you wait in the car?' Millie asked. 'I need a word with Oliver.'

She told Eric the vehicle was unlocked, that the iPad was on his car seat, and then promised almighty trouble if he beeped the horn at her. That got a grin which offered little assurance he'd taken it seriously. She watched as he headed away from the flat, across the car park, and into the passenger seat.

Oliver was a little inside the hall. 'Do you want to come in?' he asked.

'I should probably stay here and keep an eye on him.' Millie glanced back to the car, half-expecting her son to be in the driver's seat. 'How's he getting on?' Millie asked.

'We had a good day today. I've got this double-necked guitar that I let the kids use if they hit certain targets. Eric seemed really into things today, so he was allowed five minutes at the end.'

'What was he like with that?'

That got a slim smile: 'It's more of a visual thing at this stage. He played a couple of notes but was more interested in what he looked like in front of a mirror.'

That didn't *sound* like the Eric Millie knew. He was confident around adults but never much of a show-off. Perhaps playing the guitar would change that?

'Have you spoken to Georgia?' Millie asked.

'Not really since yesterday. Only to ask how she was.'

'How was she?'

'Busy with her daughter. This seemed like a mystery we'd never figure out.'

Millie let that sit for a moment. She wondered if, perhaps, it was a mystery that *should* be left to drift. Perhaps it was better not to know?

Except that wasn't her call. She thought of the woods, a fire. Casual assaults dressed up as spirituality.

'I discovered some things...' she said.

'About...?'

'Dashrian's dad used to run a commune in the woods at the back of Steeple's End.'

Oliver pressed into the door frame and stared. 'Commune?'

'They tried to be separate from society – but it also sounds a bit like a... *cult*.'

Millie whispered the final word. It felt as if it wasn't for her to judge. 'Commune' literally had part of community within it. 'Cult' was far more sinister.

'Cult...?' Oliver repeated that, too.

'It wasn't only Dashrian who had that tattoo,' Millie continued. 'I found another old member – someone who's alive – and they have the same tattoo, in the same place, as you and Georgia. He said everyone at the commune had it. They were called the Children of Enlightenment and the daisy was supposed to mean purity. That they were pure from society.'

Oliver was repeating words to himself: 'daisy', 'purity'. It was a lot to take in.

Perhaps she should have gone inside, if only so he had a place to sit down.

Millie glanced back to the car, where Eric was in his booster seat, swiping the iPad screen.

'I'm going to send you a couple of photos,' Millie said. 'First is of the other guy's tattoo. Second is a news article my friend found. There was a fire at the commune and people died.'

Millie went through her phone and sent the promised pictures across as Oliver poked his own device and started to read.

At least seven bodies have been found at the site of a controversial cult, following a fire in the woods outside Steeple's End.

Police say the blaze started overnight on Friday at the spot where the so-called Children of Enlightenment had set up camp.

Detective Chief Inspector Frank Grayson said: 'There is currently no indication of the cause of the inferno, although members of the camp are widely known to keep a fire going during winter months.

'I'd like to thank members of the fire brigade for their work and can report the fire is now out. We are currently trying to identify bodies, as we continue to search the remains of the site in case there is anyone unaccounted for.'

Locals have previously reported incidents of devil-worship and witchcraft at the cult, although DCI Grayson insisted there was 'little evidence' to support such claims.

Previous appeals to the council and the police to shut down the site have proved unsuccessful. Mike Evans, leader of Steeple's End council, last year indicated it was unclear whether the group had broken any laws.

He said: 'After numerous visits to the site, and consultation with our lawyers, it seems likely these people are acting within the law.'

Alan Archer, who lives on Barnacre Road, around a mile from the camp, said: 'This has been coming for years. My neighbour lost her cat to these people and nothing's ever done about it. We've reported the chants and the rituals; the fires and the spells. I've seen them sacrificing animals with my own eyes – but the police, the council, all of them, turn a blind eye.'

Millie watched Oliver as he read. She expected she'd had a similar look of horror and confusion on her own face after Guy had managed to dig out the correct paper.

'*Bodies*...?' Oliver said. 'How come I've never heard of this?'

'We're about the same age,' Millie said. 'I was maybe three or four and I've not heard of it. All I remember is being in the woods one time and Mum told me not to run off because the witch cult would get me.'

'It says they sacrificed animals...?'

'One guy said that,' Millie replied. 'My friend knew the journalist who wrote that article and reckons the police would have known if any of that was true.'

Oliver swiped between the two photos, back to the one of Nigel's tattoo. 'Why would I have this? Especially if I was only two or three when this all burned down?'

Millie almost didn't want to answer. There was an obvious explanation, though it wasn't for her to say. 'You're going to have to ask your mum...'

That got a gulp. 'Someone's going to have to tell Georgia.'

It was true – but it was also changing the subject.

'She can't ask her parents,' Millie reminded him, although she suspected he knew.

Oliver was biting his lip. 'I, uh... lied about the Center Parcs thing. She's not on holiday. That's the problem. She pretty much never goes out. I don't know the name but it's a medical thing. She gets her shopping delivered and she'll sometimes let Roger, her second husband, drive her places, if they *really* need to go.' He nodded inside his flat. 'Sometimes here – but not much further. She can drive but I don't think she's actually driven herself anywhere in years. Since Dad died, she only feels safe at home. It's not easy to bring up something that's going to make her anxious...' He rubbed his ear and then ran a hand through his hair.

Millie took a moment to check the car, where Eric was still tapping away on the iPad.

'I'm going to have to take a run-up at it,' Oliver said with a sigh. 'I'll go and see her tomorrow...' He bounced on his heels, geeing himself up, before repeating 'tomorrow' to himself.

Millie knew what was coming a moment before it did.

'Do you want to come along? My girlfriend's away all week and I can't really ask Georgia. You seem to know a lot more about all this than anyone else...'

Millie understood *why* he was asking. Nobody wanted complicated conversations with their parents, especially by themselves.

'I can't ask her for you,' she replied.

'I know. I'm not saying that. It's just... if you were maybe there, it might help...' He was squirming and then the reason became clear. 'She used to love your dad when he was reading the news. He'd always do that spot on a Friday, where he'd be off reporting on a rugby team, so he'd be in the pack. Or there'd be some sort of lifeboat fundraiser, so he'd be out in the boat...'

Those segments had become a part of Millie's life growing up. Every Friday, in the local 'And Finally...' section, her dad would end up bungee jumping, or trying lawn bowls, or darts. Else he'd be mixed up with the touring Irish dancers, or on set with some period drama that was being filmed in the area. A lot of his fame seemed to come from those moments. The big news stories came and went – it was the nonsense that stuck in people's heads.

'I'll tell her we're friends,' Oliver added. 'She'll be so happy to meet you and will want to talk about your dad. That'll make her relax a bit and then I can... ask about the tattoo...'

Millie could just about stomach people bringing up her dad – but full-on conversations about either of her parents were out of her comfort zone, down the road, on a plane, and then halfway around the globe before she could even think about such a thing.

'I know I shouldn't ask...' Oliver finished.

Millie was too far in and she knew it. 'Text me the address and a time,' she said.

Oliver let out a loud sigh of relief. 'Whenever works for you. At least we won't have to check whether she's in.'

He laughed humourlessly and then tailed off.

'I'm going to be in Steeple's End in the morning,' Millie said. 'Shall I talk to Georgia?' She wondered if this was another thing that Oliver wanted her to do. That was the problem with involving herself in other people's business.

'I'll call her in a bit and say I'm going to ask Mum tomorrow. I promised I'd keep her up to date. I can send her the photos you sent me.'

They were back at a dead end, at least for the present.

Oliver gulped, gave another 'thank you', and said he'd see her the next day.

Millie drifted back to her car and slotted into the driver's seat, before telling Eric to put down the iPad.

'Did you enjoy the double-necked guitar?' she asked.

A grin wrapped itself around his face. 'Can I get one?'

'Maybe when you've mastered a regular guitar.'

He nodded enthusiastically and then: 'Am I going back to Alex and Rachel's?'

Millie considered correcting him to say 'Dad', but – as with every other time in the recent past – she didn't bother. Calling his dad by his first name had started as a rebellion because Rachel wanted him to call her 'Mum'. Now, it was entrenched.

'After you've eaten,' Millie replied.

'Why doesn't Rachel pick me up anymore?'

Millie didn't particularly know the answer to that. She'd vowed to be available to her son whenever she possibly could. 'Don't you like me picking you up?' Millie asked.

Eric thought on that for a second, except he wasn't *actually* thinking about that. When he replied, it was casual and throwaway: 'It's probably because Rachel's having a baby.'

THIRTEEN

Millie almost asked her son to repeat himself. 'She's... what?'

Eric was scratching a scab on his knuckle that Millie hadn't noticed before. 'Rachel's having a baby,' he said.

Millie had no idea. She didn't know if Eric was being casual because he assumed she knew, or because his youth meant he had little concept of how big a thing it was.

It probably shouldn't have been a surprise. Alex and Rachel were newlyweds – and had no obligation to tell her what was going on outside of Millie's time with Eric.

'I'm hungry,' Eric said, with the same casualness as he'd announced the pregnancy. 'What's for tea?'

Millie drove her son back to her house and cooked him fish fingers, while he played Xbox in the living room. He'd somehow managed to persuade his parents he needed a console in each of their houses. As she cooked, Millie clasped her phone, wanting to call Jack to tell him that Rachel was pregnant. Or Luke. Or Nicola. Or all of them. She could start a group WhatsApp labelled 'IMPORTANT' and let them all know in one go. Would it be a boy, or a girl? Alex always wanted a girl, though that had seemingly been forgotten when Eric came along.

Time passed, though Millie's thoughts barely flickered – and then she was on her old doorstep, ringing the bell and waiting.

Rachel answered the door and Eric bundled past her with a mumbled 'hi'. It was rare Millie ever got out of the car when dropping him off, which left Rachel now tapping her foot, eyebrow raised.

'Did you want something?' she said.

Millie risked the briefest of glances across Rachel's midriff. She wasn't yet showing, although, silently to herself, Millie was delighted that the other woman might soon be fat.

I hope she's enormous, Millie found herself thinking. *I hope there's a twelve-pounder in there and the doctors won't let her have a Caesarean.*

'Is Alex in?' Millie asked, remembering why she was at the door.

'Why'd you want him?'

'For a quick chat.'

'About what?'

'About things to do with our son.'

'Like what?'

Millie sighed. They were destined to do this forever and ever, amen. 'Can you just get him?' she asked.

For a moment, it felt as if Rachel would simply close the door. Then she rolled her eyes, let out a sighed 'Whatever', and disappeared inside.

A minute or so later, Alex appeared. He was still in his work suit, the top two or three shirt buttons undone.

'Can we have a talk?' Millie asked. 'A proper one? Maybe go for a walk?' She stepped aside, letting Alex see the road at the end of his drive, as if he wouldn't understand otherwise. His eyes were slightly glassy, stare unfocused, and she wondered if he'd been drinking. Or, more to the point, how much he'd already had.

'Talk about what?' he asked huskily.

'That's kind of the point of talking. We go for a walk and I tell you what I want to talk about.'

'Can't you just say it here?'

She wasn't in sight but Millie could sense Rachel's presence somewhere along the hall.

Millie remained quiet but took a half-step back until Alex huffed an annoyed 'fine'. He sighed his way back into the house, leaving Millie waiting, and then re-emerged moments later with a jacket. He first tried putting it on upside-down and then wrestled angrily with it, muttering under his breath, until he finally managed to get it on correctly.

Millie would have laughed in the old days. They both would've – but they were long past that.

They didn't need to discuss a route. They'd bought the house together as a place to raise a family and both knew the area. Millie led them away from the old house that *she* chose, onto her old road, in the safe area, in the catchment of the best primary school, that *she* wanted.

Alex had his hands buried in his pockets as he kept a steady quarter-pace ahead.

'Eric told me that Rachel's pregnant,' Millie said.

Alex didn't miss a step. 'I was going to tell you,' he said. 'I was planning on it but, um...' He blew a raspberry with his lips. 'Is this what you want to talk about? We could've done this at the house.'

Millie let it go for a moment. This was the big moment. The sentence she'd rehearsed in her head over and over. 'I want you to reconsider custody of Eric,' she said.

It sounded anticlimactic now it was out, except, this time, Alex *did* miss a pace. He was suddenly a quarter-step behind as Millie led them into the alley that would bring them out by the Co-op and pizza shop.

Alex quickened his stride to get back alongside her: 'I

thought we'd been through this,' he said. They had, of course. Always his rules, his decisions. Millie played nice as her solicitor had said it was the only way of changing things in the future.

'Things will be different in nine months, or eight months, or whenever.'

'It's not like it's one child in, one child out.'

'I'm picking up Eric from school and clubs two or three times a week anyway – then feeding him and dropping him back. You're only dropping him off at school and then putting him to bed.'

They were at the end of the alley and Alex jumped ahead. He leaned on the barrier that prevented motorcyclists from using the alleys as cut-throughs, then stretched his legs to block the exit. On the other side of the road, the lights of the Pizza Palace blazed.

'You wanted access,' he said.

Millie considered barging past. It was a small power play of his but she didn't doubt it was deliberate. Perhaps it was because the wind was behind him but Millie could smell the hint of alcohol on her ex-husband's breath.

'I *still* want access,' Millie said, calmly. 'But you're using me as a free taxi and now I know it's because Rachel's pregnant.'

Alex started to reply but she held up a hand and stopped him.

'I don't mind – but if I'm going to be picking up Eric and feeding him more days than not, plus taking him every other weekend – and you're going to be busy with a new baby – I hoped you'd reconsider things...?'

Millie was breathless after getting it all out. She'd been silently running it through her head when driving across town. Now it was in the open.

Alex swayed a little on the barrier and then stood upright. 'Why would I do that?'

There was something spiteful in the 'I'. As if he'd be doing *her* a favour, instead of thinking of their son.

Millie was ready: 'He doesn't even call you "Dad".'

Alex rocked on his heels, eyes narrow. His fists clenched and for a moment, only a moment, Millie felt vulnerable.

There was movement over the road, someone heading into the pizza shop and she turned deliberately to look. Letting Alex know they weren't alone. Perhaps that was why she wanted to walk in the first place?

'What's that got to do with anything?' Alex said, though his lips barely moved.

'Eric told me he'd rather live with me – and I *know* he's said the same to you. I've been waiting almost six months for you to acknowledge it.'

That got a dismissive shake of the head: 'You told him to say that.'

'I didn't – and, even if I did, it wouldn't mean anything unless that's what he wanted. And you know, deep down, that's what he wants.' A pause. 'He wants to live with me. Why can't you just let him?'

Alex didn't reply.

Over the road, someone who looked barely old enough to pass a driving test was levering a pizza box into a compartment on the back of a moped. Millie knew he had to be at least sixteen, maybe seventeen, but he shared the same dreamy, rather-be-somewhere-else airiness that Eric had when he wanted to be on his Xbox.

It wouldn't be long, a blink, and Eric would be a teenager. Then doing his exams. Then maybe looking to go to university, or taking a gap year feeding chimpanzees somewhere. Or, perhaps, simply locking himself in his room with his Xbox.

She could miss it all.

'Is this to spite me?' Millie asked.

The reply was instant: 'Not everything's about you.'

'I'm not saying it is – but I'm asking if *this* is about me.'

Alex took a breath but didn't answer. In a way, that was the answer.

He scratched his head and then angled around Millie, back into the alley. 'Rachel will be worried,' he said.

'*Worried?* You've been out the house five minutes and we're barely off your street.'

Alex wasn't waiting. 'See you around,' he said.

'Will you think about it?'

Millie's ex-husband had already tucked his hands back into his pockets as he bounded back the way they'd come. Moments later he was gone, leaving her question hanging and unanswered.

FOURTEEN

DAY FOUR

Isaac was up on Rishi's shoulders, being paraded around the streets of Steeple's End like a conquering king. The tide was in, lapping at the steps that led up to the High Street, while groups of children sat on the edge with cheap fishing nets dangling in the water.

'We never come here,' Rishi said as they walked. Millie and Jack were a pace behind. 'It's so close but we never come.'

It was at least the third time he'd said it.

'We have our own beach,' Jack replied, which was exactly the sort of defensive thing someone from Whitecliff might say. Who cared if there was a beach along the coast, when your own hometown had a perfectly decent one?

Rishi wasn't from Whitecliff and seemed oblivious to the pointless rivalry. 'This is nice, though, isn't it?' he continued. 'I like how it's smaller, with its own cove. The boats are so pretty.'

It was true that the Steeple's End harbour was tidier and smaller than the one at Whitecliff. This was pure fishing territory, while the one along the coast had boats that were falling apart and had seemingly been moored since Thatcher was in power.

'We never go to *our* harbour,' Jack said, grumpily, which left Millie smiling inwardly and biting her lip.

'That's because it's not this nice,' Rishi replied.

'It also doesn't smell of fish.'

Rishi didn't appear to notice the passive aggression. He lifted Isaac down from his shoulders and took out his phone. 'I read there's a soft play round here somewhere...'

He began swiping the screen as Millie and Jack waited. Isaac was six and far more interested in the boys sitting with their legs dangling in the ocean, their fishing nets at their side.

'You need to book,' Rishi said, disappointed. 'I should've read it properly yesterday.'

'You're probably too old anyway,' Millie replied.

She expected a laugh but nothing came. It appeared nobody was listening, so she tried something else.

'Why don't we go to the Nemesis Café?' she asked. 'It's on the other side of the market...'

She hadn't specifically suggested Steeple's End as a reason to see Georgia again, but the tattoo thing had been nagging on her mind.

'What if there are nuts in their recipes?' Rishi asked.

There was an exchange of glances between Rishi and Jack, something unsaid.

'How about I go with Jack and order something?' Millie suggested. 'You can hang around here and let Isaac watch the boats – and then we can eat on the seafront?'

Isaac had already taken a step towards the boys with the nets, before Rishi reached and took his son's hand.

'Good idea,' Rishi said. 'I'll check the menu online and text you what I want. Just make sure whatever you get hasn't been in contact with any nuts. Make sure you ask. If I were you, I'd—'

'We'll sort it,' Jack said. He nudged Millie's arm and then set off in the wrong direction.

Millie hesitated for a moment, wondering if she should tell

him, before following and figuring they'd have to go the long way round.

'This is what it's like *every day*,' Jack said, the moment they were out of earshot. 'He's paranoid about being anywhere indoors when he's not in charge. Sometimes *outdoors*. We were at a car boot sale the other week and he made us walk in single file along the middle of the lanes.'

Millie didn't reply instantly. She knew Jack well enough to let him fume to himself for a moment. As he continued towards the docks at the end of the seafront, Millie nudged his arm in the way he'd done to her. She nodded them into a side street and then started to lead them back towards the market.

'Isn't it better to be careful?' she asked.

'Are you saying I wasn't?'

It felt as if he'd be waiting for that, perhaps even wanting it.

'Of course I'm not,' Millie replied. 'You didn't even know Isaac had an allergy back then.'

They walked wordlessly for a minute or two as Millie guided them from one cobbled lane into another until they emerged back onto the main street, close to where they'd left Rishi.

'Sorry,' Jack said, quietly. 'Sometimes, it feels like Rish is having a go. That, if I'd paid better attention at the Wonderland, none of this would have happened.'

'None of this is your fault,' Millie replied. 'You didn't know nuts would send him into shock back then. All you can do is try to be vigilant now.'

'I am – but Rish is off the scale. He didn't want to come today. I had to talk him into it and he only agreed when Isaac heard us going on about boats.'

It felt like a moment to listen, so Millie did precisely that. As she directed them through the streets, Jack vented about his partner's overprotectiveness – and how Isaac wasn't going to have any sort of social life if things went much further.

She tried to change the subject as they entered the indoor market, nodding to the plaque about lottery funding and asking if he'd ever been before it was done up. There wasn't much of a reply, though Millie felt her neck prickling as they continued through the aisles. The space was tight with people and it was impossible to ignore as shoppers brushed past. Millie tried to focus on the route and ignore how vulnerable she felt. She had no idea whether the robber had been released after she had failed to identify him. He could be beside her. Behind her.

Millie felt eyes on her... and then looked up to realise there were. She and Jack were at the front of the hydroponics stall – and Daniel was watching from behind the counter.

'Hello, again,' he said, the starer from the other day.

Millie mumbled a 'hi' and gave a narrow smile as she weaved around the back of a woman with a pushchair. She wondered if he'd tried calling Guy's landline since she gave him the number.

At least that was something to focus on.

Millie breathed out a long gasp as they reached the far end of the market. She edged into a gap between a pair of women and then almost threw herself into the sunshine on the other side.

If Jack noticed how uncomfortable she'd been, then he said nothing – although that might have been because they were in front of the café window. Rows of intricate, bright cupcakes were in a line, along with a rack of buns iced with bright, white icing.

Jack was staring – but so was Millie. It was only when the 'Fancy seeing you here' came that she realised Georgia was halfway through clearing the nearest table.

'I told my friends they had to visit,' Millie said, before looking to Jack. 'Did Rish text you his order?'

'I got something.'

'Do you want to go in and order for everyone? I'll have whatever you're having... plus an iced bun.'

Jack eyed Georgia for a moment and then took the hint as he disappeared into the café.

Georgia added a stack of crusty coffee mugs to her tray and then balanced it as she spoke: 'Oliver called last night. We talked for an hour and a half. I couldn't believe it: a cult! I tried googling them but there's almost nothing online. He sent me the pictures you gave him. He says he's going to ask his mum later, so I guess she's back from Center Parcs?'

Millie stacked a pair of saucers onto each other as a way of not answering. Georgia offered a 'thank you' and then finished piling up her tray. She glanced inside, possibly checking to see where her boss was, and then continued.

'He said you're going to be there because his mum was a fan of your dad...?'

'I figured it might help.'

Georgia risked another glance towards the inside of the café and then sank onto the chair. Millie sat on the one next to it.

'I don't understand any of this cult stuff,' Georgia said. 'My mum and dad definitely weren't involved. They were in the *actual* church. I went to Sunday school every week until I was about twelve. They had been going for years. Dad was one of the elders. There's no way they were Children of Enlightenment on the side.'

Millie had no answer for that. It felt as if running away to join a commune in the woods was something that would have been noticed.

Georgia was scratching her ear as she nodded towards the inside of the café. 'Was that your boyfriend?' she asked. 'Or husband?'

'Just friend.'

'Oh... sorry. I thought, um...' She tailed off and then: 'I do need to get back. It was good to see you. I hope you enjoy your lunch.'

Georgia lifted the last of the cutlery onto her tray and then balanced it on her elbow with the sort of precision that should probably be an Olympic event. She somehow managed to grab an empty jug from a different table – and then nudge open the door with her hip, before disappearing inside.

Wait staff were *seriously* underrated. They could perform impressive gymnastic feats, while balancing a metric ton of delicate crockery, all while smiling with feigned sympathy at a person who was spitting fury because there wasn't enough milk in their tea.

Millie remained in the chair until Jack emerged from the café with a couple of paper bags, one of which he handed to Millie. 'Did you remember my iced bun?' she asked, sticking to the priorities.

He dug into his bag and pulled out a small box, which he opened to reveal a pair of perfectly iced buns.

'I can't believe you're cheating on Rish like this,' Millie said.

Jack grinned and, for the first time since they'd arrived in Steeple's End, it was genuine. He took out his cake and then slid the box across the table to Millie.

'I won't tell if you don't tell.'

Millie waited until Jack was chewing and then: 'I asked Alex for full custody of Eric last night.'

Jack immediately began coughing. He patted his chest as his eyes flared, until he managed to get down the mouthful. He reached into his bag, pulled out a bottle of Pepsi and gulped.

'You did that on purpose,' he said.

'Did what?' Millie replied.

Jack patted his chest once more and then licked his fingers. 'What did Alex say?'

'No.'

'Did you expect anything else?'

Jack took another bite of his bun and Millie waited until he'd started chewing.

'Rachel's pregnant.'

He immediately lurched and began coughing again. He patted his chest hard and then swallowed down the bite with more of the Pepsi.

'*Pregnant?*'

'That's what Eric said. Alex reckoned he was planning to tell me... but I guess he'd have waited until she actually had it.'

Millie risked a bite of her own bun. There were currants baked into the dough and the royal icing melted in her mouth. She was suddenly nine or ten again, scoffing a similar bun at the Whitecliff Carnival as her mum used a stinking wipe to scratch the skin from her face in an attempt to clean her up.

'And you think they might give you custody because they'll have one of their own...?'

Jack sounded sceptical.

'I don't know,' Millie replied. 'Maybe.'

Jack pressed back in the chair and paused before taking a bite of his cake. 'You're not going to spring something else on me, are you?'

Millie grinned and Jack risked it. This time, she let him chew in peace. She could see him thinking.

'You know it'll never happen,' Jack said. 'He'll keep custody out of spite. It doesn't matter if he's miserable, or if two children are too much. It won't make a difference. They'll never let you win.'

'It's not about winning,' Millie replied.

'Maybe not for you...'

Jack was halfway through his bun and Millie chewed thoughtfully on hers. She knew Jack was right. It wasn't about custody, or Eric. It never had been. Alex had cheated on her with a man, even though he didn't know that she knew. It seemed so quaint that she wanted to protect their son, so hadn't confronted him. Then, while struggling with the knowledge of that, she had fallen into her own affair, which had been revealed in a horribly public way. Eric certainly hadn't been protected then. And now Alex was remarried, to another woman, and living in some sort of domestic bliss: real, or otherwise.

They finished their cakes and then Millie led them back to the front, this time avoiding the indoor market.

Rishi was waiting on a bench, a couple of metres from the boys with the fishing nets. Although they were a few years older than Isaac, they had seemingly taken him as one of their own. His shoes were on the path behind as he sat with his feet in the water, a net in his hand, the widest of grins on his face.

Millie and Jack slotted onto the bench next to Rishi, who acknowledged them with a smile of his own.

'Everyone's so friendly here,' he said, nodding to the boys. 'They noticed him watching, so invited him over.'

'Has anyone caught anything?' Jack asked, sounding needlessly grouchy.

'Don't be such a grump,' Rishi replied.

'I was only asking.'

'It's not about the catching.'

'What is it about, then?'

That got a sigh and a roll of the eyes.

Rishi picked up the bag Jack handed him and glanced inside. 'Are you sure there are no nuts in here?' he asked.

'I ordered ten packets of dry-roasted peanuts to go, so I don't know.'

The two men glared at one another and, when Jack said nothing more, Rishi pulled out a sandwich and separated the bread to sort through the contents.

Millie could sense Jack trying to catch her eye, so she ignored him, and instead started on her own sandwich. She hadn't expected tuna, and didn't particularly want it – but she had told Jack to get her whatever he was having, so it was hard to argue.

Rishi gave Isaac his food, which the boy immediately shared with one of his new friends.

The three adults sat together on the bench, with Millie in the middle in more sense than one. There was an angry silence around her, which left Millie staring across the water towards a couple who were struggling to get themselves onto a pair of paddleboards. The man had the balance of a one-legged drunken reveller as an earthquake raged. Every time he mounted the board, he immediately toppled into the water with a splash. The fact his girlfriend or wife was openly mocking him didn't help his mood as he banged the surface with his fist and tried again.

'I think that man's watching you,' Jack said. It sounded as if he was trying to speak without moving his lips.

Millie had no idea what he was on about, or whether he was talking to her or Rishi.

'Where?' she asked.

'By the post box.'

Millie angled herself slightly to take in the spot at the edge of the water, where a man was leaning on the scuffed red box, staring directly at them. He waved – and there was no doubt it was at her – especially when he beckoned her across.

'Do you know him?' Jack asked.

'Unfortunately,' Millie replied, as she brushed down her lap. 'I'll be right back.'

FIFTEEN

'We should clear the air,' Craig said, as Millie approached. He only stopped leaning when she was upon him – and then he tapped the corners of his mouth. 'You have something there,' he said.

Millie brushed away what was probably icing. 'How long have you been watching me?' she asked.

'Not long. I was putting something in the post box and then turned and noticed you there.'

Millie wasn't sure if she believed him, or why she was bothered – other than that she still wasn't happy that Craig had turned up at her door on Christmas Day, claiming to be Guy's son. She wondered if he lived in Steeple's End, although she wasn't interested enough to ask.

'I dunno what Guy's told you about me,' Craig said. He let it hang, as if expecting Millie to fill the gap, which she didn't. When it was clear she wasn't going to reply, he continued. 'I can guess. It's about me taking advantage of Aunt Carol, isn't it?'

'Did you?'

Craig turned to take in the bay: him on one side of the post box, Millie on the other. Across the water, the man who'd been struggling with the paddleboard was finally standing. He swept his oar into the water and started drifting after his partner.

'My dad was a joke,' Craig said – and, from what Millie had seen and heard from Nigel, she could only agree. 'He was always walking out on Mum,' he added. 'Even when he was home, he was boozed up. So, yes, I went to stay with my aunt sometimes. She said I was welcome any time, and they always had plenty of room.'

Millie wasn't sure what to say, or why he was telling her – but she could feel an empathy she didn't expect. If someone like Nigel could dump his family and run off to join a cult in the woods, why *wouldn't* his son crave something close to family?

'Guy was always a slave to his job,' Craig said.

'He still is.'

'He'll never stop. On the day he dies, he'll be chasing a story, or trying to figure out how his phone works. You know it's true.'

Millie had only known Guy properly for a year and a half but she doubted he'd had a day off in that time. Evenings, weekends and holidays were spent writing, researching, checking and exploring. And indulging her, of course. The only other thing in his life was the dog.

'Aunt Carol was lonely,' Craig continued. 'There was a time when she was talking about training as a vet but she gave up any hope of a career because Guy expected her to be a housewife, like some nineteen-fifties woman in an apron. He wanted food on the table. For the house to be cleaned while he was out.'

It stung. Guy had never struck Millie as particularly old-fashioned, or the sort who believed women had their place. From the conversations they'd had, he was progressive as anyone she knew... except that didn't mean he'd always been like that.

'I bet he didn't tell you that,' Craig said.

'Why would I believe you?' Millie asked.

'Why would I lie?'

'You lied to me about him being your dad...'

Craig was quiet for a moment, probably considering how best to reply.

Across the path, Isaac was still sitting on the edge of the water with the other boys. He was waggling his fishing net up and down, eagerly chatting to his new friends. A little past him, Jack was trying to catch her eye. Wanting to make sure she was OK and likely wondering to whom she was talking.

'My business went under during the recession and I messed up a couple of relationships,' Craig said. 'Aunt Carol offered me money a few times but it was *offered* as a way to help. I've made mistakes but so has everyone. Then Guy found out and accused me of stealing. Said he knew people in the police and that he'd be having a word, things like that. So I got out of town. What would you have done?'

Millie didn't answer. It still didn't feel like the Guy she knew, and yet could anyone *really* be known and understood in only eighteen months? And maybe it *did* sound a bit like him. He did know a lot of people and undoubtedly knew higher-ups in the police.

'It sounds like you think we talk about you a lot,' Millie replied. It was cold and she knew it.

'Because you wouldn't be the first person he's poisoned against me.'

'What's that supposed to mean?'

'He told my ex-wife I was paying child support to someone else.'

Across the bay, the man on the paddleboard was back in the water. His partner was sitting, straddling her board as she tried to drag him towards his.

'I can't work out if I'm meant to feel sorry for you,' Millie replied.

'It's not like I'm proud of it – but it was none of his business.

It's always the same stuff with him. Says I'm a leech, that I mess everything up. That I only ever come home when I want something. He was always trying to turn Aunt Carol against me, just because he never wanted kids – but she was happy to have me around.'

Millie didn't reply, didn't know how. Did it change anything if it was all true? She wasn't sure. Except, perhaps it was a reminder that she'd let down her guard recently. She'd been too trusting. There was still the fact that she'd been betrayed by the person sitting on the bench not far away – and she had said nothing about it. Pretended she didn't know.

Her other friend, perhaps her *best* friend, Nicola, had also betrayed her. They acted like it hadn't happened. It was a pattern.

'He's not who you think he is,' Craig said.

'You told me he was your dad and I know he's not.'

'I wondered how you'd react, that's all.'

'I'll assume that's what you're doing now.'

Craig was shaking his head furiously. 'Nah, if you only knew the things he's done.'

'Like what?'

'I shouldn't say. I know you look up to him, like he's *your* dad.'

That stung, too – probably because it was true.

'You don't know anything,' Millie said defensively. She took a step away from the post box, back towards the bench on which Rishi and Jack were still sitting. She felt Craig reach for her, though she was too far away.

'Look,' he said, 'I didn't plan to run into you. I'm here for the day, catching up on some old business. I saw you out and figured it was a chance to talk one-on-one. I just thought you should know a few things.'

Millie rolled her eyes. Regardless of what he claimed his

intentions to be, Millie knew some old-fashioned stirring when she saw it. She had an eight-year-old son, after all.

'Do you want anything specific?' Millie replied.

'I was actually on my way to find lunch somewhere.' A shrug. 'Do you know anywhere good?'

Millie didn't know why she bothered but she told him about the Nemesis Café anyway. He said he'd check it out – and then Millie returned to the bench as Craig disappeared into the network of side streets. She scanned the water, looking for the man on the paddleboard, except he was back on dry land, fighting with what looked like the zip of his wetsuit.

'I was trying to get your attention,' Jack said.

Millie was still stewing over what Craig had told her, wondering how much – if any – of it was true. 'I didn't notice,' she replied dismissively.

Except Jack wasn't making small talk or fishing for details. 'Someone's been charged with your robbery,' he said excitedly. 'The person they arrested the other day. I just saw it on Facebook. I guess they got their man…'

SIXTEEN

Oliver knocked on his mum's front door, before unlocking it and letting himself in anyway. 'It's me,' he called, as he held open the door for Millie to enter.

An 'in here, love' echoed back, and Oliver directed Millie through a side door, into a cramped living room. It wouldn't have been so poky if it wasn't for the fact a showroom's worth of furniture had somehow been crammed in. There were two sofas and three armchairs, a coffee table, magazine rack, dining table, six chairs, an empty birdcage, at least four uplighter lamps, two electric heaters, and the smallest television Millie had seen in at least two decades. She had to squeeze around a drinks cabinet to get into the room, and then hovered awkwardly on a small patch of feathery carpet in between the coffee table and one of the chairs. It was an obstacle course.

Oliver said hello to his mum and then turned. 'Millie, this is my mum, Linda. Mum, this is David Westlake's daughter, Millie. Remember him? From the news?'

Oliver's mum was in one of the armchairs, with a cross-stitch hoop on her lap. She had to be in her seventies, yet squealed like someone a fraction of her age.

'I used to *love* your dad,' she said, as she clapped her hands together. She turned to Oliver. 'You didn't tell me you were bringing a guest.'

'I wanted it to be a surprise.'

Millie wasn't sure she approved of being anyone's surprise – but it was a bit late now.

'I met your dad once,' Linda said. 'I used to work as a cook at the community centre and he opened the playground. Such a nice man.' She looked to her son. 'I used to tell you that whenever he came on, didn't I?'

Oliver nodded to acknowledge the point – and Millie did what she always did in such situations. There seemed little point in stealing other people's memories to say what he was like away from the public eye, so she smiled and nodded.

'It was *awful* what happened to him and your mum. I can't *think* what could've led them to do that. I was telling our Oliver that it must've been an accident. Something like that. There's no way they would've killed themselves. Why would they?'

There was more gentle nodding and mumbled semi-agreement from Millie. What else was she supposed to say?

'I don't think we'll ever know what happened,' Millie offered, which felt like the best compromise. Bland and non-committal.

Linda said they should sit, and it wasn't as if they didn't have a choice. Millie ended up on one sofa by herself, as Oliver took one of the armchairs. Everything was so compact, their knees were touching.

'I heard you'd been in a robbery,' Oliver's mum said. Millie could sense Oliver squirming and wondered how much else he'd been telling his mother. Despite the events of the past few days, she didn't really know him. 'It's awful out there, isn't it,' she continued. 'Muggings. All the street crime they're always going on about. You never know when someone's got a knife, or a gun. Didn't used to be like that.'

'It's not that dangerous, Mum,' Oliver said.

'You should read the papers. It's full of it.'

'That's because they don't report all the normal things that happen. If ten thousand people have a perfectly normal day, they're not writing about that. They write about the one thing that stands out.'

That got a dismissive *pfft* and it felt as if that particular conversation had been had many times before.

Linda placed the cross-stitch hoop on the arm of her chair and turned to Millie. 'Do you want something to eat, love? What do you like? I've got some cauliflower in.'

'Nobody likes cauliflower, Mum.'

'I wasn't asking you.'

'I'm not hungry,' Millie said.

'You sure? Roger pickles his own onions, so I could do something with that...?'

Millie remembered that Roger was Linda's second husband, Oliver's stepdad, though she had no interest in what he did with his, ahem, onions.

'I ate not long ago,' Millie said, not that Linda appeared to hear. She had heaved herself up and was already off towards the door at the back of the room.

'Tell you what,' she said. 'I'll put some sardines under the grill.'

Before Millie could protest, the woman had hobbled out of the living room and, presumably, into the kitchen.

'You've got to let her do her thing,' Oliver said. 'When I was a kid, all my friends would want to come over because Mum would insist on feeding them. They'd eat here, then go home and have a second tea.'

'Cauliflower?' Millie replied. 'Pickled onions? *Sardines?* What sort of meals were you eating?'

'Bad ones.'

Millie laughed at that. 'I didn't realise you'd been telling her about me...'

'I haven't... not really. It was an accident. We were on the phone and she was on her usual rant about everything being dangerous – you just heard a bit of it. I accidentally said that a friend of mine had witnessed a robbery. That made it worse.'

There was a bump from somewhere near the back of the room and then the patio doors slid open. A man stomped his shoes outside and then took them off as he entered the living room with them in his hands. He was almost out the other side when he realised Oliver and Millie were camouflaged in among the clutter of furniture. He jumped a little, blinked, and then straightened as if to pretend it hadn't happened.

'I didn't know you were coming round,' he said, talking to Oliver. Millie assumed it was Roger, the aforementioned onion-pickler. The man nodded towards the yard behind. 'Just been checking my potatoes,' he added. 'How's work?'

Stepfather and -son made small talk about Oliver's job and Roger's vegetable garden. Neither particularly seemed interested in what the other was up to, but there was a forced polite-ness that made it feel as if neither of them had too much in common.

Oliver nodded towards the kitchen. His tone was a whisper: 'How's she been?'

A shrug, and Roger lowered his own voice: 'The same. Still trying to get her to talk to the doctor about it all. Trying to get her to stop reading the news. She hears about some burglary in London and thinks we're at risk here. She had me out of bed at three o'clock the other night because she was convinced the patio door was unlocked. Then there was a car-jacking on *Corrie* the other night and she told me I should lock the doors when I drive, just in case. It never ends...'

He finished with an exasperated sigh and a glance towards

the kitchen. It was a conversation Millie had never heard, and yet the faces and tone of the two men made it feel as if she'd experienced it many times over.

Roger held up a muddy hand. 'I need to clean up. If you're gone by the time I'm back down, then it was good seeing you.' He gave a slim smile to Millie, muttered a 'nice meeting you', even though they hadn't been introduced, and then headed through one of the doors that led off the living room. There was a *stomp-stomp-stomp* of him going up the stairs, and then a woody creak of floorboards above.

Oliver sat quietly and Millie understood why he'd lied about his mum being on some jolly at Center Parcs. Why he'd wanted Millie to come to the house. He was going to have to ask his mum about the Children of Enlightenment, and his tattoo. It wouldn't have been easy at the best of times, let alone when she was a frightened hermit.

It was a few minutes until Linda limped back into the room, with two plates of sardines on toast. Millie tried to bat hers away under the pretence of having just eaten but the older woman was having none of it. A couple of lap trays were rustled up from the mounds of furniture and, before Millie knew what was happening, she was somehow being force-fed a meal she didn't want, and didn't particularly like.

Linda was back in her chair, cross-stitch in hand, when Oliver cleared his throat and risked a sideways glance to Millie.

'I have to ask you something,' he said.

Linda was pushing a needle through her canvas and gave a breezy 'uh-huh...?'

'I found a tattoo behind my ear. A flower, or a daisy. Something like that...'

Millie watched as the needle paused for the briefest of moments on its way through. 'When'd you have that done?' she asked.

Oliver put down the lap tray on the nearest table. 'I *found* it,

Mum. I never had it done. It must've been there a long time. I was wondering if you ever noticed it?'

Linda continued working but it felt conspicuous and unnatural. Nobody would try to ignore such an oddity.

'A tattoo?' It was as if she'd never heard the word. 'You know how I feel about that sort of thing. And piercings. I don't understand it myself. You see people with rings through their noses and eyebrows and you wonder where it'll all end.' Without missing a beat, she looked up to Millie. 'I bet your dad didn't have anything like that, did he? I wish he was still on the telly. The woman they have now talks too quickly. I can't understand a word she says. I'm always saying—'

'Do you know anything about the Children of Enlightenment?'

Linda had been halfway through her assessment of the current newsreader's performance – but she froze mid-word, the needle mid-poke. It was impossible not to notice the shift, as if the patio door really had been left open.

And then, as instantaneously as it had arrived, it passed.

'The what?' she said.

'The Children of Enlightenment.'

'Is that a TV show, or something? I told you, I don't watch that sort of stuff.'

Oliver waited patiently. He had a bite of his toast and Millie did the same. The fish was salty, the butter slathered on the bread like cement on a brick.

'It was some sort of cult thing from years back,' Oliver said. 'The people in it had the same tattoo I do. It's a little flower on the back of your ear. Somewhere you wouldn't know to look.'

Linda continued working her cross-stitch as if nobody had spoken.

A good thirty seconds passed until Oliver added: 'I was wondering if you knew anything about it?'

'About what?'

'About the Children of Enlightenment. They were in Steeple's End, so maybe you knew someone who was a member, or—'

'Of course not.'

It was too quick a reply, too care-free.

'It's just—'

'Oliver, I told you I don't know anything about it.' Linda slammed down the hoop into her lap. 'Why are you asking?'

'I told you: because I have some sort of tattoo behind my ear that I didn't know was there.'

That got an annoyed huff. 'It's probably a freckle or a birthmark. I think you always had it.'

Oliver fully moved the food away and leaned in, trying to get his mother to look at him. 'It's not, Mum. I asked a tattoo artist and she said it's definitely a tattoo. Someone *branded* me.'

Linda's fingers were twitching, even though she hadn't picked up the cross-stitch. 'Why are you telling me? If you choose to do something like that to your body, it's up to you. You know my opinion on the matter.'

Oliver started to say something more but his mum pushed herself up and swept her cross-stitch to the side. The sound of creaking pipes echoed from above.

'I should check on Roger,' she said, as she headed for the door.

'Mum—'

Linda ignored her son as she closed the door behind her. Moments later, the stairs creaked – and then the floorboards above. Oliver was staring into nothingness and then wide-eyed his way around to Millie.

'She's never like that,' he said.

'Do you mind if I say something?' Millie replied. She got an open-mouthed shake of the head, so she added: 'It's just... she definitely knew what the Children of Enlightenment was.'

Oliver stared, dead-eyed, mouth open. Like a contestant on a quiz show, who didn't know the answer. 'I know,' he whispered.

SEVENTEEN

It was starting to get dark when Millie's doorbell sounded. Eric was at his dad's, Luke had his own plans, Nicola was in Spain, she'd seen Jack and Rishi that morning, and she had no clients bringing dogs in her diary for that evening.

There wasn't anyone else who might visit.

Millie moved through the house, switching on the light in the hall, and leaving the chain clipped to the door as she cracked it open.

A woman was on the other side, her arms folded across the front of her jacket. She was somewhere in her twenties, slim and angular. Millie had no idea who she was.

'Are you Millie Westlake?' the woman said.

'Who's asking?'

'Why'd you tell the police it was Nick?'

She was pointing, though her tone was more frustration than anger.

Millie started to close the door. 'I think you've got the wrong person.'

'You were in that shop, weren't you? The one that got robbed...?'

Millie stopped and levered the door back to the end of its chain. 'How do you know that?'

'It's on Facebook,' she spoke as if explaining that water was wet.

'What do you mean?'

'There was a post about someone being charged for the robbery. People were commenting to say you were the witness. That you'd been there when it happened. I mean, everyone knows who you are. It's Whitecliff, innit...'

Again. Water was wet.

Whitecliff *was* a small town – and Millie had reached notoriety in recent years. People knew who she was and where she lived. Even if Heather, Chris, or someone directly involved at the shop hadn't mentioned her name, someone in the police could've done. If not them, Jack or Oliver might have told someone. Everything always seemed to end up on Facebook sooner or later, even if it was some old person posting 'how do i do a google?'

'Who's Nick?' Millie asked.

'They charged him for the robbery. You told the police it was him and now he's going to prison.'

'I didn't tell them anything,' Millie replied. 'I don't know who Nick is. The robber was wearing a balaclava. I told the police that. They know I couldn't identify anyone.'

The woman sank lower on her heels, deflating with a huff like a balloon going down. 'Oh...'

Millie unclipped the chain and opened the door a little wider. 'What's your name?'

'Karen.'

She said it almost reluctantly, which perhaps wasn't a surprise. The non-lunatics named Karen had been given a rough ride since that name had been given over to describe the privileged.

'Who's Nick to you?' Millie asked.

'He's my, um... friend.'

Millie almost laughed. The lingering pause before 'friend' said much more than the actual word.

'His solicitor said there was a line-up,' Karen added.

'There was – but I didn't identify anyone.' Millie didn't know if she was supposed to keep that to herself, though nobody had told her differently. 'Maybe there was more than one line-up?' she added. 'Someone else might've done one.'

Karen pinched her nose and twisted slightly on the spot. 'Can I come in? I wouldn't normally ask. I thought you were the one who'd ID'd him. I don't know what's going on now.'

It was against her better judgement but Millie held open the door and allowed Karen to duck inside. She led her along the hall, into the kitchen, where she ended up asking if the other woman wanted tea. It was a reflex. Then she was filling the kettle and digging out teabags from the cupboard. Of the friends who visited, it was only Nicola who drank tea.

Karen was on one of the chairs around the kitchen table, her head low.

'The robbery wasn't Nick,' she said, as Millie slotted in across from her.

'How do you know?'

'What time did the robbery happen?'

Millie ran back over the events of the day. She hadn't been looking at a clock but she'd picked up Eric from Oliver's and had stopped at the shop on the way back.

'About five o'clock,' Millie said. 'Maybe a little earlier.'

'Nick was with me between four and six.'

'Ah.' A pause. Two hours of friendship and all that. 'Did you tell the police that?'

Karen let out a low breath and stared off towards the window at the back of the kitchen, and the garden beyond. She didn't reply but she didn't need to. Millie knew. She'd probably known with that pause before the word 'friend'.

'Which of you is married?' she asked.

The reply didn't come for a while. The kettle fizzed and bubbled, so Millie filled a pair of mugs and made herself a tea, even though she knew she wouldn't drink it all. Karen asked for 'loads' of milk, so Millie sloshed it in and then passed across the mug.

'My husband would kill me,' she said quietly – and there was something about the way her voice cracked that made Millie think it might not be a simple turn of phrase. 'He works on the oil rigs. Four weeks on, four off. He doesn't know about Nick... obviously.'

Millie wasn't sure what to say. It explained why Karen didn't want to go to the police.

'I've seen you around a few times,' Karen added, moving on.

'What do you mean?'

Karen had a sip of her tea. 'I work at the Co-op,' she said. 'The one by the Pizza Palace. My brother works in the Ladbrokes next door. You used to come in all the time, then I didn't see you for ages.'

'I split up with my husband,' Millie said.

'I know.' Karen looked up and the gentlest of grins creased her lips. 'You used to come in and buy cheese on Thursday nights. I was on the tills every week and it would always be at half-seven when I saw you.'

Millie had forgotten that until Karen brought it up, even though she didn't remember her face. 'My husband... *ex*-husband, used to work late on Thursdays,' Millie said. 'I'd end up eating loads of cheese and then buying a new one to make it look like I hadn't...'

Karen laughed: 'Everyone needs a bit of cheer-up cheese sometimes...'

Millie thought for a moment and then crossed to the fridge. She pulled out the blocks of cheddar and parmesan, then placed both on the chopping board in the middle of the table. She laid a knife in front of Karen.

'Cheer-up cheese...?'

That got another laugh, before the other woman turned serious. 'You have to tell the police it's not Nick,' she said.

'I never told them it *was* him. I've never even *met* him. They must have had a reason to arrest him? To charge him? It wasn't anything to do with me.'

Karen put down her tea and picked up the knife. She sliced a sliver of parmesan and swallowed.

'They found stolen cash at Nick's flat. I don't know the exact details but I assume it's what was taken from the shop.' A pause. 'I know how that sounds.'

She went for another piece of cheese, bigger this time. Millie had heard something about a storage locker – though Facebook rumours were always just that.

'I really don't know what you want me to say,' Millie replied.

Karen stared at the table, avoiding any direct scrutiny. 'Could you... maybe... just... sort of... say it isn't him? Like, if you have to go to court? Say it wasn't him, that the guy you saw was taller? Something like that? It *wasn't* him, so it's not really a lie...'

Millie sliced herself a cube of cheese and nibbled the edge. It took her back to those evenings Alex would work late and she'd be at home with an infant Eric, hoping he'd go to sleep. It was only later that she figured Alex wasn't actually at work many, or any, of those evenings he said he was. She wondered if, now he was married again, he was still having those late nights 'in the office'. She wondered whether Rachel knew, or cared.

'Did you see anything else?' Karen asked.

'There was a key that was dropped,' Millie replied. She fiddled with her phone and then slipped it across the table for Karen to see the photo.

The other woman narrowed her eyes and then picked up the phone. 'That's Nick's storage key,' she said, sounding surprised. She pinched in closer. 'He lost it a week or two back. He hadn't needed it so didn't notice it was gone – but he said the last time he definitely had it was at mine. I tore up the flat looking for it.' Karen slid back the phone. 'How did it end up in the shop?'

Millie didn't want to be the one who said it. There was a fairly obvious reason.

'I know what you're thinking,' Karen added. 'It wasn't him. It really wasn't. He was with me. Why would I lie?'

'Because you're seeing him and want to protect him?'

Karen shook her head quickly. 'It's not like that. We *were* together that afternoon. I'd tell the police but... my husband. You don't know what he's like, or his family.'

'Has Nick told them where he was?'

'Even if he did, how could we prove it?'

That was a fair point. The word of a random person probably wouldn't serve as an alibi – and would still get Karen into trouble with her husband. It was a big risk, without a guaranteed result.

'Can I give you my number?' Karen asked. 'You don't have to give me yours. I know you don't know me and probably don't believe me. It's just... if you think of anything else, can you text? I don't know what to do.'

Millie loaded the contacts app and passed her phone across. Karen typed in a number and then handed it back. As soon as Millie had it in her hand, it began to buzz. She assumed she'd accidentally pressed a button, but Oliver's name was on the screen.

She mouthed a 'one moment' to Karen and then pressed to answer.

Oliver didn't wait for a hello. 'You're not going to believe this,' he said. 'But Mum's gone out.'

EIGHTEEN

Millie asked Oliver to give her a minute. She put him on mute as she told Karen it was an important call. She promised the other woman she'd let her know if something with the police came up, and then led her out of the house, before returning to her phone.

Oliver picked up where he left off. 'Roger called,' he said. 'He wanted to know what I'd said to Mum because she'd been upset since we left. She started going through boxes under the bed and at the bottom of the wardrobe. Pulling things out and putting them away. Roger doesn't know what most of it was. They're all documents and photos from before Dad died. He said he was in the toilet and, when he got out, she had taken the car.'

There was an unquestionable hint of panic in his voice.

'I don't think she's driven in six or seven years,' Oliver added. 'Roger's waiting at home in case she comes back. He doesn't have a car to go looking for her, because Mum took it. He was talking about calling the police, but I don't think they'll care about a grown woman going for a drive, so I'm going out to look for her.' He paused, breathless, and then added: 'Can you come? I don't know who else to ask.'

Millie didn't need longer than a second to take in the empty kitchen in her empty house. 'Where are you?' she asked.

There was a quiet, almost embarrassed, cough. 'Outside.'

Oliver was driving along the Whitecliff promenade. It was a cool evening, not quite ready for shorts season, although that had never stopped a sizeable minority from showing off their gleaming white knees. Couples were strolling in the early-evening sun, trying to pretend the breeze wasn't biting, while groups of teenagers massed on the steps near the entrance to the pier. Some things never changed.

Traffic was crawling, which at least gave Millie and Oliver time to take in the surroundings. His mum had apparently gone off in a silver Corsa, which looked like every other car on the road.

'Was it after your dad died that she stopped going out?' Millie asked.

'That's when it got bad,' Oliver replied. He angled forward to peer into an alley and then leant back. 'It started a bit when I left home. I realised I was always visiting her and Dad. They'd hardly ever come to me, even when I only lived across town. I asked Dad and he said Mum always wanted to stay in. It wasn't as bad then. She'd still go to events, or maybe out to eat. There was a wedding or two – that sort of thing. That's when she started cutting out stories from the paper about fights in the centre.'

Oliver pulled in at a set of traffic lights and nodded across towards the pub in which Millie and Guy had talked to Nigel the previous morning.

'There's always fights,' he said. 'Especially in the summer. She'd save the cuttings until she saw me and then say I should be careful. She meant well, because I'd just moved out. I didn't know it would build into... *this.*'

The light changed and Oliver eased away. The two of them continued to look for parked silver Corsas, or anyone who looked like Oliver's mum on the pavement. After a short distance, Oliver took the turn and headed towards the centre of Whitecliff.

'She somehow got the idea that anything outdoors was this crime-filled horror show and that it was safer to stay in. Which it is, of course, but it's not really a life, is it? When Dad died, she'd only go to the Legion with her friend, which is where she met Roger. I thought he might help her get over it, and it sort of did for a bit. They went on holiday, they went to a few plays and things in the theatre. Then the old ways started to creep back.'

Oliver turned into the car park at the back of the British Legion. A dozen or so cars were speckled around the faded, barely there once-white lines. A board at the front of the club was advertising 'Legs Zeppelin' as an act for the following Friday and 'The Whom' the day after.

There was no sign of a silver Corsa in the car park. 'We might as well check anyway,' Oliver said.

The club was like walking into a different decade – and it wasn't the previous one. There was a sticky carpet and rainbow lights looped around the browny ceiling. A couple of blokes were playing pool in one corner, while small groups were dotted around the tables and booths. Oliver and Millie stood near the front door and took in the room. There was no sign of his mum and, though the barman vaguely recognised her picture, he said he'd not seen her in ages.

Back in the car, Oliver messaged Roger to say she wasn't at the Legion and that they'd keep looking. He quickly received a reply to say she hadn't arrived home. He spent a few seconds rubbing his ear absent-mindedly, likely not realising he was touching the tattoo, and then he started the engine.

As he pulled out of the car park and back onto the road, Millie remembered she hadn't told him about seeing Georgia in Steeple's End that morning. They talked for a while, and, the next time Oliver stopped, they were outside the gates of Whitecliff's main cemetery. He hadn't mentioned the destination, though it wasn't much of a surprise.

The gates were locked, though the wall at the side was barely hip height. The light was gloomy as the evening slipped, and Oliver clambered onto the brickwork, before helping Millie over the top.

A group of teenagers sat on the grass a few metres away, hidden from the outside by the wall. Crushed cans were on the ground at their side and they briefly stopped their conversation to ensure Millie and Oliver were nobody important, before continuing to drink and talk.

Oliver led Millie across the path, then onto a small trail as they navigated the tombstones until eventually arriving in front of an unassuming grave. There were no flowers, or anything else to mark the spot, only the slightly mossy stone.

Nobody was in sight and Oliver stared down at his father's name. Millie stood to his side, unsure if she should say anything. Her parents' own graves were on the other side of the graveyard, not that she ever visited.

In the distance, over the low wall, the faintest hint of orange seeped through the trees, clinging to the horizon.

'Dad hated retiring,' Oliver said. 'One of those who didn't know what to do without work. He didn't particularly want to go to the Legion with Mum, or take up bowls or golf, like some of his mates. He didn't have hobbies, he only had his job.'

'What did he do?' Millie asked.

Oliver laughed but there wasn't a lot of humour to it. He sounded more sad than anything. 'That's the thing, he worked at Morrisons – and Safeway before that. He ended up as stock manager. There's nothing wrong with that – but he couldn't live without it. He died about seven months after retiring.'

He crouched for a moment and touched the headstone.

When he stood, there was something haunted in the way he stared through Millie.

'Where next?' she asked.

'I don't know. I was sure she'd be at the Legion... or here. She never goes out. I have no idea where she might be.'

The teenagers with the beer cans in the distance had moved on to the giant bottle of cider. What a night.

'Have you always lived at that house?' Millie asked.

'Not always – but about twenty years. We moved just before I did my GCSEs.'

'What about before that?'

Oliver *hrmed* to himself and then: 'We could try our old place. It's closer to town.'

He had one final glance at his father's grave and then they turned and walked back through the graveyard. Millie got herself over the wall second time around, and then they were back in the car.

Oliver wasn't speaking but, for some reason, Millie felt the urge. 'I grew up in the house where I live now,' she told him.

'Have you always lived there?'

'I moved out when I was twenty or so. I lived in a few flats and then bought a house with my ex-husband. I moved back after splitting up with him.'

She didn't need to add that she'd inherited the place. Everyone knew.

'How did you cope after your mum and dad?' he asked.

Millie started to stumble over a reply, but Oliver continued: 'When you first picked up Eric, I knew your face. It felt like everyone was talking about you for a while. You and that MP, then your parents, and people saying that you, um...'

'...That I killed them?'

Oliver didn't answer, not properly. He took a hand from the wheel and rubbed his ear, perhaps subconsciously. 'I'm worried that, whatever this is, that it's big. That maybe I don't want to know...?' He risked a momentary sideways glance. 'I play five-a-side, I teach a bit of guitar, I've got a girlfriend, I'm supposed to be going to Mexico this summer. I kinda like my life like this. Everything's easy...'

Millie knew that feeling. Before her affair, her life had been the same way. She knew what Alex was up to behind her back and yet she had wondered if she should carry on as if she didn't. Life would have been simpler.

'People stared for a long time after Mum and Dad,' Millie said. 'Adults. Kids. It doesn't happen as much now. I know it's a cliché but you take everything day by day.'

That got a gentle snort: 'You sound like a footballer ahead of a match.'

'I lost my job after everything with Peter,' she said. It was the name of the MP with whom she had the affair. She didn't talk about it too often. 'I organised festivals and events. I booked acts. There was always an end product. I loved that – and now I'm the person who's "into weird things".'

Oliver was navigating a roundabout but then: 'I didn't mean it like that.'

'It's not a dig at you...' Millie sighed and turned to look through the side window, even though all she could see was glare and the dark beyond. 'I miss my old work friends,' she said, partly to herself. It was something she felt unable to tell any of her real friends. They knew her too well. They might think it was a slight on them, that they weren't enough.

She wondered if this was why Oliver wanted her with him. She was distant enough from his life and situation that it didn't matter whether he confessed a few things. Whether he told her that he was worried his life was about to change.

'Maybe they weren't friends if they didn't stay in contact?' Oliver said.

It was hard to argue that point, although Millie hadn't gone out of her way to contact them either.

Suddenly, it was important that she and Oliver *weren't* close friends. That, after this all ended, they likely wouldn't see much of one another.

'What would you do if someone close to you betrayed you?' Millie asked. A question she couldn't ask anyone else in her life.

'Do you mean if they cheated?'

'No... maybe... but... worse. If someone you know did something so bad it ruined your life.' She stopped and then added: 'Maybe "ruined" is too strong. That they *changed* your life – and they did it for money. They don't know that you know.'

Oliver took a few seconds to reply. 'This doesn't sound like a hypothetical...?'

Millie let that hang. Her affair had been exposed by a photographer, but Millie had always wondered how somebody else knew. She hadn't told anyone, so how could he have known where to point the camera? Luke had offered to ask a private investigator friend – and she now had an answer. Except...

'I don't think I could be friends with someone like that,' Oliver said. 'You'd always know what they did. How could you ever look at them? Spend time with them? It would all be a lie.'

The glass of the window felt cool against the side of Millie's head as she pressed against it. Oliver's words were as true now as when Luke had told her something similar at Christmas.

She knew there would be a confrontation sooner or later.

Oliver had slowed. They were on a terraced street with cars parked along both sides. The last time Millie had been in one of these houses close to the centre of Whitecliff, it had been to talk to a woman whose son had been missing for close to three decades.

It wasn't the same road, but it might as well have been. Guy told her the houses had been built for factory workers, back when there had been a town industry that wasn't tourism. He'd grown up in one himself. It had been a window to a world Millie hadn't experienced. She'd grown up with a famous dad – well, locally famous – in a big property, where she'd always had her own room and never had to share.

Oliver stopped in the middle of the road. Orangey street lights illuminated a gloomy passage along either side. Most windows had their curtains drawn, though a few had televisions beaming bright onto the street. A faint *doof-doof-doof* of someone's dance music thumped from somewhere out of sight.

'That's where I grew up,' Oliver said, pointing across Millie towards the house on her side of the street.

Number sixteen was unremarkable. There was a black siding around the white door and window frames. The curtains were pulled, with no light seeping from the inside. As far as Millie could see, nobody was home.

'The upstairs window was my bedroom,' Oliver added. 'I haven't been in since I was about fifteen but it still feels weird to know somebody else sleeps in there.' A pause. 'I used to keep five or six copies of the *Sunday Sport* under the carpet. I sometimes wonder what they thought when whoever moved in after us pulled it up.'

Millie laughed. 'They'd have guessed why they were there.'

'I suppose...'

Headlights flared behind and Oliver moved quickly ahead. They reached the corner and he turned to get out of the other car's way, before looping back around to where they'd been. He drove even slower second time, paying attention properly to the vehicles. There were a few small silver cars, but not Roger's Corsa.

Oliver's crept his car forward. 'I don't know where she might be,' he said.

A little ahead, a front door of one of the houses opened,

sending yellowy light spiralling onto the pavement. A squat shadow limped from the doorstep onto the pavement and then headed in the opposite direction.

Millie almost said it, though Oliver had been watching as well. 'That's her,' he said.

The front door closed and, with no vehicle behind, Oliver continued idling. His mum had emerged from a house six doors down from the one in which he'd grown up. Considering she seemed to have something wrong with her hip, she was moving as quickly as it appeared possible. After passing a couple more doors, she disappeared into the shadows of the alley that would lead to the path that ran along the rear of the houses.

Oliver edged ahead but then headlights flared and an engine growled. Moments later, a small silver vehicle pressed its way from the darkness. It turned onto the road in front of Oliver's car and headed for the junction.

Millie could sense the hesitation. 'Do we wait here?' Oliver said. 'Shall I follow her?'

'If she's driving home, you can't pull up right behind her,' Millie replied.

Oliver eased off the accelerator, as his mum went through the junction.

'Shall we knock on the door?'

'It's nine o'clock,' Millie replied. 'You can't knock on a stranger's door at this time.'

Ahead, the red rear lights of the Corsa were disappearing around a bend.

'What do I do?' he asked.

'Check in with Roger tonight and make sure she gets in safely,' Millie said. She was watching the front door of the house from which Oliver's mother had appeared. 'And then you can knock on number seven tomorrow.'

NINETEEN

DAY FIVE

Barry bounded along the hedgerow and darted underneath the stile. His snout was close to the ground, tail wagging enthusiastically from side to side.

There was nobody else on the moor as Millie and Guy walked at each other's side after the dog. In the distance, over the ridge, the black sea stretched into eternity. The sky was a pale grey, with the merest hint that the sun was trying to force its way through.

Guy eked his way over the stile, grumbling about his knees as he lowered himself on the other side. Millie followed and felt her own hips click as she touched down. It wouldn't be long until she turned forty and she'd have psychopaths telling her that was when life would begin.

Shakira was correct that hips don't lie – but wait until she hit forty, and then she'd know the truth.

Barry led the way, following the trail away from the moor and into the woods. Guy and Millie followed.

'How did Oliver take the news about his tattoo and the commune?' Guy asked.

'I'm not sure how *he* took it. His mum doesn't like going outdoors – but she went for a drive for the first time in years last night. We found her at a house a few doors down from where he grew up. Oliver's going to knock on the door this morning to see who lives there.'

'That could be dangerous…'

Millie checked the time on her phone. From what he'd said the night before, Oliver would be calling at number seven any moment now.

Not that she wanted to talk about him, or the tattoo. That wasn't why she'd agreed to help walk Barry.

'What are you working on at the moment?' she asked, delaying.

'A bit of local politics. I got a tip that one of the local authority grants might've ended up with a company run by a councillor's brother. It could be legit, so I'm looking into it. I'm waiting on a couple of emails and a freedom of information request. We'll see what comes…'

Millie had the sense that he likely *knew* what was to come and was making his final checks before publishing. Millie let it sit for a few moments as they continued crunching across the ground.

'I saw Craig in Steeple's End yesterday,' Millie said. She was trying to sound as if she had only just remembered such a thing, and not that this was the reason she was in the woods with him.

Guy trod around a large root and called for Barry. The dog was up the track – and slowed, though he didn't stop. He peered over his shoulder, wondering why he wasn't allowed to explore by himself. Guy told the pup to wait and then, as they neared, the dog ambled on.

'What was he doing there?' Guy asked. For a moment, Millie thought he was talking about the dog.

'I don't know,' Millie replied. 'He said he wanted to tell me a few things about you...'

'Did he now...?'

It came out in a rush: 'He said you were a workaholic, who expected Carol to be a stay-at-home wife to do all the cooking and cleaning. That she gave up a career as a vet for that. And that you never wanted kids, which is why you resented Craig being around.'

Barry had dug out a stick from the undergrowth and was busy tearing away strips of soggy bark, before spitting them on the ground. He waited for Millie and Guy to pass and then picked up what was left of the wood, then trotted ahead with it in his mouth.

'It's partly true,' Guy said. He didn't sound offended or surprised. 'I can't really deny I'm a workaholic but I never asked Carol to give up her career. She had a few problems with the person running things, which is why she dropped out of her veterinary course.'

Guy crouched and picked up a long stick, with which he started to walk. It was such a perfect height that it was almost as if it had been cut for him personally.

'There were times when I was selfish,' he added. 'When I put work first and didn't have the tact to pretend otherwise.'

He slowed, stopped, waited for Millie to turn and face him.

'You learn as you get older,' he said. 'Which isn't an excuse but I've never pretended to be perfect.'

Millie could *feel* his words as much as she'd heard them. She wanted to believe him and she did.

When they set off side by side again, it was slower.

'Craig did ask us for money more than once,' Guy said. 'That's always what he wants. *Always*. And he's a thief, although I can't prove that part.'

'I thought you had a two-source rule about making accusations?' Millie was teasing, although, maybe she wasn't.

'That's a rule for *publishing*,' Guy replied. 'There have been lots of things I've known to be true, even though I wouldn't have been able to prove it. I *know* Craig's a thief, regardless of whether I can prove it.'

Millie tried to remember the conversation from the day before. There was something else she'd meant to ask.

'He said you'd told his ex-wife about him making child payments to someone else...?'

Guy didn't skip a beat. 'That's true. He married someone who didn't know he had a child with another woman – but, as bad as that is, that's not why I told her. He took six grand from Carol, which he used to pay off his old partner, so she wouldn't take him to court. In the meantime, he was telling his wife he was skint. So, yes, I told her – and I'd do it again.'

'There was more...' Millie said. She was beginning to see that Craig was trying to turn her against Guy, for whatever reason. It had started at Christmas, when he'd pretended he was Guy's son – and it was continuing now.

'You can ask,' Guy replied. 'I won't be offended and I don't have anything to hide.'

'He said I didn't really know you, or the things you've done.'

'What things?'

'He didn't say...'

Barry had dropped his stick. After his initial burst of energy, he'd seemingly burned himself out and was now trotting at their side.

'I can't defend myself against that,' Guy replied.

'I know...'

Millie had gone through her list of questions and was out the other side. She had thought at the time that Craig was likely stirring, although his motivation was harder to figure out. Was it simply that he didn't like Guy?

As she checked the time on her phone, Millie realised she'd missed a message from Oliver.

Nobody home. Might try again later

There was a gap of four minutes and then a follow-up.

Fancy it?

Millie left it on read. She wondered if Oliver actually *had* knocked on the door by himself. It didn't feel as if he'd done much on his own since he'd shown her the mysterious tattoo. Not that it was necessarily an issue. When she'd been at the nursing home and Ingrid had told her she had seen a woman pushed from the roof of the house in the valley, Millie hadn't tried to solve it on her own. Whenever Millie wanted to look into anything strange now, she always spoke to Guy.

'A woman came to the house last night,' Millie said. 'Told me she's having an affair with the man who's been charged with the robbery at the shop. She's married, so can't tell the police he was with her, plus she has no way to prove it anyway. She wants me to tell the police it wasn't him.'

They walked on a few paces. The ground was damper, the trees thicker, the dappled light darker. Barry was now a pace behind.

Guy took everything as calmly as if he'd been asked how he took his tea. 'Does she know why he's been charged?'

'I showed her the photo of the key and fob – and she says it's his. I assume the police tracked the storage unit to him. She also said they found the missing money in his flat…'

Sometimes, Millie was sure she could see Guy thinking. His left eye and nostril twitched as he chewed on that side of his mouth.

'I learned a lesson very early in this job,' he said. 'This was back when we used to run a photo feature every week. We'd print a picture of the beach in the summer, when it was full of tourists and sunbathers. If people came to the office and could identify themselves, we'd give them a voucher for free chips. It was sponsored by the chip shop and the voucher was for fifty pence off, or something like that. There was a limit of one per household. They'd obviously make way more than that ever cost them, so the advert paid for itself.'

'Is that what you learned? How to scam a newspaper's advertising department?'

A laugh: 'I think it was the second summer we were running it when we got to the office and there was this bloke banging on the door. He was demanding to know who'd taken the photo and, more importantly, when. It turned out, in the background of the picture, there was a couple sitting together on a bench, sharing an ice cream. Problem was, they were each married to different people.'

'Oh...'

'We didn't run any more photos after that,' Guy replied. 'And I learned not to get involved in domestics, even if accidentally.'

'What happened to your photographer?' Millie asked.

'Nothing. We told the guy we'd call the police if he didn't leave. He stormed off and that was the last we saw of him.'

Millie thought on the story for a moment. It wasn't as if she *wanted* to be involved in whatever was going on between Karen, her husband on the oil rigs, and alleged robber, Nick.

'What if he didn't rob the shop?' Millie said.

'You haven't told anyone he *did*.'

'But I found that key. It's not like I saw it fall. It could have been dropped earlier and then lay there as other people stepped over it. If it wasn't for me, the police wouldn't have it, and Nick wouldn't have been charged.'

'The police would have checked the cameras for that. Plus they'd have asked when they were questioning him about where he was during that day. They'd have tried to account for every hour. If he'd been in the shop at any point that week, they'd know.'

Millie had forgotten about the cameras. She wondered what Nick had told them about where he was if he was unable to use Karen as an alibi. Whatever it was hadn't helped.

They had reached a board with a map, on which a large yellow star marked where they were. Next to the map was a bench and a bin, under which Barry was sniffing. Guy creaked his way onto the bench and offered a 'sorry'. Millie settled at his side. It had been good to unload everything but there was one final thing.

'Do you remember when we were in your kitchen and I first told you what Alex had done? Why I had the affair?'

'Of course.'

'I told you somebody had betrayed me. That they must have tipped off a photographer to catch me with Peter.'

'I told you it would be very hard to find out who because journalists don't burn sources.'

'Right... it's just I know who it was. I found out a few months ago. I've got the emails.'

'Oh... wow. I knew you were good at this but I didn't know you were *that* good.'

Guy was impressed, which didn't happen that often. Millie could have corrected him that she hadn't been the one to get the emails and that it had been Luke – but she didn't.

'I don't know everything. I don't how they knew where Peter and I were going to be when the photographer caught us. I never told anyone where we were meeting.'

'What are you asking?'

Millie realised she was chewing the inside of her mouth on one side. Perhaps she was inheriting Guy's traits?

'Nothing,' she replied. 'I wanted to tell someone. I'm going to say something soon and let them know I know.'

Guy didn't reply immediately. She liked it when it felt as if he was considering what she'd said. She valued it.

'That's brave,' he said. 'But... there's no going back after.'

Millie reached down and ruffled a hand through Barry's fur. He was huffing gently. 'I know...' she said and then quieter: 'I know.'

TWENTY

Millie wasn't on the volunteer schedule at the nursing home but, being a Sunday, none of the managers were in anyway. That left Jack in some sort of control as the most senior person on the floor – although even he had seemingly run out of things to do. Millie had spent forty-five minutes checking in with a few of the residents, before delivering a bit of mail that hadn't been sorted in the prior days.

That done, she was in the shelter at the back of the home, Jack at her side, as they watched a flock of seagulls circle the valley below.

She told Jack how she'd read to Ingrid in her room. The older woman was having one of her bad days, where her joints wouldn't do what she wanted them to. Millie had the sense that Jack wasn't really listening. He was staring into the distance, fingers interlinked, thumbs pressed together, as if about to give a sermon. It was Sunday, after all.

He didn't say anything after Millie had finished speaking and, before she could ask what he was thinking, he told her.

'I'm thinking of applying for a new job,' he said.

'Where?'

'There's a Hilton opening down the coast. It's sort of in the middle of all the resorts but not near any of them. More of a base than anything. It's got its own beach.'

Millie had heard of it. There'd been the usual planning permission complaints in the news, and then the promises of jobs, and then votes and protests, then the counter-protests – and so on. Then everything had gone quiet. It was always the way.

'They're hoping to open for summer,' Jack said.

'Isn't it about an hour's commute?' Millie asked. 'That's a lot of extra time every day. I'm not saying you shouldn't go for it but two hours is a lot to lose...'

Jack didn't reply and Millie suddenly realised why.

'You're not going to commute, are you?'

He sighed and it felt as if he didn't want to say, even though he'd brought it up. 'I don't know. I'm thinking about things. I put in my application, so I'll see what comes.'

Millie almost replied, though she stopped herself. He'd gone from thinking about something to having already applied. It felt as if, assuming he was offered a job, his mind had been made up. She nearly asked how Rishi felt about things, except she wasn't sure she wanted to hear the answer.

'I need to tell you something,' Millie said.

Jack clasped her wrist dramatically. 'You're not pregnant are you?'

'Do I *look* pregnant?'

He eyed her tummy. 'No... I mean, I thought with you and Luke and everything...' A pause: 'Has he asked you to marry him?'

'Of course not.'

'You've not asked him have you? Come on, Mill. I know it's the twenty-first century but—'

'Obviously not – and how come, when I need to tell you

something, your first guess is pregnant, and your second is marriage?'

'Because you don't pre-announce something unless it's big. I don't say, "I need to tell you something... I'm having fish finger sandwiches for tea".'

It was a fair point... although it left Millie with a sudden craving for fish finger sandwiches.

'I know who sold me out for the affair with Peter,' Millie said. 'I've got copies of the emails that were sent to the paper.'

Jack had turned sideways to face her and she could sense his mouth was open, even though she was watching the seagulls and the valley. A few of the larger birds had swooped to ground level and were pecking at something Millie couldn't see.

'Do you know?' Millie asked as she turned to Jack, who gulped.

'I thought you were about to tell me.'

She paused. 'It was Rish.'

There was a twitch of the eyebrow. Perhaps something, perhaps nothing. Had Jack known all along?

'Have you told him you know?' Jack asked.

'I wanted to talk to you before. We were friends first and I know you better.'

Jack huffed out a long breath and they watched the seagulls together for a while. 'Rish...'

The birds had all descended close to where the larger gulls had been pecking. There was a hint of something dark on the ground, perhaps a badger, or a mole. Millie didn't know what seagulls ate, except for tourists' chips.

'How would he have known about you and the MP?' Jack asked.

'I don't know. I guess that's one thing I'll ask if...'

Millie wasn't sure where that sentence was going, but maybe she did. Was there anything to gain from confronting Rishi himself? Perhaps it was about telling Jack all along? Without him, she and Rishi would never have met. If Jack and Rishi split up, it was Jack with whom she would side – even if he was in the wrong.

'Could the emails be faked?' Jack asked.

'They're not – and why would anyone do that?'

'Where did you get them?'

It was a fair question, considering what Millie was accusing Jack's boyfriend of doing – except she didn't want to answer.

When it was clear a reply wasn't coming, Jack went for something else. 'How long have you known?'

'Since Christmas.'

'Whew...' Jack let out a low whistle and pressed back onto the seat. 'Why didn't you say something sooner?'

'I wasn't sure what to say. I still don't really know how to talk about it.'

'Why now?'

That was a good question and Millie didn't really know the answer, other than that it had been building. Five months was a long time to hang onto something that felt as if it had guided her life.

'I suppose I couldn't let it sit any more,' Millie said.

'Do you want me to talk to him?'

'No.'

'Are *you* going to talk to him?'

Millie went back to watching the gulls. Whatever they'd been eating had been successfully pulled apart. The bigger birds were back in the air, presumably with full bellies, as the small ones pecked at whatever was left.

'Maybe,' Millie replied. 'Probably not.'

Even as she said it, she wasn't sure. She had so many questions for Rishi about how he'd known and why he'd done it. Except knowing those answers wasn't going to turn back the clock and make things any better. It had been done before he and Jack had adopted Isaac and their lives were different now.

'Do you want me to break up with him?' Jack asked.

'Of course not.'

'So why tell me?'

That was a fair point as well.

'Because I don't know what else to do,' Millie said. She sank forward, resting her elbows on her knees. 'It changed my life. I might still be with Alex if not for that. I would've still had Eric with me. I'd have never gone back to Mum and Dad's...'

Millie never had the affair because she wanted to break up with Alex, not then, and certainly didn't want to lose custody of their son. She knew the risks of both happening – and had done it anyway.

'Did you hear back from Alex?' Jack asked. 'You said you'd asked him for custody...?'

'I figured I'd let it sit,' Millie replied, although she knew he wouldn't come back to her without being pressed again.

The gull party was over, with the birds back as a flock and heading towards the seafront to mug some tourist.

'I have to get back to work,' Jack said. 'I don't know what to say about Rish. If you change your mind and want me to talk to him...?'

Millie took his hand and squeezed. He gripped her fingers back, gave a slim smile of acknowledgement, and then disappeared back into the home. Millie continued sitting by herself for a while. She thought she might feel relieved to have shared what she knew with both Guy and now Jack... except, if anything, she felt worse. She certainly didn't want Jack to break up with Rishi because of her and yet, what was she hoping to achieve by telling him?

After a few minutes more, she headed back through the home, offering a couple of goodbyes, before getting into her car. Millie skimmed around the town centre, avoiding the weekend traffic and tourists. She wasn't in the mood for stopping and stewing. It was a longer, though uninterrupted trip – and she had already indicated to turn onto her driveway when she realised a woman was leaning against the gatepost. Millie stopped and buzzed down her window.

Karen had her arms crossed over her front, the way she had when she'd turned up at Millie's door the night before. She was wearing the same jacket and gave an apologetic smile.

'What are you doing here?' Millie asked.

'I have a favour to ask.'

'You already asked it last night. I told you, I can't lie to the police.'

A shake of the head. 'Will you meet Nick? He's out on bail.'

Millie asked Karen to move aside and said she'd be back. She parked on the driveway, turned off the engine, and then returned to where the other woman was standing at the end of the drive. Millie felt watched, although that wasn't a new feeling. Her neighbours either had consistent breezes focused entirely on their front curtains, or the Neighbourhood Watch members were a bit too Noseyhood Watch.

'I can't talk to him,' Millie said. 'I'm a witness in a case where he's been charged. If he's on bail, he could be sent to prison just for talking to me. In any case, what could we possibly say to each other?'

Karen gulped and winced at the same time. Her eyes flickered over the top of Millie's shoulder.

'I sort of figured you'd say "yes",' she replied.

A second glance had Millie turning to look – and there, sitting in the passenger seat of a car parked across from her house, was an unshaven man with messy dark hair.

'He only wants to say hello...' Karen added.

TWENTY-ONE

After a beckoning wave from Karen, Nick got out of the car and headed across towards them. His limp reminded Millie of watching Oliver's mother hobble around the night before – except, if anything, Nick's was more pronounced.

Considering he was someone for whom Karen was putting her entire life on the line, it was hard not to see Nick as... underwhelming. He was short and broad, with patchy black hair and slightly crooked features. Like an art project where the paint hadn't dried properly.

The curtain over the road was flickering, so Millie ushered the pair of them onto her drive and into the house. Moments later, the three of them were around her kitchen table. Nick was looking sheepishly at the floor, while Karen was eyeing Millie hopefully.

'I know for a fact you're breaking your bail conditions,' Millie said. She was putting on the same voice she used to tell off Eric, even though she wasn't sure she actually felt it.

'They didn't tell me that,' Nick replied.

'I've been arrested,' Millie told him. 'I've been bailed. I *know* they tell you to stay away from witnesses and anyone who might be involved with the case. You'll be banned from that shop as well.'

Nick was quiet and had, presumably, been hoping she wouldn't know the law. If not that, he'd been bullied into coming... which suddenly seemed likely from the way Karen was trying to make eye contact with him. Millie knew that look. She had it in her own locker, when she was trying to remind Eric to thank someone, without actually telling him.

'Why are you here?' Millie asked.

'You've got to tell the police it wasn't me,' Nick said.

'I never told them it was,' Millie replied. 'And I went through this with Karen last night.'

'I know – but you could tell them it's definitely *not* me.' He looked up and pointed to his face. 'I've got green eyes. Maybe the person you saw had blue? Or brown? Maybe he had a different accent? What did he say? I'll prove it to you.' He cleared his throat and then, in an accent that felt as if it belonged in a Guy Ritchie movie, bellowed: 'Gimme the money!' before he returned to his own voice to add: 'Did it sound like that?'

Millie almost laughed at the absurdity. She wondered if this was along the lines of what he'd said in the interview room. If it was, it was no wonder he'd been charged. It was hard to know what he was hoping to achieve, other than having her tip off the police about the bail breach. Not that she would.

'They found the stolen money at your flat,' Millie said.

'I don't know how that got there.'

'I found your key and storage fob at the shop.'

'I don't know how that got there either – except I lost it a week or two ago. The last time I had it was at Karen's flat.'

There was a moment of tension in the glance between them and Millie saw the hint of a conversation they would have had recently, and more than once. Karen would have said she never saw the key, he'd have said he didn't know where else it could be, she'd have replied that he should have looked after his things better... and so on.

That one look had Millie knowing there was no acting. Regardless of absent husbands, or other complications, they were a proper couple. Only those who'd shared the most intimate times of their lives could have such lengthy arguments with the briefest moments of eye contact.

'Were you at the shop any time that day?' Millie asked.

'I don't think I've *ever* been there. I told the police that. It's not on my way to work, it's not close to my flat. There's a petrol station I use if I need bits and pieces. I'd have no need to go anywhere near there.'

'Where did you tell them you were during the robbery?'

There was another moment of side-eye between the couple. 'That I was at home by myself watching cricket on TV,' Nick said.

'So you definitely lied to them...?'

'It's not like I could tell the truth. I figured if I stick to one story, they can't catch me out. They asked about who was playing and all that – but I knew the answers, because I watched the highlights.'

'Sounds like that didn't work out...'

Nick sank a little lower. 'They reckon I could go to prison...'

'For a first offence?' Millie had already said it when she realised.

A quiet filtered through her kitchen, with only the vague, distant sound of an idling lawnmower.

'What else have you done?' Millie asked.

A glimmer of anger burned through Nick's clenched teeth. 'Not what *else*. I didn't do this.'

Karen stretched across and patted the top of his hand. 'It's nothing bad,' she said.

'Easy for you to say. You're not going to prison.' He let out a long sigh as Karen withdrew her hand. 'I used to steal from shops when I was younger,' he added. 'I kept getting away with it but it all got a bit out of hand. I was caught with an iPad and tried to run – but accidentally knocked over this old woman. I didn't even see her. She dislocated her hip and fractured her knee. I ended up being charged for theft and a couple of counts of assault. I got a suspended sentence...'

That complicated things. Millie didn't know *that* much about the justice system – but she did know people were likely to go to prison for another offence, if they were already on a suspended sentence.

'I haven't done anything like that in years,' Nick said. 'I was almost at the end of my probation period. I was stupid then.'

Millie didn't point out that an affair with a married woman probably wasn't the smartest move.

'I *can't* go to prison...' Nick rubbed his eyes and stared towards the window and freedom beyond.

Millie didn't know what to tell him. She believed that he wasn't the man under the balaclava and yet it didn't feel as if there was anything she could do to prevent the injustice.

'Maybe you could tell us what you remember?' Karen said. 'All of it from the beginning. There might be something that helps...?'

Millie squeezed her eyes tight until green and pink stars swarmed. She didn't want to do it and yet: 'I've been forgetting bits of it,' Millie replied.

Neither of them spoke, and so she told them how she'd gone into the shop to get ketchup. That she'd picked up some cut-price crisps at the door. Someone had come in behind her and brushed past. He'd gone to the counter and asked for money, then turned and jogged out the shop. Crisps had tumbled to the ground and then she'd seen the key fob on the floor. The guy behind the counter had called the police, and then they'd arrived and there had been interviews and...

'I think that's it,' Millie said. 'But I might have misremembered. Sometimes I wonder if I saw a knife. Other times I think he kept his hand in his pocket.'

Millie opened her eyes and the brightness of the kitchen seeped through the swirling disappearing stars. She could hear Karen's breathing.

'Did you say he jogged out of the shop?' she asked.

That was something Millie definitely remembered, because she'd thought the robber was going to collide with the stack of crisps. 'Yes,' she replied.

Something had changed. Karen and Nick both snapped around to look at each other.

'Nick can't run,' Karen said.

'What do you mean?'

It was Nick who replied. 'When I collided with that old woman, I tripped over her as well. I fractured my patella and had to have keyhole surgery on my knee. I'll probably limp the rest of my life. Some days, I can't manage stairs. I've not been able to run or jog for almost three years.'

He'd certainly limped out of the car – which would have been quite the set-up for this, considering he couldn't have known what Millie was going to describe.

'How could your keys have got to the shop?' she asked, to a pair of blank faces.

When no reply arrived, she crossed to the counter and the basket that Heather had left. Aside from a single bread roll, there was nothing left – except the business card that had been tucked into the side.

'Do you know a Heather Speed?' Millie asked, reading the name on the card. 'She delivered this after the robbery as a thank you for giving a statement. It's her shop.'

Millie wasn't sure what she expected – but she received two more blank faces.

'I don't know anyone called that,' Nick replied.

'Did you say her last name was "Speed"?' Karen asked.

'Because my brother, Jordan, has a friend called *Chris* Speed. I dunno if he's any relation...?'

Millie stared. 'Chris Speed was working behind the counter,' she replied. 'His mum owns the shop and brought me the gift basket.'

Karen shrugged but Millie had spent so many hours thinking of Rishi and how he could have known about her affair, that she already had an idea.

'Does anyone know about you two?' she asked.

Karen shook her head and then looked to Nick.

'I haven't told anyone,' he said. Karen looked sceptical for a moment but then he added: 'I didn't even tell the police!'

Millie was trying to put together the pieces. Brothers and friends and oil rig workers and...

'I had an affair,' Millie said. 'I didn't think anyone knew – but then it turned out they did...'

TWENTY-TWO

Millie was in the passenger seat of Oliver's car. They were parked a few doors up from the house in which Oliver had grown up, almost half a street off the one from which they had seen his mum emerge.

A set of curtains had fluttered a couple of times as the nearest homeowner checked to see who had parked outside their house. Nobody had assigned spaces on a street such as this, not that the residents seemed to know or care. When it came to parking on terraced streets, wars had been started over less.

'Do you think I should knock?' Oliver asked, for the second time.

'I can't answer that,' Millie replied again.

Oliver made no movement to get out of the car. He craned sideways, looking along the street towards the door on which he was debating knocking.

'Have you spoken to your mum since last night?' Millie asked.

'Roger wouldn't put her on. He said she was upset and needed to sleep.'

'Did you tell him you'd followed her here?'

'No, I asked whether she was home and didn't let on I knew where she'd gone. He's convinced she disappeared because of something I said... which I guess is true. When he asked, I told him I wasn't sure what happened – and we haven't spoken since. He knows I'm lying.' He wriggled in his seat, angling to look along the street again. 'Do you reckon whoever lives there has been in the same house all this time?'

'It's a bit of a coincidence if they haven't.'

'True... it's just I didn't know Mum was friends with anyone that far along the street. We knew our neighbours on each side – but I've not heard anything about them since we moved. I didn't think Mum kept in contact...'

They waited a short while and then: 'Do you think I should knock?'

Oliver realised what he'd said a moment after and chuckled to himself. A few seconds later and he opened the door, quick like ripping off a plaster. He was already three doors down when Millie caught him. He bounded ahead, weaving around the recycling boxes that had been left out for morning collection, until he was standing outside number seven. It was a plain white door, with a 'NO FREE NEWSPAPERS' card taped to the glass.

Oliver snapped the letterbox back and forth a couple of times, sending a pair of booms echoing inside. A friendly 'coming' was called – and, not long after, the door was pulled open to reveal a woman who was probably in her late seventies. She was stooped, with a hunched back, and the type of walnut wrinkles that had almost folded on top of each other.

She and Oliver looked blankly at one another and then: 'I don't buy anything on the doorstep,' she said.

She started to close the door but the reply came just in time: 'I'm Oliver Higgins.'

The door froze in place, the woman's crinkled knuckles

white against the frame. It was obvious, though Oliver said it anyway.

'You know who I am, don't you?'

The woman stared, mouth bobbing as she struggled to figure out what to say. 'I'm not great with names nowadays,' she replied. 'It sort of rings a bell.'

She shifted the door a fraction more but Oliver wasn't done.

'You know my mum,' he said: a fact, not a question.

'I don't.'

'I never told you her name.'

'Oh... I mean I don't think I—'

Oliver indicated diagonally across the street. 'We used to live at number sixteen when I was growing up. She was Linda Higgins then.'

The woman was shaking her head. 'Sorry...' was the only word she got out before snapping the door in place. There was a loud clunk of the deadlock sliding into place and then footsteps disappearing along the hall.

Oliver reached for the letterbox but Millie caught his wrist before he could snap the flap.

'Not now,' she said quietly.

'But she definitely knew who I was.'

'I know... but standing here banging on her door isn't going to get you anywhere. Someone will call the police.'

Oliver sighed and let his head hang. He seemed somewhat defeated, As he leaned against the wall, Millie moved around him and crouched. She removed the lid of the recycling box and started fishing inside, before removing a packed-flat cereal box, some flyers from the supermarket, and a couple of envelopes.

'What are you doing?' Oliver hissed.

Millie ignored him and pulled out half-a-dozen cans which had the labels meticulously removed, an empty bottle of own-brand Coke, and then a handful of papers that had been ripped in two. Millie glanced around, feeling watched, even though she couldn't see anyone in the windows.

'Here,' Millie said, passing Oliver one of the torn pages as she returned things to the box.

It was a letter from the council, informing residents that there would be tree trimming occurring in the week just gone.

Oliver scanned the page, confused, until Millie said: 'Margaret Garrison.' They hadn't known the woman's name before.

'Oh...' Oliver said, catching on. 'Didn't you say you had a friend? Someone who knows everyone?'

TWENTY-THREE

Oliver was standing at Guy's gate, one hand poised over it. 'Should I open it?' he asked. 'It looks like it might fall apart if I touch it...'

'There's a trick,' Millie replied. She lifted up the wood and wrestled it inwards, before standing aside to let Oliver onto the path.

'I didn't know anyone lived up here,' Oliver said, as he turned to take in the clutter that littered Guy's garden. 'I didn't know there were any houses. I drove past that track a few times and assumed it was to get into the woods.'

They stopped at the front door and Oliver read the faded notes. They had been written on lined paper, then taped to the frame.

No estate agents!
No lawyers!
Not for sale!
No solicitors either!

Millie was so used to them that they didn't register when she visited now. Oliver seemed less certain.

'Aren't lawyers and solicitors the same thing?' he asked.

'I asked that once and he gave me a long answer about how "lawyer" is an umbrella term without a specific legal meaning. I think it was more that someone had come to his door insisting they were a *solicitor*, not a lawyer.'

'Why?'

'Something about people trying to buy his house because they want the land.'

Oliver glanced sideways nervously. 'Are you *sure* he won't mind us coming?'

'As long as you're not a secret lawyer...'

Oliver had moved aside, and Millie pulled on the handle to open the unlocked door. Oliver let out a 'whoa' at the breadth of stacked papers as they entered. They were floor to ceiling in some places, along with stacks of abandoned notepads and various pages and papers.

Oliver trod carefully as Millie guided him part-way along the winding path and into Guy's study. He was tapping on a keyboard, squinting at the fat-back monitor, as Millie entered. He looked up as if he'd expected her the whole time and didn't flinch at the sight of a newcomer.

'You should really start locking the door,' Millie said.

'It's only you that ever comes. Besides, I have a vicious guard dog.'

Barry the labradoodle had pushed himself up from a spot next to the radiator and trotted across to the door. He gave the merest brief glance to Millie and then started sniffing Oliver's shoes.

'Is he actually vicious?' Oliver asked, as he failed to hide the tremble in his voice.

'Terrifying,' Millie replied.

'Rumours are he once licked a small child to death,' Guy added.

Oliver lowered his hand hesitantly. Barry gave it a nudge with his snout and then returned his attention to Oliver's shoes.

'This is Oliver,' Millie told Guy.

'The man with the tattoo! We meet at last!'

With the attention from the dog and Guy's out-of-character enthusiasm, Oliver's insistence on visiting had seemingly waned to the point that he'd forgotten why they were there. He aimlessly stroked the hair on the back of Barry's neck, while taking in the room. In fairness, it did look like something that would end up online after a serial killer was taken into custody. One wall was taken up by an enormous map of the area, which was covered with crosses, dots, arrows, and large red type that said things like 'here' and '2003'. There were piles of old newspapers and a couple of mounds of notepads, plus so many pens, it was like a stationery shop had been burgled.

It was a lot to take in for the uninitiated.

Oliver was still clutching the stolen, ripped letter but he let Millie take it, before she passed it across to Guy.

'Do you know a Margaret Garrison?' she asked.

Guy scanned the page and then examined Millie over glasses he wasn't wearing. There were a couple of moments of psychic connection, in which he asked whether she knew taking someone's mail was illegal, and she replied that the rip should make it clear it had been thrown out.

Guy looked back to the page, then his map, and then Millie again. 'There was a Garrison who used to be part of Whitecliff Athletics Club,' he said. 'Tim, or Tom, or something like that. I vaguely remember him winning the seniors' category in the Sandy Mile years ago.'

The inevitable 'What's the Sandy Mile?' came from Millie. Sometimes, Guy would drift off onto long tangents about things like a shop that had gone out of business before Millie was born.

'It used to be a one-mile race on the beach, on the closest Saturday to the first of April,' Guy said. 'Runners would finish at the pier and, because it took place on the sand, sometimes amateurs would beat some of the best runners in the county. It was this massive free-for-all.'

He looked from Millie to Oliver, wondering if either of them knew what he was on about.

'I used to be really quick as a kid,' Oliver said. 'I ran one- and two-hundred metres for the county when I was about twelve, something like that. I don't really remember why I stopped.' He tailed off, as if this was something of which he hadn't thought in a long time. 'What happened to the race?' he added.

'I'm pretty sure it died out because they couldn't get a sponsor – but there were a few injuries because running on the sand isn't easy. It was getting to the time that people started paying attention to things like health and safety. We're talking thirty-odd years ago. More.' Guy picked up a paper from the nearest pile, checked the front, then put it down again. 'Wrong year...' he muttered to himself, before looking back to Millie. 'The paper used to carry photos of all the winners – so, if it's the same Garrison, I'll have him somewhere.'

Guy breezed past them into the hall and started plucking papers from the various piles, before continuing into the kitchen. Millie was used to this sort of aimless hunt, though Oliver seemed far more confused. He mumbled a 'What's going on?', to which Millie replied with a shrug and a grin.

After flipping through a pair of notebooks and another newspaper, Guy muttered something Millie didn't catch, then led them back into the hall, and into a room Millie had never seen before. There was a double bed in the middle, the covers unmade and screwed into a knot. The mattress looked almost flat – and Millie doubted it had been flipped, let alone replaced, at any point in the previous decade or so. There was a dresser with a dusty mirror on top – and then the usual amount of clutter that occupied the rest of the house.

Millie stood in the doorway as Guy began checking the newspaper piles. 'I moved the older stuff in here after Carol...' he said. He was on his way down to check the bottom drawer of the cabinet when he clasped his back and stood abruptly. 'How about you go through the papers in here?' he suggested, talking to Millie. 'The Sandy Mile was always front page, with more on the inside. You'll know it when you see it.' He turned to Oliver. 'I'll set you up in the office and then I can do the hallway. I know I've got it somewhere...'

Without waiting for a different option, Guy moved around Millie and led Oliver back through the depths of the cottage. Millie heard a door opening and closing.

She was alone in Guy's bedroom and it was impossible to pretend it didn't feel odd. In the house she'd inherited, she could barely bring herself to enter the bedroom that used to be her parents'. It still hadn't been cleared fully. Now she was in somebody else's.

Millie was used to Guy's train of thought being disrupted by barely remembered news articles from years before. He'd find what he was after, which would trigger another memory that would involve him listing family members, previous addresses, and all sorts of other information that might be useful.

Oliver didn't know any of that. From his perspective, they hadn't even explained who Margaret Garrison was. Millie allowed herself a laugh as she pictured his confused face when Guy gave him the task of going through a dozen piles of newspapers.

Millie approached the nearest stack of papers. The one on top was dated a couple of months before the day she'd been born – and had a front-page story about the tourist board expecting record numbers of visitors. It felt like the sort of

article that might have been written every year since Whitecliff
Pier was built.

The date was roughly around the time when Guy said the
Sandy Mile races were happening, so Millie continued through
the pile. The papers themselves were crisp and tea-coloured,
though, mercifully, in sequential order.

It was strange that such a thing should be in someone's
bedroom. Millie wasn't surprised that they'd only ended up in
there after Guy's wife had died. She wasn't convinced by
anything Craig had told her about Guy not being who she
thought he was – and yet he must have been difficult to live
with. There were more than forty years' of newspapers in this
cottage, not to mention the notebooks and other clutter.

Millie had checked close to thirty front pages before she
found a duplicate... and then another. She almost laughed. Not
only was the cottage full of tens of thousands of papers, Guy
had even kept multiple copies of the same issues.

She wondered how Oliver was getting on in the study
which, if anything, was far messier than the bedroom. Millie
knew first-hand there was little order to anything in there. Guy
would find something he needed in another area of the cottage,
take it into the office for his immediate piece of work – and then
it would be left.

A small stack of papers had spilled from under the bed, so
Millie knelt and pulled them out. They were from the late
eighties, so perhaps too recent for the Sandy Mile. Millie
checked the front pages anyway and then slipped them underneath the frame. She was about to stand when she spotted the
crusty suitcase. The leather was brown and well-worn: the sort
of thing that Millie had seen fly-tipped in a hedge at least once.

She knew she shouldn't, and wasn't entirely sure why she
did... except it was right there. Millie dragged out the suitcase
and flipped the lid. She wasn't sure what she expected, probably nothing... except it wasn't nothing.

It was... cash.

Lots of it.

There were mainly twenties and tens and, without delving too deep, Millie counted four-thousand pounds. At first she thought they might be long-time savings that Guy didn't trust to a bank – except they were the newer plastic notes that had launched within the past few years. It was possible that Guy had traded in his old notes for new ones – but, if he'd gone to a bank for that, why wouldn't he have paid it into an account?

Millie continued counting until she was roughly halfway through the mound.

Eleven grand.

There was a bump from the hall, so Millie quickly shoved everything back under the bed, before standing and snatching the nearest newspaper.

Nobody came in, although she heard the steady *click-clack* of Barry's nails as he prowled the house looking for food, attention, or both.

It was impossible for Millie not to think of Craig casually telling her that Guy wasn't who she thought he was. Who kept twenty thousand or so under their bed? Why did someone who was self-employed as a journalist have that much money?

Millie couldn't think of an answer.

TWENTY-FOUR

The buzz of her phone made Millie jump. A message from an unknown number was on the screen and, when Millie opened it, there was a photo of a half-eaten Cornish pasty, on top of a Nemesis Café napkin.

Great recommendation! – C

It took Millie a few moments to realise it must have been Craig who'd texted. She'd suggested the Nemesis Café and, seemingly, he'd gone. It was too late in the day for the photo to have been taken there and then, and she wondered if it was from the day she'd seen him in Steeple's End. If so, why had he held onto it? Then she wondered how he had her number – because she certainly hadn't given it to him.

Somehow, he'd been thinking of her at the same time she'd been thinking of him.

Millie considered replying, asking what he'd meant when he'd told her about Guy. Then she figured it was what he wanted and locked the screen instead.

Her mind was on other things as she started on the pile of

papers closest to the dresser. The issue on top was from when she would have been three. A councillor had proposed banning alcohol on the pier, which had led to protests and counter-protests.

The more things changed, the more they stayed the same.

Millie checked more papers, where there were stories about council meetings, a Home Secretary visit, police arrests after a fight on the pier, the impact of rising potato costs on the local chip shops and then...

It was there.

Olympic hopeful wins Sandy Mile

Millie skimmed the article, which was about an athlete she'd never heard of winning the race by close to twenty seconds from his nearest rival. She figured she'd got the wrong year – but then she read the final line.

... the winner of the over-40s race was Timothy Garrison
from Whitecliff Athletics Club. Pictures and full coverage on
p17–20.

The pages felt brittle as she turned inside until she was looking across a series of dotted black-and-white photographs. The runners had worn the tiniest of shorts and the photos were borderline top shelf. There were pictures of the mass start, plus the winner reaching the pier first. There were podium photos, a few from what looked like a children's race – and then one of a man holding a medal. A woman was at his side and a younger girl on the other.

Over-40s winner Timothy Garrison celebrates with his wife,
Margaret, and daughter, Samantha

Now she was looking for it, Millie could see the gentle resemblance of the woman in the photo to the hunched lady who lived at number seven. There was something in the way they pressed their lips together that was the same. Samantha Garrison was probably fourteen or fifteen and had that teenagery rolled eyes look, of wanting to be somewhere else.

Millie took the paper through to the kitchen, where Guy and Oliver were now in opposite corners, working their way through piles. Barry was near the back door and Millie opened it to let him out.

For a moment, she thought she'd ask about the money, except it felt like something for when it was only her and Guy. There would be a simple answer.

'I've found something,' she said.

Oliver was closest, so she passed him the paper and pointed to the photo of the trio. He stared at it for a few seconds and then looked up with a crinkled forehead.

'I *do* remember a Samantha,' he said curiously. 'Sam. She babysat me a few times when I would've been six or seven. She would have been maybe mid-twenties? Something like that? I remember because I didn't know girls could be called Sam before her...'

It was the sort of vague, recovered memory that happened to Guy all the time when faced with a story such as this.

Oliver passed the paper to Guy, who scanned the photograph.

'I guess we did know them,' Oliver said, sounding more surprised than anyone. He looked up to Guy: 'Do you remember anything more about the Garrisons?'

It got a slow shake of the head. 'I don't think I do,' Guy replied. 'I don't remember a Margaret Garrison, or a Samantha.'

Millie realised Oliver was watching her. 'What do we do now?' he asked.

. . .

Millie had Oliver drop her off at the end of the road where she and Alex had once lived. There was a dejected sense of confusion to Oliver as he drove away. Millie told him that she'd be in touch if she or Guy thought of anything more they could do that didn't involve directly confronting his mother. He was reluctant to do that, given what had happened the first time. If Margaret Garrison refused to say why his mum had visited, Millie wasn't sure what more could be done.

There were lights on inside Alex's place. The house that Millie had never quite been able to think of as anything other than hers. She'd chosen it, after all.

It was Rachel who answered the door. She was in a set of floaty pyjamas, her hair in a loose ponytail.

Her face fell as she realised it was Millie. 'I thought you were the Deliveroo bloke,' she said, failing to hide her disappointment.

'Is Alex in?'

'Why?'

'Do we have to do this again? You ask what I want, I say I want to talk to Alex. You ask why, I say I'd rather tell him. We go back and forth for five minutes and then, eventually, I talk to him anyway.'

Rachel rolled her eyes. 'You know we're married, don't you?'

'I was at the reception, remember? When you made a mess of your dress...'

It was a low blow, considering Eric had 'accidentally dropped' a glass of red wine over the bride. That was the phrase Rachel had been telling relatives to explain what happened. In reality, Eric had thrown it on her in a pique of stepson rebellion.

Rachel's eyes narrowed and Millie could feel her trying to think of a cutting comeback. 'You're such a slag,' she managed, before turning and heading into the house.

Millie laughed at the absurdity of it all. If in doubt, there were few insults better than calling someone a slag. It was teenage stuff.

When Alex appeared on the doorstep, he was unshaven in lounge pants and a top that had a print of a suit with a dickie bow. He peered over Millie's shoulder towards the road.

'We thought you were the Deliveroo guy,' he said. 'Eric's in bed, if that's why you're here.' He checked his watch purposefully, needlessly making the point.

'What are you getting?' Millie asked.

Alex blinked wearily at her and fought away a yawn. 'There's a new curry place on the hill...'

'Prawn Madras,' Millie replied and, for a moment, Alex narrowed his eyes, wondering how she knew. 'It's what you always ordered,' Millie added.

'What do you want?' he asked, wearily.

Millie nodded towards the inside of the house. 'I take it you didn't tell her what we talked about the other night.'

Alex took a small step forward and pulled the door behind him, so that it was almost locked in place. He was wearing a pair of Uggs –shoes he'd called 'ridiculous' when Millie herself had once bought a pair.

'Why are you here again?'

'I told you the other night. I want custody of Eric. I want *you* to give me custody.'

Alex was quiet for a moment. He was biting his bottom lip and then brushed something away from the fake pocket of his top.

When he spoke, it was with a wistful sigh. 'Did you ever think it would come to this when we got married?' he asked.

He was looking directly at her, staring into Millie's soul for what felt like the first time... ever. They'd not had any sort of connection such as this since the separation – and probably a year or two before that.

Millie stumbled over her words. 'Of course not,' she

managed. 'I *chose* this house, remember? You wanted to move closer to the bypass onto that new estate. You said it would take twenty minutes off your commute each way – but it would have added twenty-five minutes to Eric's journey to school.'

Alex was nodding slowly. 'I'd forgotten that. I drive past those houses every day. There was something on the news the other day about the foundations sinking on a few of them...'

For the briefest of moments, Millie had the life she'd left. She'd be in her pyjamas waiting for a curry to arrive as Eric slept upstairs. She'd be having aimless conversations about sinking foundations and commute times.

Then she was back.

'You can't have custody,' Alex said.

'Why? I know you don't really want him.' Millie had rehearsed this part. 'I'm not saying you don't love him – but I know you don't want this seven days a week. You didn't when we were together. You wanted me to be a stay-at-home mum.'

'No, I didn't—'

Millie cut him off with a stare. That was the other thing about Craig telling her how Guy had wanted Carol to remain at home while he worked. It had felt too close. Too familiar.

Alex shrank under her gaze. He hadn't *specifically* told her to stay at home – but he and his mum had dropped enough hints. There'd been the throwaway lines from his mother about Alex 'making enough for both you', or how she was convinced Alex had 'become a success' because he had such one-on-one attention as an infant. Then there was Alex himself claiming he saw a piece in the *Spectator* that children earned more in later life if they had a full-time parent during their first four years. He never suggested *he* should be the one to be a full-time parent.

Alex was pressed back into the doorway, wanting to escape.

'It's because you can't bear to see me win anything, isn't it?' Millie said. 'Even if "win" is the wrong word. Even if it's what

Eric wants and, deep down, it's what you want, you still won't
let me have anything.'

Alex was quiet. He glanced over her shoulder again and
then checked his watch. 'Don't tell me what I feel,' he said.

'We were together long enough. I do have some idea about
the person I married.'

Alex leaned in and his voice was a ferocious whisper. 'You
humiliated me, Mill. The first I knew of your affair was from my
mum because she read it in the paper. I had to pretend I was
fine in front of everyone. My workmates knew. Our clients. The
partners.' He nodded over the road. 'Our neighbours.'

'And this is your revenge? Because of that, you'll keep our
son hostage, even though he won't even call you "Dad"?'

Lights swung around behind Millie, sliding across the driveway. It was almost dark and she'd somehow not realised. The
curries had arrived.

'I'm going inside,' Alex hissed. 'If you want to have this
conversation again, get your solicitor to talk to mine.'

He called a 'hi' to the delivery driver, who was lifting a bag
from the passenger seat.

Millie didn't bother with a 'bye'. She walked to the end of
the road and cut through the alley. She emerged opposite the
Co-op where Karen worked and then got a taxi from the rank
outside. The driver wanted to tell her about his son getting
picked for the town's Under 15's rugby team, so Millie let him
as they crossed town. She mumbled a few 'that's good' but
otherwise switched off.

For some reason, despite all evidence and history, she'd
thought Alex would agree to her having custody this time. She
stewed and re-ran the conversation, wondering if she'd handled
it wrong. If a word here or there might have made a difference.

The taxi pulled in at the end of her drive and Millie gave
the bloke a tenner, told him to keep the change and then headed
for the door. She was so lost in her thoughts that she almost trod

on the person sitting on the step. If it hadn't been for the smell of nicotine, she probably would.

'Jack...?'

He stubbed out his cigarette on the ground and stood, while picking up a small rucksack. 'I was wondering when you'd get back,' he said.

'Why are you smoking?'

'Because I like it and I wish I'd never given up.'

It was honest, if nothing else.

'Why are you *here*?'

'Because I've left Rish.'

TWENTY-FIVE

There was little point in Millie pretending she was surprised. It was the sort of news she'd somehow been expecting, while also convincing herself it couldn't happen.

'Is this because of the emails I told you about?' she asked.

Jack shrugged. 'Sort of. Yes.' A pause. 'No.' He nodded at the door. 'Can we go in? I've been sitting on your doorstep for an hour. I've smoked half a pack and need a coffee.'

Millie eyed the scorched, ashen remains on the path and found herself wondering who was going to clear it up. Almost certainly her.

She unlocked the door and led Jack into the kitchen. After filling the kettle, she set it boiling as Jack went through her fridge and cupboards.

'Why do you never have anything in?' he asked.

'Because it's only me who lives here. Luke brings supplies when he comes over.'

Jack slumped onto a chair as he thumbed a two-finger KitKat he'd found. 'Can I have this?'

'Fine.'

'What about the other seven?'

'Have them, too.'

Jack stood again and grabbed the full packet of KitKats, before falling back onto the chair. He ripped the paper and foil and bit the chocolate in half, without bothering to separate the fingers.

'That's unforgiveable,' Millie said, deadpan.

'Leaving Rish?'

'Biting a KitKat in half without pulling it apart... but, yeah, Rish...'

Jack wasn't in the mood for jokes. He had the other half of the chocolate and then separated the fingers on a second bar. 'Do you remember when these used to be bigger?' he said. 'Everything's smaller now. Wagon Wheels used to be the size of your head, now they're like a two-pound coin.'

Millie waited as the kettle began to bubble. 'Is this because of Isaac?' she asked.

She wanted an answer, a quick 'of course not'. She wanted a furious denial. Instead, there was nothing except the snap of KitKat fingers.

And, from nowhere, it was Millie who was on the warpath. All the time, the effort, the pain, the thought she'd put into getting custody of Eric – and here was Jack walking out on his six-year-old.

'You're a disgrace,' Millie said. There was such fire in her voice that Jack's head snapped up, wondering if this was some weird joke. 'There's this young boy who's up for adoption. He's living who knows where – and has no idea what it means to be safe and loved. Then he finds two people who give him that. He goes to school and he starts to settle. There are two people who he thinks will look after him – and you've gone and walked out. How do you think he feels?'

Jack had his mouth open as if about to fire a reply. Millie couldn't remember either of them ever being openly angry with the other. They were listeners, not ragers – but not now.

When Jack replied, his tone was more of a sigh. 'He doesn't know yet. He was in bed...'

'How do you think he *will* feel?'

Jack's eyes were closed as if hiding. 'We can't stay together just because we adopted a child.'

'So why adopt in the first place? It's not like you went ahead with it years ago.'

Millie knew the answer, she always had. She'd been Jack and Rishi's character witness for the adoption agency. She knew then that Jack wasn't sure – and she should have said.

'Because Rish wanted children,' Jack replied. 'I didn't want him to leave me.'

The kettle snapped off and Millie furiously sloshed boiling water into a mug. She was so annoyed, so careless, that she scalded her hand. When she plonked the mug in front of Jack, along with the jar of instant granules, more spilled over the edge. She was too furious to stir them in for him. As for milk, he could find his own.

'So now you're leaving him. And instead of going your own ways a year and a half ago, there are now three of you who are going to be miserable? Worst of all, there's a six-year-old...'

Jack dunked a KitKat in his tea and slurped down the sticky remains. 'Can I stay?' he asked.

Millie suddenly realised why he had a rucksack with him. Somehow, she'd missed its significance.

'Fine,' she said, although she didn't feel it. She probably should have said 'no' and wasn't entirely sure why she hadn't, other than that they were friends.

They sat at the table, not talking. Jack took intermittent sips of his tea as he worked his way through the KitKats. There wasn't much to add.

When he finished eating all eight chocolate bars, he rubbed his eyes and half turned so that he wasn't facing her.

'It sounds like you're stringing Luke along,' he said.

This was *also* the sort of conversation they never had.

'We're both adults,' Millie said. 'Sometimes *adult* relationships don't work. It's not like we're planning to marry. We see each other a few times a week. We eat and watch TV. Six-year-olds don't get the luxury of choosing their relationships...'

Jack was quiet again and Millie could sense him searching for something that would turn it around on her. He wanted to stay in her house – but only if they were both in the wrong. If they were both broken.

'Did you kill your parents?'

The question echoed, as if the ghosts of her parents were repeating it. Jack had never asked Millie outright. The only person she cared about who had was Guy – but he'd immediately told her not to answer.

Jack was still going: 'They died of an overdose, both of them, and I found the pills hidden in the living room. Plus, you went from a divorce, to living with your parents to all this. You don't have to work if you don't want. You get to *volunteer* at the place where I *need* to work because you can afford to.'

It sounded spiteful and brutal. Millie had never heard things like that before. She thought she was helping, but perhaps it *was* a slap in the face that she could afford to help for free, while those around her needed the hours.

She suddenly wondered if she and Jack *were* truly friends.

This felt like something that had been festering.

'Do you really want to know what happened to Mum and Dad?' Millie asked.

'Yes.'

TWENTY-SIX

'No,' Jack added, and then: 'Maybe.' Another pause. 'I don't know.'

'Pick one,' Millie replied.

Jack yawned and scratched his head. He reached for another chocolate bar, even though he'd eaten them all, and yawned a second time. 'It's been a long week,' he said. 'Isaac's still having night terrors and, if anything, it's getting worse. Rish sat up with him most of the night Wednesday.'

'That's not a reason to leave.'

Jack didn't reply to that as another yawn came and went – and then Millie joined in. It was infectious.

'If you need to ask about Mum and Dad,' Millie said, 'then you might as well choose your own answer. If you really think I did what you said, then why are we hanging around almost every day? You can't think much of me...'

There was no reply to that, which is what Millie wanted. What was there to say?

Jack had found another KitKat among the debris of wrapping. He bit it in half, munched, then had what was left.

'Are the sheets still in the dresser?' he asked.

Millie pushed herself up. 'I'll make up the bed for you.' She rounded the table and squeezed his shoulder. 'Like old times,' she said.

'Less alcohol now.'

Jack stood and, before Millie knew what was happening, they were hugging. She could feel the dampness of the sweat through his top pressed against her.

'I'll do it,' he said. 'I think I want to go to bed now, if you don't mind.'

Millie let him go and he stepped towards the doorway.

'Alex will never give you custody,' he said. 'You must know that. People do crazy things when affairs are involved. It's not about Eric, it's about you.'

Millie was temporarily speechless, as she hadn't told Jack about being at Alex's place an hour before. She'd come to the same conclusion.

'If you ever want custody, you'll have to do more than ask,' Jack added.

Millie replied that she knew and then Jack drifted into the hall and up the stairs. Millie listened to the bathroom door opening and closing, and then, not long after, the spare bedroom.

He was right that people did crazy things when affairs were involved – but, as Millie considered it, she wondered if it wasn't the point he thought he was making...

TWENTY-SEVEN

DAY SIX

Jack was waiting in the kitchen for Millie when she came down the stairs the next morning. His eyelids were heavy and he had the type of expression that looked as if it might be interrupted by a yawn at any moment.

'I was going to make you breakfast,' he said. 'But you only have Crunchy Nut Corn Flakes in the cupboard – and I reckon you can pour those in a bowl yourself.'

Millie filled a glass with water from the tap. Jack waited until she was settled and listening.

'I'm going back to Rish,' he said, while staring at a spot somewhere close to the toaster. 'I slept on it... sort of. Actually, I didn't sleep much but you're right about Isaac. It's not fair. I already texted Rish to say I'll see him later.' Jack made a point of looking to the clock on the microwave. 'I've got work this morning,' he added. 'I need to go to the flat to get changed.'

There was an assumption that Rishi would accept the U-turn, which he probably would. Millie wasn't quite ready to let it go. 'If you're only going back for Isaac, then you can't spend ten years being miserable. It'll rub off on him anyway.'

'You were the one who wanted me to go back.'

'No. I said you shouldn't have taken on the responsibility of a child if it wasn't what you wanted. He's only six and already vulnerable from being up for adoption in the first place. He needs to feel loved and safe – and that's not what he's going to get if you're unhappy.'

For a moment, it looked as if Jack was going to reply but then he simply yawned. 'I need a shower at mine,' he said. 'Are you in today?'

He was talking about the nursing home, and whether she was volunteering today. It was impossible not to remember the resentment from the night before. That she could pick and choose her moments to work – but that he *had* to.

'No,' Millie replied.

'I'll see y'around then...'

Jack picked up his rucksack from the floor and headed through the house. A draught billowed momentarily as the front door opened and then closed.

Millie had no idea where the past few hours left them as friends. Perhaps, somehow, they were in a better place because of all the honesty? Or, perhaps, their friendship only existed because of the bottled-up lack of truthfulness.

More importantly, Millie wasn't sure where poor Isaac would be left.

She shouldn't have given them the character reference. Shouldn't have insisted Jack was ready for parenthood. She'd known at the time it was a mistake but she'd done it for the sake of their friendship. And now...

Millie's phone buzzed, with Oliver's name on the screen.

You up?

Before she had the chance to decide whether she wanted to reply, the phone was ringing. Millie answered, partly against her better judgement, and Oliver was straight into things, without even the briefest of hellos.

'I found a Sam Garrison,' he said. 'I was googling around and there are a few Samantha Garrisons in America but I couldn't find anyone around here. There are loads of Sam Garrisons all over the place – but most of them seem to be men. Then I remembered that her dad won that Sandy Mile and I wondered if she was into running. I went onto the athletics club website and scrolled through all the results – and there's an S Garrison listed in a load of races from the past ten years or so.'

It was a lot of information to take in first thing in the morning. Oliver was speaking with the speed of someone already on their fourth coffee.

'How do you know the "S" stands for Samantha?' Millie asked.

'I didn't at first – but I was clicking around, looking for anything extra, and there's a meet the coaches section on the website. I went on that – and there's a Sam Garrison who coaches the under-elevens.' He was speaking faster and faster and finished with a breathless flourish:

'She's a primary school teacher in Whitecliff.'

'Have you slept?' Millie asked.

The question left a gasping Oliver momentarily silent. 'I was up early,' he replied.

Millie was trying to remember if there was a Miss or Mrs Garrison who taught at Eric's school. Whitecliff was a small town and Millie could have probably named all the primary schools if she thought about it.

'Where does she teach?' Millie asked.

'Ridge Road Primary.'

It wasn't Eric's.

'I found an article from last Christmas about a nativity play,' Oliver added. 'There's a photo of Willow class, with their teacher, Miss Garrison. She looks fifty-something, so she's the right age to have babysat me...'

Millie understood the excitement but it was a bit of a stretch from Oliver's strange daisy tattoo, to Oliver's mother, to a woman who once lived down the road, to that woman's grown-up daughter. It was sounding a bit stalkery. She almost didn't want to ask the next question.

'What are you planning to do?'

'I was going to wait until school's finished and hang around the gates, or the car park. Maybe—'

'A childless man standing outside a school doesn't sound like a good idea...'

Millie realised a moment too late that he knew that.

'I thought *we* could ask if she's heard of the Children of Enlightenment,' Oliver said. 'Or maybe just if she knows my mum? Or if she remembers babysitting me? See what she says...? There has to be a reason my mum went to see Margaret Garrison after I asked her about the commune.'

Millie's sigh probably said enough.

'My girlfriend's back from holiday tomorrow night,' Oliver added, and there was a definite sense that, once she'd returned, some degree of sanity would prevail. She was on holiday – but this investigation was his.

'If Sam doesn't want to talk, we can leave it there and that'll be the end,' he added, still breathless. 'I just think... I think she might want to talk to me if I show her the tattoo...'

It was wishful thinking, like believing a lottery win was destined because someone had found a pound on the pavement outside the shop.

Millie knew he was going anyway – and, if it was without her, she might not find out what had been going on. She couldn't leave things now.

'What time?' she asked.

'I checked the school website and they finish at three-thirty.

Maybe we can meet just across from Ridge Road? Or go
together...?'

He definitely wanted company – and, after all the talk of
people doing unexpected things on the back of affairs, it was
going to be quite the day for confrontation.

·

TWENTY-EIGHT

Millie was leaning on the fence opposite the Co-op. It was around the corner from where Alex lived and the place where, as Karen had pointed out, Millie used to go for cheer-up cheese. She wondered if Karen was behind the counter at that moment and whether she should have a look. Perhaps it would be better to run her idea past Karen first, instead of going for outright confrontation...

Or not.

When Millie crossed the road, it wasn't the Co-op she entered. Instead, she went into the Ladbrokes next door. She'd never been in a betting shop before, even though there now appeared to be one on every corner. Not to mention, every television break was littered with endless shouty men banging on about throwing their life savings on whether a goal would be scored.

The inside was bright and white, like an Apple store but with lots more televisions. Digital boards were displaying odds, while men – all men – stood watching horse races. Millie was the only woman in the place, which might usually have brought some attention, except nobody was interested in anything other than the screens.

There were a pair of counters at the far end, each protected by what looked like extra thick glass. Employees were standing behind each counter, which is when Millie realised she *wasn't* the only woman in the shop. The other was typing something into a computer as the man at her side stared blankly towards Millie.

Millie approached the counter and took in 'JORDAN' on the man's name tag. He was probably in his mid-twenties, and had patchy bumfluff on his chin, plus hair that looked like someone had cut it with a knife and fork.

She saw it in him the moment she said 'hello'. Jordan's eyes widened and his mouth opened. Karen's brother recognised Millie, even though they'd never met.

And Millie knew.

Alex was so betrayed by her affair that he was determined not to give her anything when it came to custody of Eric – even if it was better for him. That was because people did the strangest of things when it came to affairs and betrayal.

Jordan had a similar build to Nick but it wasn't even that which told Millie who he was. It was the way he was staring at her, not only with recognition – but terror. She was the last person he'd expected to walk into his workplace.

'Jordan, isn't it?' Millie said.

He blinked and coughed, then stumbled over a 'yeah...?' that sounded like a question. Millie pointed towards his name tag and he followed her finger, before righting himself. 'Oh, right... yeah. I'm Jordan. How can I, uh... help?'

For a moment, Millie could see the relief within him. He was off the hook and it was a coincidence Millie had walked into this particular shop.

'I think I know your sister,' Millie said. 'Karen, right? She works at the Co-op next door...?'

'Yeah, uh... Karen...?' It sounded like another question.

The woman behind the counter had stopped what she was doing and was now watching the exchange with curiosity.

'Just saying "hi",' Millie added.

'Can I help you with anything?' he said.

'I think you already have.'

Millie turned and headed for the door. She wasn't sure what she'd expected before entering the shop. She hadn't even been certain that Jordan would be on shift. Then, when he was, she didn't know what she'd say.

In the end, none of it mattered – because he'd told her himself without saying a word. The man under the balaclava, the man who'd robbed the shop, was unquestionably friends with Chris from behind the counter.

Karen's brother, Jordan.

TWENTY-NINE

Ridge Road Primary School was on the outskirts of town, at the edge of a new estate that was still being built when Millie was young enough to have attended.

There was a single building, with a padded play area. It was a far cry from the huts in which Millie had been taught, not to mention the tarmacked playground, from which she still had a scar on the back of her thigh after a childhood tumble.

Millie and Oliver were watching from her car as a steady stream of parents collected their children from the gates. Some headed off to their vehicles, while others walked to the bus stop at the end of the street. From the safety of the driver's seat, Oliver's plan didn't seem quite as mad as it had sounded that morning.

Oliver had been quiet on the journey over, not that Millie blamed him. It had been a long few days – and he still had no clear answer to what was on the back of his ear. If anything, he had more questions and he'd managed to fall out with his mother.

'I guess you've done this quite a few times,' Oliver said.

'Ambush teachers outside their school?' Millie tried to make it clear she was joking but it sounded harsher than she meant.

'School pick-ups,' Oliver replied.

There hadn't been as many as Millie would have wanted, considering Eric was mainly collected by Rachel. There seemed little point in complaining about that in the moment. Oliver didn't wait for a reply anyway.

'My girlfriend's started to talk about having a baby,' he said.

'That makes it sound a lot like it's something she wants, not you...?'

Perhaps it was because of everything that had happened in the past day, but Millie felt sensitive over that sort of distinction.

Oliver shuffled a little, and released the seatbelt he was still needlessly wearing. 'I'd never really thought about having kids before. I'm not saying I'm against it, or that it's a bad thing.'

'How long have you been together?'

'Almost three years. We've been living together about two.' A pause. 'We got a joint bank account about three months ago.'

'Big step,' Millie said, and even she wasn't sure whether she was teasing. She and Alex had never got as far as opening a joint account – and they'd not only been married, they'd had a child. She wasn't sure why. It was one of those things they'd never got around to.

'I think she'll have a lot to say when she gets back,' Oliver added. 'All her friends on her trip are about the same age as her and most are settled. They either have kids, or they're trying. Her mum's always dropping hints about grandchildren...'

The stream of children leaving the school had slowed to the final dozen or so. The street that had previously been nose-to-tail cars was close to clear.

'Women are having babies later now,' Millie replied. 'But there comes a point when it's definitely harder to get pregnant. Your girlfriend probably feels that, after three years with you, this is her chance. If you don't want to have children with her, she doesn't have a lot of time to move on...'

Oliver was nodding. 'Mum said you have to be sure it's what you want because, once you have a child, it's not all about you any longer.'

Millie shivered at the second-hand advice. It was too close to what had been going on in her life. And Jack's.

'Let's go and find Samantha,' Millie said, as she reached for the door handle.

A modest car park was attached to the side of the school. A large 'STAFF ONLY' sign was pinned to the wall outside, and another inside. As Millie and Oliver reached the gates, a small girl exited the main doors of the school. She was in a red sweat-shirt and holding hands with a woman who Millie assumed was a teacher. The pair of them crossed the playground and stopped at a set of railings, where the teacher started talking to the girl's mother. The girl was showing off some sort of drawing or paint-ing, as the two adults chatted amiably.

Millie was wondering how long they'd have to wait for the teachers to start heading for their cars when she realised Oliver was a few paces away from her. He'd moved almost impercepti-bly. Millie stretched and pulled his sleeve. When he turned, he was blinking, as if he wasn't sure how he'd drifted away.

'Is that her?' Millie asked. It felt like fate.

Oliver nodded.

The teacher was one of those people who could have been anything from mid-thirties to mid-sixties. She had bony arms and legs and, even standing still, had a spring about her that made it seem as if she might bang out a 10K on a whim.

The parent and daughter turned and headed off towards the road, as the teacher twisted to go back into the school.

Time froze.

Samantha Garrison almost seemed to be hovering. She had

one foot off the ground and was statuesque in mid-pirouette as she stared across the car park towards Millie and Oliver.

Towards *Oliver*.

There was a rush of air and then Samantha put down her suspended foot, and turned to face them properly. A sense of self-consciousness washed across Millie as the other woman started to walk towards them. They were unknown adults hanging around a playground and it was going to take a lot of explaining. It was such a bad idea to come – and it always had been.

Samantha stopped in front of them but she was only interested in Oliver. She looked him up and down and then: 'It's been a *long* time since I saw you...'

The age difference was somewhere around twenty years and it made it look as if Samantha might have been an old teacher of Oliver's. That they had run into each other unexpectedly and would have the briefest of catch-ups before never seeing one another again.

There was silence, but Millie could feel something in the air.

'How'd you recognise me?' Oliver asked after a while. His voice was a confused croak.

'Mum said that *your* mum had gone over and then, the next day, you'd gone to ask some questions.' Samantha paused and then added: 'I figured it was only a matter of time until you came to see me. I guess I've always known you'd come one day...'

THIRTY

Oliver was momentarily dumbstruck. 'How did you recognise me?' he repeated.

Samantha took the smallest of steps backwards. 'I've always kept a distant eye. Nothing too close, or too weird. I know how that sounds but I'd look for your name online. Things like that.'

It could have sounded creepy and yet there was something comforting about it. Soothing.

'Mum pointed out you were on Facebook advertising that you did guitar lessons,' she added. 'You popped up in her feed and I thought that was nice.'

'Why have you been keeping an eye on me?'

Samantha took another small step backwards and watched a pair of teachers who were exiting the school. They waved and she waved back as they headed to their cars.

'Do you want to come inside?' Samantha asked. 'You and...?'

She glanced to Millie and Oliver said that she was his friend. Millie gave her name and then Samantha turned and led them towards the school. The three of them passed another teacher who was leaving with a giant box under her arm. Aside from a nod of acknowledgement, she paid Millie and Oliver no attention.

Samantha led them through the main doors, into a toasty reception area, and along a hall. The walls were covered with drawings and paintings, plus an alphabet trail that looped along one side and then back across the other. Alex and Rachel had assumed control of the parents' evening visits for Eric and it had been a couple of years since Millie had been inside a primary school. Everything felt that little bit too small. The door frames a few inches too short, the ceilings a fraction low. Like walking into a cave with central heating.

They reached a door with a painted tree and 'Willow' stencilled over the top. Samantha held it open for them and there were more paintings on the walls inside, plus an animal mural on the far side. Chairs that were barely knee high were dotted around a series of low tables as Samantha closed the door behind them.

'There are some adult chairs around here somewhere,' she said, as she turned in a circle. She added a 'wait here', and then disappeared back into the corridor.

Millie and Oliver were alone in the classroom and Millie drifted across to the corner, where a small lizard was lounging in a vivarium, underneath a heat lamp. The creature could have fit in Millie's palm and its skin was a greeny-yellow, with five bulbous toes on each of its legs.

Oliver was at her side. 'Did you have a class pet?' he asked croakily.

'I don't think so.'

'We had some fish. I remember we went back on a Monday and one of them was a lot bigger than it had been the week before. Our teacher said it must have eaten a lot at the weekend. It was about twenty years later that I realised it must have died and she'd bought a new one...'

The lizard turned to give them a bit of side eye, though otherwise seemed unworried by their presence.

'Do you know what it is?' Millie asked.

Oliver nudged the card at the side of the tank, which had 'Echo' printed on it. 'Gecko,' he said.

The door sounded behind them and Samantha was back with a pair of stacked plastic chairs. Except for the size, they were identical to the small ones in the classroom, as if she'd enlarged them somehow.

'These were the best I could find,' Samantha said, as she pulled them apart and placed them next to her desk. A moment later and they were sitting at her side, like a pair of naughty kids who had been held back a few decades.

Samantha unlocked her desk drawer and removed a bag of chocolate eclairs. She held them up and, after receiving two shaken heads, dispatched it back into her desk.

They were doing well to avoid the reason they were there... and then all pretence was gone.

'Do you already know about the Children of Enlightenment?' Samantha asked. It was casual, as if enquiring whether they'd seen the rain that morning.

Oliver stumbled at first, which wasn't a surprise. They had spent close to a week going in circles and, now, someone seemingly wasn't trying to hide.

'I didn't,' Oliver replied, 'Not until a few days ago. I heard they were some sort of church, or commune, or—'

'Cult,' Samantha said firmly. 'They were a cult.'

She let it sit and it felt more final when she'd said it. There were none of the niceties of saying it was a friendship group, or an innocent gathering. There was no question.

'We're talking thirty-five years ago when I was twenty or twenty-one,' Samantha continued. 'I'd never had a proper job and had been living at home. I know you won't remember but there was a big movement around nuclear disarmament – and I'd started going to a few protests, where I met this boy. There was a bigger rebellious community in Steeple's End, so we moved there together. We ended up living in a squat on the edge of town with a few others.' She laughed gently, perhaps fondly, at that and held up her hands to indicate the space around them. 'I didn't put any of that on my CV when I got into teaching...'

Samantha asked if they wanted some water. Millie and Oliver both said no but she stood abruptly anyway and let out a gentle cough, before disappearing back into the corridor. A minute or so later and she was back with a plastic cup, from which she was sipping.

When she sat, she continued the story as if she hadn't moved. 'I got pregnant within maybe a week of moving to that squat,' she said. 'Predictable, I suppose. I was eight months in when my boyfriend walked out. That was probably predictable as well. His parents ran this mail order company in Brighton and they'd been trying to get him to go back ever since he'd left. I'm not sure he ever told them he had a girlfriend, let alone that I was pregnant.'

'What did you do?' Millie asked.

'The squat was barely liveable. It was just about OK for adults but I couldn't raise a child there. People had been leaving anyway, because our protests hadn't been getting anywhere. Nobody had a job, or money, and there's only so long you can live like that. I was at the point where I figured I'd have to go home. They wouldn't have said it, because they weren't like that, but it would've meant admitting Mum and Dad were right that I shouldn't have left in the first place.' Samantha tailed off momentarily, before adding: 'Nobody likes admitting their parents are right...'

A gentle moment of silent acknowledgement passed between them. Nobody would deny that.

'Then I met a man on the Steeple's End beach,' Samantha said. 'Down where the boats are moored. Do you know it?'

Millie and Oliver both said they did. It hadn't been that long ago that Millie had watched Isaac sit with his legs dangling in the water as other boys let him use their fishing nets. That was before Jack had walked out and then gone back. Too much had happened.

'I still wonder how everything happened,' Samantha said. 'I was clearly, and obviously, *very* pregnant. This man asked when I was due and we started talking and then, somehow... I was out in the woods with him. There were tents and a fire pit. There was a vegetable patch and other people my age... and it was so different to what I was used to. There were a couple of these cabins they'd built, and they said I could pick a bed, which I did. There were blankets they'd woven and a crib that someone had made. It was all really... *nice.*'

She paused for another drink of water and Millie could feel how a young, heavily pregnant, woman could have been drawn in. Especially if the alternative was returning home to admit that person's parents had been right all along. Millie had spoken to Jack about similar things the night before in regard to Isaac. People craved safety and security, especially at vulnerable moments.

'They said I could stay,' Samantha continued. 'There was no rent, no bills. One of the women living there used to be a midwife – and she was great. I had my baby there and then started being a nanny for the other children. For those first few months, it was everything I wanted...'

It was impossible to miss how ominous that sounded.

'That doesn't sound like a cult,' was the first proper thing Oliver said since they'd sat. As Samantha had been speaking, he'd shifted closer to the edge of his seat and was almost balancing in a crouched position.

'No...' Samantha said. 'It took me a long time to see everything properly – and sometimes I wonder if I ever figured it out. Over those months, there were a few weird things that I was finding harder to ignore. The man I met on the beach was called Jaelryn...' She must have seen some degree of recognition in Oliver's face because she added a surprised, 'You know him?'

'Only the name,' Oliver replied.

'I suppose that's the bit that's hardest to describe. Jaelryn had this sort of... magnetism. A charisma. Words don't really exist to describe it because it's more of a feeling that you have from being around someone. I suppose the closest thing is when you're really young, three or four, and your mum or your dad is your whole world. You believe everything they say, and you trust them and...'

She tailed off, though it felt as if she'd been understood. Millie certainly knew what she meant. There was a time when her father had been the centre of her universe.

'Jaelryn would pick different women,' Samantha said. She was staring at the floor now. 'Sometimes girls. Sometimes young girls. They'd be with him in his tent for a few weeks here and there – and then he'd move on. I know how that sounds, how you think someone should have done something. But you *wanted* him to choose you.'

Millie didn't want to ask – and she didn't need to, because Oliver said it: 'Did he choose you?'

That got a gentle shake of the head. 'I kept waiting. I can't really remember those feelings now, other than that I *wanted* him to choose me. There was always another girl.'

She stopped for a sip of her water, before peering over to the gecko. She stood and crossed, then unlocked the cupboard underneath, where she pulled out a tub and a pair of tweezers. The lizard knew what was happening because it was immediately off its rock and underneath the hatch that Samantha slid aside. She plucked a mealworm with the tweezers and lowered it into the creature's waiting mouth.

It was gone in barely a second.

Samantha resealed the vivarium and put the tub and tweezers back in the cupboard. When she sat, there was something resigned about her voice. 'Jaelryn wanted us to all be able to identify each other,' she said. 'He said it was part of giving ourselves over to Enlightenment. It's nonsense but it made sense at the time.'

She touched her ear and Millie knew. Perhaps she'd known since Samantha had told Oliver she'd been keeping an eye on him. She wondered if Oliver knew as well. He was still perched on the very edge chair.

'Jaelryn branded people,' she added – and, this time, Oliver touched his own ear. Almost imperceptibly, Samantha nodded. 'Nothing obvious, nothing big. Just enough.' A pause. 'He called it The Blessing and he wanted to brand my baby...' She took a breath and then a drink, before staring across towards the lizard.

'I'd been there for about a year by then and had been having a few doubts. When he said he wanted to put that mark on my baby, on Victoria, I suppose I finally saw everything for what it was. It was a cult in the woods. It was a man and his women. And the children were being brought up to think it was normal. So I waited... and then I took Victoria and I ran.'

Millie had been wondering whether Oliver knew what she was really saying. He might have been thinking one thing but then Samantha had said 'Victoria'. She'd had a daughter.

There was a silence and both women watched him until: 'I don't think I understand,' he said.

Samantha bowed a fraction. Smiled like a mother seeing their newborn for the first time. 'I didn't only take *my* baby...'

THIRTY-ONE

Oliver was suddenly on his feet and pacing. He strode to the animal mural, turned and came back. He scratched his back ferociously and then his neck, as if something invisible was crawling across him.

Samantha hadn't moved. She waited until Oliver was back on his chair before continuing.

'I took two others,' she said. 'I was still working as the nanny. We had no clocks, or watches, so all we had to go on was whether it was light or dark. It used to be so quiet out there. You couldn't hear the traffic and there were no street lights. I waited until it was night. And waited some more. It was silent. I grabbed Victoria and the two youngest babies. And then I ran as best I could. Part of the reason nobody really bothered us was because there was no official track to get from the village to our site. I wasn't completely sure where I was going – except Dad used to go night running. He told me as long as I noticed where the sun had gone down, then I could figure out what was north, south, east and west. I suppose it stuck, because I knew Steeple's End was east of the site, which is where the sun rose.'

Millie nodded up towards the poster on the wall next to the

board that showed the positions of the sun and Samantha nodded in acknowledgement.

'I've had that up in every class I've ever taught...'

'I take it you found the town?' Millie asked.

'I called home from the payphone that used to be outside the market. I didn't know then but it was two-thirty in the morning. I had to try three times until Dad picked up. The second he heard my voice, he asked, "Where are you?" and it was like he'd been expecting it the whole time I'd been away. He must have driven like a lunatic – especially in those old cars without power steering. It felt like he was there five minutes later. He didn't question the three babies; he drove us all back to Whitecliff...'

There were footsteps from the corridor and Samantha went quiet. The footsteps echoed closer and closer, then further and further away. A creaky door eked open and shut from somewhere in the distance.

'I knew they'd look for me,' Samantha said. 'Jaelryn wasn't violent but... well, he was – but it was all in private. His son, Dashrian, was the sicko who did the dirty work. I once saw him punch someone so hard that he was knocked out cold. That was because the man had stopped digging the vegetable patch to have some water.' Samantha sighed and finished her drink. 'I can't remember why we all thought that was normal...'

She was lost in the thought for a few moments, which wasn't surprising.

It was Millie who asked the obvious question. 'If you knew they'd come for you, why did you go home? Did they know where you lived?'

'Sort of,' Samantha replied. 'They knew my name and I assumed there would have been ways to find out who my parents were. Jaelryn always seemed to know things and I wondered years later if it was because he knew someone at the council? Or the DVLA? That sort of thing. Someone with access to addresses. Truth is, I didn't know if it would be safe.

Dad picked me up that night but I didn't stay with them.' Her gaze flickered across Oliver. 'I lived down the road...'

It took him a few seconds to catch on: 'With... with my Mum and Dad...?'

Samantha nodded. 'I didn't go out for weeks,' she said. 'Months, I suppose. My mum would sometimes say she thought someone was watching the house but she never actually saw anyone. Over time, I wondered how much of things with Jaelryn was a feeling, compared to a fact. Perhaps he *didn't* know all those things about people? Perhaps he *never* came looking for me? Or, if he did, he had no idea where I came from after all...? I wondered if it was all an illusion, that he wanted us to think he had more power than he did.'

Millie wasn't sure Oliver had been listening. He'd been fidgeting, mouth opening and closing as he waited for a moment to speak. 'You said there were three babies...?'

'Yes.'

'Me...?'

It was massive, perhaps the biggest moment of Oliver's life, and yet it happened with a nod. Huge and tiny at the same time.

'Georgia?' he asked.

'Those weren't your names then,' Samantha replied. 'You were Lek, which means small person. You were tiny back then.'

Oliver had a moment to gulp it in. He was taking things remarkably well, considering.

'She was called "Sook",' Samantha added. 'It was something to do with nature. Jaelryn gave everyone new names. I was "Rinzen", which he said meant clever.' A pause. 'I've never looked it up...' She repeated 'Rinzen...' to herself and then added: 'For a while, I was looking after the three of you at your parents' house. They were helping, obviously. When we thought it was safe, when we'd not heard anything in months, I got a flat on the other side of town, nowhere near my mum and dad. I couldn't keep all three of you there, so your parents took you. They'd been looking after you a lot anyway. Some of Mum and Dad's friends took Sook... took *Georgia*. I hid with Victoria.'

Oliver was nodding along but didn't seem to know what to say. Millie didn't blame him. Entire parts of his life were unravelling at a speed he couldn't possibly have fathomed.

'When was the fire?' Millie asked.

'Maybe a year later?' Samantha replied, not questioning how much they already knew. 'Perhaps not quite that long. Mum called and asked if I'd seen the news. It had been on breakfast TV and they'd flown a helicopter over the site. I could picture the tents and the cabins as they used to be – but they were all gone. There was just smoke.'

It was only at that moment when Millie realised her father had almost certainly reported on the fire. He'd been the local TV newsreader at the time.

'They said Jaelryn was dead,' Samantha added. 'And I couldn't believe it. Even though I'd been out for a year or so, he felt like the sort of person who couldn't die. As if he'd be around forever. I was planning to move a long way away, to have some sort of normal life where he'd never find me... and then it was over.'

'Have you ever run into anyone from the camp?' Millie asked.

A shake of the head. 'Never. I don't think anyone ever knew how many people died and how many had already left. It's not like there was a register. I always half-expected it...' She nodded to Oliver. 'It's why I kept my distance from you. Sometimes, I couldn't resist. You probably don't remember but I babysat you a few times.'

'I remember...'

They looked to each other and Millie couldn't read what either of them was thinking. Samantha was the woman who stole him from his parents, or the woman who rescued him from hell. Or she was both.

She'd waited thirty-five years to tell the story and now, surrounded by chairs that were too small, and a lizard that ate worms, it was out.

'Who was my real mum?' Oliver asked.

The hairs rose on Millie's arms. It felt like a dangerous question, a dangerous moment.

Samantha didn't flinch, and it was as if she'd been rehearsing this conversation those entire three-and-a-half decades. 'She was called Caroline. She would've had a name that Jaelryn gave her but I've forgotten. She was a little older than me but I always thought she was younger. She used to talk about horses. She was into the Badminton Horse Trials, even though I think she'd only seen it on TV before coming to camp.'

'And my dad...?'

It was an even more dangerous question and Millie knew the answer from the way Samantha breathed in. From the way her eyebrow flickered.

Oliver answered himself: 'Jaelryn...?'

A nod.

'She'd been with the Children of Enlightenment for longer than me. Jaelryn was always harder on his own kids.'

Oliver was blinking rapidly, as if trying to force the information to go in. 'What happened to Caroline... to Mum?'

Samantha breathed in again and the answer was there. 'When Jaelryn finished with the girls, they were sent back to the rest of camp. They were meant to fit back in, and take on whatever role he gave. Your mum... Caroline, she, um... didn't take it well.'

Oliver's chair creaked and he was on his feet again, standing over them now. 'What happened?' he asked, and there was a panic.

'After she'd given birth, she wouldn't do what she was told, so Dashrian told her she couldn't eat. Jaelryn always left that sort of thing to his son – and that was always Dashrian's rule: no work, no food. Except nobody *ever* refused to work, until your mum...'

Oliver was pacing again.

'I don't know why nobody stepped in,' Samantha said. 'Maybe they did and I didn't see? After a while, when she still wasn't allowed to eat, Dashrian took her into his own shack and then... we never saw her again...'

The room was cold, plus simultaneously light and dark. The sun was up and Millie could see and yet there were shadows everywhere.

'She was so tiny,' Samantha continued. 'She'd gone so long without eating that, in the end, she couldn't, even if she wanted to. Dashrian told us she starved herself and, somehow, it all felt normal. As if she brought it on herself.'

Oliver had stopped striding. He was sitting on one of the small tables, chest rising and falling. Millie wondered if she should go to him and tried to think of what could be said. Except there was nothing.

'I know it's a lot,' Samantha said. 'That's the other reason I've left you alone. I didn't know what to do. I was twenty or twenty-one at the time, a kid. I knew I needed to get Victoria out of there and, in the moment, I grabbed you as well. And Sook— *Georgia*. You were all so small. Then there was the fire and I had no idea who was in it. I heard that Dashrian might have been living in Steeple's End for a few years after, so I assumed he *wasn't* in the fire. I've never been back to Steeple's End since I left. Not once. There've been school trips, things like that, but I've always avoided the place.'

'We were told Dashrian died,' Millie said.

There was quiet in the room. Quiet in the school. It felt as if everyone had gone home, including whoever locked up.

Nobody spoke for a while and then, little more than a whisper: 'Thank you,' Oliver said. He repeated it, louder. He and Samantha were watching each other across the room and Millie was the invader.

'You don't have to say that,' Samantha replied. Her voice was a croak now.

There was another moment of quiet and then Oliver glanced across to Millie and caught her eye. 'You OK?' she asked.

He laughed gently, more of a snort, perhaps. 'I mean, my dad was a cult leader, my birth mum was starved to death, the people I thought were my parents aren't actually mine, and I'm branded by a symbol of it all. Other than that...'

He snorted a second time and Millie smiled kindly at him. She didn't know what to say.

'Your mum and dad looked after you,' Samantha said. 'That's the other reason I kept half an eye on you. I wanted to know you were safe and that I did the right thing.'

In a blink, Oliver had moved across the room and was holding hands with Samantha. They didn't speak but they didn't need to. Millie felt her chest tightening; a lump growing in her throat.

'I'll have to tell Georgia,' he said.

'Let me give you my number,' Samantha replied. 'Tell her to call if she wants to talk. Or meet.'

Oliver handed her his phone and she typed her number into it, before handing it back.

It felt like an end of a sort, but perhaps a beginning as well.

Except Samantha wasn't done.

'There's one more thing,' she said. 'My daughter, Victoria, she doesn't know any of this. Jaelryn never branded her because I ran away before that could happen and her dad wasn't one of the Children. There didn't seem to be a reason for her to know. If you or Georgia ever want to talk to me, I understand, and I'll answer anything I can. But you can't involve Victoria. This is nothing to do with her.'

'Does your husband know?' Oliver asked, before quickly correcting himself: 'Or partner, or...?'

A shake of the head. 'I never really got on with men after everything that happened. It was just me and Victoria for a long time, now it's just me' – she held up her hands again, meaning the class – 'and my kids.'

Millie had the sense that Samantha was one hell of a teacher.

'Is it really OK?' Samantha asked. 'You know your parents love you. The ones who raised you. You'd have never had that from Jaelryn. You'd have been in that fire.'

A short while passed and then Oliver said a quiet: 'I know...'

'I need to tell you one more thing,' Samantha said – and this time it felt different. She was the one fidgeting and looking to the furthest corners of the room. 'They found bodies after the fire – but nobody ever knew how many, or who was who. Nobody ever came to find me – but I never went looking, either.' She stopped and then added: 'Do you know what I'm saying?'

Oliver nodded slowly – and Millie knew as well. Samantha had spent thirty-five years keeping her head down but, in the past week, Millie, Oliver and Georgia had done the exact opposite. She had spent all those years anticipating Oliver or Georgia coming to ask questions. Perhaps she wasn't the only one who'd been waiting.

THIRTY-TWO

Millie was exhausted by the time she arrived home. The listening had taken it out of her. The burdens weren't hers, even though it felt as if they were. She considered messaging Oliver to ask how he was feeling, even though they'd only said their goodbyes minutes before. Then she wondered quite how all those feelings could be boiled down to a short reply. He'd told her he was going to give himself an hour and then visit his mum to tell her everything he'd found out.

That would be a big conversation.

He'd also asked Millie if she'd go with him to visit Georgia the next day. Given everything they'd experienced in the past week or so, Millie wasn't going to say no.

In among all that, his girlfriend would be back from her holiday and there would be a lot to explain.

Millie had unlocked her door and was about to head inside when an engine rumbled behind. As soon as she saw Jack's car, she assumed he'd had yet another change of heart. There was no way she was going to let him stay with her again, not after everything they'd spoken about the night before and that morning.

Except it wasn't Jack who clambered out of the driver's seat, it was Rishi.

Millie couldn't remember the last time she'd seen him without either Jack or, in particular, Isaac. Those days of her dropping in on Jack and Rishi, or vice versa, had been long gone since the adoption. Then Isaac's nut allergy had been discovered and now nothing happened with Rishi unless it was planned in advance, and everything had been scouted.

Rishi worked as a barista and was still in his coffee shop uniform as he strode towards her. Luke's 'I can't believe you still hang around with that guy' rattled through Millie's mind as he got closer. This was the first time it had been only them together in a long time. No Jack. No Isaac. No Luke.

There were dark rings under Rishi's eyes and what looked like dried tear stains around his cheeks.

'Can I have a word?' he asked – and there was an urgency that Millie wasn't sure she'd ever heard from him before.

Millie let him inside and then they were in the kitchen, sitting around the table as she seemed to be doing a lot recently.

Rishi didn't wait for any offers of food, or drink, or concern.

'Did Jack stay here last night?' he asked.

'I assumed he'd told you...?'

Rishi didn't seem to be listening. There was a hint of desperation. 'I know Jack's more your friend than me – and you don't have to say but... do you know what's going on with him? We haven't actually argued, not really, but he stayed here last night – and he's been distant for weeks. Months. I try to talk to him but he always says he's fine. It's at the point where Isaac's starting to notice. He's been asking what's going on.'

Millie didn't feel ready for another deep conversation, not after the afternoon she'd had with Oliver. She needed a few hours in front of something mindless.

'I think you need to talk to Jack,' she replied.

'I've tried – lots. He always says there's nothing wrong. It's like a shotgun, reflex thing. I'll ask if there's anything wrong and, before I've finished the sentence, he's telling me he's fine.'

Millie didn't know what to say, not really, because Rishi was right about one thing: Jack *had* been her friend first. She'd met Rishi through him.

And then she did know what to say. There wouldn't be a better time.

'Why did you do it?' she asked.

Rishi was halfway through a sentence about something else, but stopped. 'Do what?' he asked. 'Did Jack say something?'

'Why did you sell me out?'

He stared. Blinked. His mouth opened. Closed. Opened again. He was caught and he knew it. Plus he had quite the cheek coming to ask for help after what he'd done.

'How did you even know about me and Peter?' Millie asked. 'It's not like you and I ever had a conversation about us, let alone where we were going to be.'

Rishi continued to stare. His nostrils flared a little.

'I've seen the emails,' Millie said and, before she knew it, she was stomping into the living room. She opened the drawer of the bureau, in which her father used to keep the family passports, and grabbed the printouts.

Back in the kitchen, Rishi hadn't moved, and she slammed them on the table in front of him.

'There,' she said.

Rishi glanced down to the papers and then picked them up. He scanned the top few lines, or at least that's what it looked like to Millie.

'I can actually live with not knowing *why* you did it,' Millie said. 'I just want to know how you knew.'

Rishi looked up to her and then shifted to the next page, then the next.

'Tell me!' Millie was furious now. The absolute gall of the man to come to her for help. All those times he'd been in her house, or she'd been at their flat. She'd sat next to him, eaten with him, drunk with him. And all the way through, he'd known what he'd done.

Rishi lowered the papers to the table. 'I don't know what this is,' he said quietly.

Millie poked the email address at the top. 'That's your email,' she said. 'You've sent me things and it's the same.'

'I know... but I don't know what you're showing me.'

She jabbed the page harder. 'That's *you* emailing a photographer to tell him where Peter and I are going to be. That's *you* asking for five grand as a tip-off fee and him negotiating you down to three, if it makes the front page... which it did.'

Rishi didn't bother scanning the pages again. 'Mill... I didn't send these emails. The first I knew of you having an affair with that MP was when I saw it online. I could never understand why it was anyone else's business.'

Millie reached for the pages once more but, for the first time in months, felt something faltering.

'What's the point in denying it?' she asked, though even she heard the wavering tone.

'I didn't know you were having an affair, Mill – and, even if I did, I wouldn't care. You know me. Lastly, even if I *did* know and *did* care, I would never have bothered contacting papers, or photographers, or sticking it on Insta, or any of that.'

Millie realised she was sitting, although she didn't remember slotting back onto the chair. She picked up the pages and flipped through them, as she had plenty of times before. 'But it's your email...' she said. 'It's not just these printouts, I've seen the original headers, with the date stamps. It's definitely you.'

She was trying to convince herself but the fire had gone.

'Who else could've accessed your email?' she asked. It felt like a curtain had gone up because, with that question, she knew.

Rishi did as well.

There was only one person with whom Rishi shared a laptop. It sat under the coffee table at the flat he shared with...

Jack.

'What do we do now?' Rishi asked, and there was a sombreness about him. A deep, knowing, regret that nothing was ever going to quite be the same.

Millie's phone started to ring. It was on the table, though she didn't remember putting it there. She was going to let it ring off, except it was 'Guy Home' on the screen. He wasn't the sort to call for a chat, or to check in. It was only ever because there was something she needed to know.

Millie picked up and gave a chirpy, forced 'hello?' that she didn't feel.

There was no answer at first.

'Guy...?'

There was a gentle moan from the other end, and then a croaky: 'Help.'

THIRTY-THREE

Guy's front door wasn't simply unlocked, it was open. Millie almost tripped over the step as she dashed inside, calling Guy's name. She had told Rishi she had to go, and then torn across town with little regard for things like speed limits, or traffic lights. It wasn't like her and she simply didn't do that sort of thing... except she had.

'Guy...?'

There was no reply but some of the papers that had been tidily stacked in the hall were now speckled across the floor. The cottage was always messy but there was at least some order to it.

Not now.

Millie checked the study, where the drawers of the various desks had been left open, and more piles of papers had been knocked to the floor.

'Guy...?'

A gentle tip-tap of claws echoed on the wooden floor and Millie headed back into the hall to find Barry. The labradoodle's hackles were high, teeth on show, until he realised it was Millie. He instantly turned and led her into the kitchen.

Guy was sitting on the floor, head resting against the wall, with the corded phone hanging from the receiver above. Barry padded towards him and lay on the ground, resting his head on Guy's knee. Guy looked up to Millie and attempted a smile but groaned instead.

'Can you help me up?' he asked.

Guy was seventy but rarely seemed old with it. He walked every day, he'd hurdle stiles and bound across moors. He worked, to some degree, seven days a week and had few problems remembering names, especially with prompts.

For the first time Millie could remember, Guy seemed his age. Older.

She hooked a hand under his armpit and pulled, before taking Guy's weight as he used her to keep himself up. They hobbled to the table, where Millie helped him onto a chair.

'Can you put the kettle on?' he asked.

Millie filled it at the tap and then lit the hob, before slotting into the chair at Guy's side. His arm was hanging limply and she lifted it, before holding onto his hand.

'What happened?' she asked. 'Did you fall?'

That got the beginnings of a laugh, which morphed into a cough. 'I'm not *that* old.' His voice was husky and he wasn't doing a good job of proving his youth.

Millie waited as Barry did a loop of the table and then lay across Guy's feet.

'Craig,' Guy said.

'Craig... what?'

Guy wriggled and managed to lift his top, where a series of a purply-yellow marks were already beginning to show around his breastbone. When he tilted his head, there was dried blood creasing his hairline. He lowered his top and pressed back into his chair.

'I'll take you to casualty,' Millie said, before remembering that she'd left her bag in the car... and, most likely, the keys in the ignition.

She was already on her feet when Guy coughed a 'no'. 'I've had worse,' he added.

'You can't mess around with head injuries.'

'It's just a scratch.'

'How do you know? You can't even see it.'

Guy smiled very gently, acknowledging the point. 'They're run off their feet as they are,' he said. 'No point in bothering them with this.'

If Guy was one thing, it was stubborn. In many ways, he was the opposite of her father – but not with things like this.

Millie lowered herself back onto the chair. 'What about the police?' she asked.

That got a shake of the head. 'Carol wouldn't want that.'

'She's not here.'

It came out more forcefully than Millie wanted, although Guy didn't react in any way other than repeating a simple: 'No.'

The kettle was beginning to rattle on the stove, so Millie picked a mug from the draining board and dropped in a teabag. She added the water and Guy's customary six sugars, before putting it in front of him.

'I need you to check something for me,' he asked.

'Anything.'

'Under the bed...'

They had never spoken about the cash Millie had seen under Guy's bed but he spoke as if she knew. Millie wondered if that was why he'd left her in there to go through the papers, when he'd taken Oliver into a different part of the cottage. Perhaps he wanted her to know?

'What am I looking for?' she asked, wondering if he'd spell it out.

'There's a suitcase...'

Millie headed through the cottage, around the broken piles

of papers and into the bomb site of a bedroom. There was more mess than anywhere else in the cottage, with the dresser tipped onto its front and the bed itself shunted to the side. The suitcase in which Millie had seen the cash was on the bed, unzipped, open, and empty.

Back in the kitchen, Guy was lifting his mug in slow motion. He glanced over the top towards Millie, who gave a straightforward 'empty', to which Guy gave a gentle nod. He sipped his tea and lowered the mug.

'I figured,' he said.

'How much?' Millie asked.

Guy didn't answer at first. His breaths were raspy daggers and when the reply eventually came, it was more of a croak. 'About eighteen thousand,' he said. 'I haven't counted it in a while.'

It was impossible to forget what Craig had told her about Guy not being who she thought. That he had secrets.

Millie slipped back onto the chair across from Guy. 'Where did that amount of money come from?' she asked, unsure if she wanted the answer.

It got a shrug. 'Nowhere, really.'

'No one comes up with that amount from "nowhere".'

Guy sipped his tea and groaned as he wriggled in his chair. He said there was paracetamol in his study's desk drawer and asked if she'd get them for him.

Millie went back through the cottage again, first heading to her car to retrieve her keys and bag, then back inside to the study.

She was expecting to find a blister packet or two in the drawer – but there was a large tub of pills, the type of which had been banned years before to try to discourage overdoses. It rattled as Millie picked it up, and there had to be a good few hundred pills. Millie wondered where he'd bought such a large amount, though the answer was on the faded label. It had a use-by date that expired before Millie had become a teenager.

She almost laughed.

Back in the kitchen, Guy fished a trio of tablets from the tub and swallowed them with his tea. Millie didn't feel the need to point out they were out of date, nor that two was supposed to be the limit.

'My dad used to keep cash in his mattress,' Guy said. 'He literally slept on his money and always said he never trusted banks. I suppose I inherited a bit of that.'

Millie let that settle for a moment. It was a cop-out and they both knew it.

'You've been a reporter for most of your adult life,' Millie said. 'Are you trying to say you've covered all those news stories, met all those people, and you don't trust banks...?'

Guy bit his lip and, as his face creased, Millie spotted a crinkle cut in among the wrinkles at the corner of his eye. More dried blood was beginning to flake.

'Carol used to say the same thing,' he said. 'Then Northern Rock happened. We had our savings with them and, though we didn't lose everything, we lost a bit. The government covered the savings, but we had shares and they were worthless. After that, I suppose I convinced myself anything was possible. We still had bank accounts but...'

Millie still wasn't convinced. Guy wasn't a conspiracy theorist, or someone who'd bang on about the government coming for them. She couldn't work out whether she believed him.

'How did Craig know?' Millie asked.

'He didn't, not really. He'd have known there was some cash around, because there always was. Carol would give him a few hundred, or a thousand, in notes – and he'd go away for a bit. He wouldn't have been expecting *that* much.'

Guy touched the spot on his hairline where the blood had dried. He checked his finger, though there was nothing on it.

'What did he actually *do*?' Millie asked.

'Came asking for money. I told him to go and...' Guy lifted a finger a fraction, pointing up and indicating the cottage. Perhaps everything in general. There was rarely a mobile signal where he lived so, unless he was standing next to the landline, Guy would have had no way to call for help until afterwards.

'Any idea where he's gone?' Millie asked.

'We won't see him for a bit. He gets his money and disappears until it runs out. I guess this will last him a while...'

'You have to tell the police.'

A shake of the head.

'This isn't just a low-level assault. It's a full home invasion and burglary.'

'I let him in.'

'You didn't let him knock you to the ground and steal your money.'

Guy sighed and wrapped his hands around the warmth of the mug. 'I'll be all right. I do have a bank account – and the mortgage on this place was paid off years ago. The redundancy pay-off was generous.'

'Guy...'

His name felt different in Millie's mouth. She felt his equal and yet, now, she couldn't understand him at all.

He didn't reply and so: 'How was Barry?' Millie asked. The dog was still on Guy's feet, though his eyes shifted towards Millie at the mention of his name.

'Poor thing was scared,' Guy said. 'Woofed a bit but hid behind the table. He's always been a lover, not a fighter.'

Millie reached and nuzzled the back of Barry's ears. He purred, like a kitten, at her touch. 'Poor fella,' she said to herself.

They sat for a few minutes as Guy continued to drink his tea. He winced and moaned as he moved. Unless he went to the hospital, Millie wasn't sure what else she could do.

When Guy finished his tea, he put down the mug and pushed it away. 'Can you do something for me?' he asked.

'D'you want another?'

A shake of the head. 'Just... sit with me. If that's OK? Not all night, just... for a while.'

Millie touched his hand. 'Of course.'

THIRTY-FOUR

DAY SEVEN

Millie scanned the sandwich board and figured the 'Johansson' was as good as it was going to get. It contained three types of cheese, red onions, and some pickle – which felt like it would have enough of a punch to wake Millie up.

Every sandwich on the board was named after a major celebrity, even though Millie would have gambled everything she owned on the fact nobody listed had ever visited Whitecliff, let alone this random sandwich shop.

'I can't decide between "The Rock" and "Cruise",' Luke said. Both were crammed with various types of meat, which had Millie rolling her eyes at the predictability of it all.

Luke gave her a wink, before they put in their orders and retreated to a small two-seater table in the window.

'...So is Guy all right?' Luke said, picking up the conversation they'd been having before they got to the front of the line.

'I don't know,' Millie replied. 'He's a typical, well... man. Older man. He says everything's fine and seems to think a couple of paracetamol every few hours will sort him out. I sat with him for about an hour and a half last night, until neither of us could stop yawning. I told him he should sleep at mine, or let me stay there but he was having none of it. He took Barry to bed with him and I locked all the doors when I left.'

Millie tried and failed to fight away a yawn. The mention of the word had brought it on. Her eyes watered as a second one rippled across.

'Why won't he go to the doctor?' Luke asked.

Millie gave him The Look. 'It was only about six weeks ago you almost cut off your thumb. You covered it in kitchen roll, wrapped it up with electrical tape, and carried on working.'

A glimmer of a grin crept across Luke's face. 'Good point.' He flexed his thumb to prove it was still there, still working.

'I called him this morning,' Millie said.' He says he's fine. Reckons he's going to do some work from home. I told him to take some time off but he goes, "What else am I going to do?" – and there wasn't a lot I could say to that.'

Another yawn sneaked through, as Millie made a half-hearted attempt to cover her mouth.

'Why won't he tell the police if so much was stolen?'

'I don't know. He says it's because his wife wouldn't approve of getting his nephew in trouble.'

'Didn't you say his wife died a few years ago?'

'Exactly...'

Luke let out a low whistle. 'I don't think I know many people who'd write off eighteen grand...'

Millie had been thinking the same. If it had been a few hundred, she might have understood the reluctance. But for that much money, it was hard to get her head around, without considering the obvious.

'Guess he doesn't want the police to know he had eighteen grand knocking around,' Luke said, plucking the thought from Millie's mind. It sounded more like stating the obvious than anything malicious.

She didn't get a chance to reply because a waitress had appeared with two plates of sandwiches. She didn't ask who ordered what as she placed Luke's 'The Rock' sandwich in front of him.

There was a gentle clinking of cutlery and plates but the sandwich shop was small and most people took their food away with them.

Luke had started eating, as Millie took small bites of hers. Since ordering it, she figured the onions were a luxury her insides would end up making her pay for later in the day.

Luke put down his sandwich and gulped away a burp. 'Sorry,' he said. 'I don't usually eat this early.' He made a point of looking up to the clock above the counter. 'Why are we here at half-eleven...?'

Millie had another bite. 'I've got to be in Steeple's End for three,' she said.

'OK, but why *here*,' Luke replied.

He wasn't stupid. Millie's choice of place to eat wasn't close to her or him, nor anywhere near the middle. It was out of both their ways – and she couldn't exactly pretend they were there to experience the quality of the food. A cheese sandwich was a cheese sandwich, even if it was named after Black Widow.

Millie took her time in swallowing the next bite as she stared through the window, across the road towards the Co-op and the betting shop.

'Do you trust me?' Millie asked.

Luke had been mid-mouthful and did that thing of swirling a finger in a circle to indicate he'd reply when he was done. The twirling went on for a couple of seconds too long until he got it down.

'What kind of question is that?' he replied.

'An honest one.'

'Are you about to tell me you're a spy, or something? Or that you invented Bitcoin?'

Millie wasn't hungry any longer. She used a trio of napkins to wrap up her sandwich and then dispatched it into her bag.

'I'll have it later,' she told him, before nodding across the street. 'I need you to trust me and go with something,' she said. 'I'm going to go into the Ladbrokes in a bit.'

'You've not got a gambling addiction, have you?' It was a joke, albeit one about which he sounded unsure.

'Not that. It's something else but it's complicated and would take a really long time to explain. I just... want someone there. Just in case.'

Millie could feel Luke watching her, even though she didn't shift her gaze from the shops across the street.

'In case of what?' he asked.

'I don't know. Maybe nothing... but that's why I want you to trust me.'

She twisted back to him and looked him in the eyes as he nodded.

'Sure. I mean... as long as you're not gonna rob the place, or whatever...'

Luke grinned and so did Millie, then he grabbed a handful of napkins and began tidying up his own food.

'You wanna go now?' he asked. 'Too early for me to eat this anyway. I'll drop it in the van...'

Millie thanked him and then they were outside. He unlocked his work van and slipped the sandwich into the glove-box, before they crossed the road together.

The betting shop was quieter second time around. One man was sitting on a stool, staring up at the racing – but, aside from him, the only others inside were the same employees Millie had seen behind the counter on her last visit. Both looked up as Millie and Luke approached, though Millie only had eyes for Jordan. She watched his stare flicker sideways, towards Luke, wondering who he was.

'Can I have a word?' Millie asked, when she got to the counter.

'Now?' Jordan replied.

'Yes.'

'Here?'

The woman at Jordan's side cleared her throat with a deliberateness of someone who simply couldn't help sticking their oar in.

'Maybe outside,' Millie replied. 'Out front.'

Jordan laughed a little, in the way people overrun with nerves did. He asked his colleague to cover and then there was some sort of double door system, in which he had to hover between them in order to leave. Millie waited with Luke at her side. When Jordan got through, he ducked, avoiding any chance of eye contact with Luke – and then scuttled through the door at the front.

Millie preferred public, even though she'd half expected Jordan to refuse to talk to her.

The three of them ended up standing next to a bin that had a mound of crushed Quavers dust on the ground at its side.

Jordan was staring at the floor, perhaps the disintegrated Quavers, almost certainly expecting what was coming.

'Where did you get Nick's key?' Millie asked.

'Who?' Jordan replied quickly. 'What key?'

Millie waited. She was used to this sort of thing with an eight-year-old. The denial would be instant and then they'd talk themselves into trouble.

'I don't know anything about a key,' Jordan added.

'I'm assuming you got it from your sister's house,' Millie replied, before nodding to the Co-op. 'Is Karen at work today?'

Jordan turned towards the place where his sister worked and then lowered his head again, like a scolded puppy.

'We both know what you did,' Millie said. 'And why.'

'I don't know what you're on about. I don't know who you are.'

Jordan risked a sideways glance to Luke, who was a good six or seven inches taller than him. Luke was doing his best at looking like some sort of bouncer. He was pushing himself up and down on his toes, his chest peacocked out. Millie knew him well enough that the false tough guy act was laughable. It was hard to take someone seriously when you knew how ticklish they were – except the reason she wanted him there was to play the role he was.

'I'm going to talk to the police and tell them Nick definitely didn't rob the shop,' Millie said. 'I'm going to tell them I remember as clearly as possible that the robber had blue eyes. Definitely not green, definitely not brown. One hundred per cent blue.'

Jordan couldn't keep looking at the ground. He risked another sideways glance at Luke and then focused on Millie with his blue, blue eyes.

'I don't know what you're on about,' he repeated.

'Of course you don't. You better hope the police don't find fingerprints, or anything else, from when you dumped the cash in Nick's flat. You better hope nobody leaves them an anonymous tip, telling them who was *really* under the balaclava. Saying they should probably start asking questions about whether that person actually has an alibi...'

Jordan was sweating. Millie watched a pinprick creep down from his ear and loop around his neck before seeping into his branded polo shirt.

'I think you've got the wrong person,' Jordan replied. He was nothing if not consistent.

'Maybe you should go back to work,' Millie told him. 'But you should know that your sister can see *whoever* she wants, *whenever* she wants. None of that is any of your business, even if you're good friends with a certain someone who works on an oil rig...'

The last line was a bit of a guess, although it was the only reason Millie could think of for why Jordan had done what she was convinced he had.

Jordan gulped and took a small step towards the shop, before stopping.

'We're not friends,' he said firmly.

'OK...'

'He'd kill her if he knew. I'm doing her a favour.'

'That's an elaborate way to do a favour...'

Jordan began to say something and then stopped. Millie realised she'd somehow over- and underestimated him at the same time. He'd staged the robbery with his friend behind the corner shop counter to set up his sister's lover... but Millie believed him when he said he was trying to save his sister. In a warped, weird, way, perhaps it was about protection?

'Why didn't you just tell them to stop?' Millie asked.

Jordan poked a thumb towards Luke, before immediately dropping it as he apparently realised what he'd done. There was a hint of defiance to him. 'Would you?' he asked. 'If your brother, or whoever, told you to stop seeing each other?'

He had a point there. Millie didn't have brothers or sisters – but, if she did, she knew she wouldn't listen to them about things like relationships.

'Wasn't there a simpler way?' she asked.

That got a shrug. 'I should get back.'

Millie figured she'd let him go but Jordan had only taken two paces when he stopped again.

'Maybe the person's eyes were brown...?' he said. 'If you talk to the police, I mean...'

Millie knew what he meant. Nick's eyes were green; Jordan's were blue.

'You should go back to work,' she said – and, this time, slowly, reluctantly, he did.

As soon as the betting shop door closed, Luke breathed out. His chest sank and his belly sagged.

Millie laughed. 'I did wonder how long you'd keep that up,' she said.

Luke was gasping. 'Do I need to know what that was all about?'

'No, but you looked lovely with your chest all puffed out like a little robin.'

Millie pinched his side and he squirmed from the tickle.

They walked side by side along the pavement, past the Co-op, until they were opposite Luke's van.

'He was the robber,' Millie said, though she figured Luke would have worked that out for himself.

Luke turned to look back towards the Ladbrokes. 'Did you figure all that out yourself?'

'Pretty much.'

'How?'

'It's a long story,' Millie said – which was true. Some of it was what Karen and Nick had told her, when they'd been in her kitchen. Much of it was due to the reactions of people after her own affair, mainly Alex and his refusal to give her custody. Jack, too, although that was a conversation for another time. She'd still not spoken to Rishi after rushing off the night before.

'Why?' Luke asked.

'Only he can answer that,' Millie replied. 'But he was trying to frame his sister's secret boyfriend. He must've known he was on probation.'

'What's that got to do with an oil rig?'

Millie laughed. 'I'll tell you all of it... just not now.' Another yawn was battling its way out and Millie let it go.

'What are you up to in Steeple's End?' Luke asked. 'I've not been in years.'

Millie looped her arm into his and rested her head on his shoulder. 'That's another long story,' she said.

'Are you ever going to tell me all these long stories?'

Another yawn. 'Soon,' Millie promised.

THIRTY-FIVE

It was mid-afternoon and the Nemesis Café was winding down after its lunch rush. Millie and Oliver were sitting at a table outside, tinkering with hot drinks they'd ordered but which neither of them were drinking. It didn't feel like a time for food or drink – plus Millie still had a sandwich in her bag.

Oliver hadn't said a lot since Millie had picked him up. She'd asked how things had gone with his mum and he replied that she'd confirmed everything Samantha had told them at the school.

'She said she planned to tell me when I was older,' Oliver had said in the car. 'But there never seemed a time. She didn't want to disturb my exams, and things like that. Then I was suddenly eighteen. Nineteen. It felt a bit late... and so she never did.'

'Did she know about the tattoo?' Millie had asked.

'She knew there was a mark when I was a baby. She figured it would fade over time. It's not like she was watching me in the shower as I got older. She couldn't have known it was still around for sure, and it's not as if I brought it up.'

'Until you did,' Millie had replied.

Oliver had been quiet for the journey after that, which wasn't a surprise. He had a lot to process – but at least he'd have one other person who knew how he felt... after they told Georgia, of course.

Millie and Oliver waited as she went about finishing her shift. She'd cleared some plates and cups, saying she'd be about ten minutes.

When Georgia emerged from the front door, there was such concern in her face that Millie assumed she must have found out what they were about to tell her from somewhere else. She ducked and looked underneath the tables, then stood and scratched her head.

'Someone broke into the back room,' Georgia said. 'It must have happened after lunch. They took my bag, my keys, my purse. There was only about forty quid in it, so they didn't get much...' She held up her phone. 'The only reason I've still got this is I keep it in my apron.' She sighed. 'There's always something, isn't there? I'm going to have to cancel all my cards. There was *so much* in there.'

There was no particular reason to think it – but Millie remembered that she had told Craig about the Nemesis. He'd sent her a photo from when he'd visited – and robbing people was what he did, after all. Could he have come back?

'Did they take anything else?' Millie asked.

'I don't *think* so. My boss's bag is still there. I don't know why they'd only take mine...' She turned in a circle, flustered, before swiping something on her phone screen, and then looking up. 'You said you had news...'

Georgia was talking to Oliver, except he was frozen in invisible headlights and still dealing with things himself.

'We can do it another time if you need to sort this out first,' Millie said. 'It's going to be a lot to take in...'

A shake of the head. 'Might as well get everything in now,

then I can pick up Isla, and start cancelling my cards. I'll probably have to call the police too. Get it all done in one.'

Millie wasn't convinced it was the best time, or place, but there seemed little point in arguing.

Between her and Craig, they explained everything Samantha had told them about the Children of Enlightenment and how she'd saved three babies, then hid them. How Oliver and Georgia were two, and that the third was Samantha's own daughter.

'She said we should give you her phone number,' Oliver explained. 'You can talk to her if you want, or see her. Ask any questions, hear it yourself...'

Georgia was sitting and had taken everything in with little more than a thumbing of her ear. Millie wondered if having other things on her mind was a help. People could only deal with so many simultaneous crises. Perhaps it would hit harder later?

Georgia asked about Oliver's mum and he repeated the things he'd told Millie. 'I've been thinking about it since last night,' he added. 'The real parents are the ones who brought us up, aren't they? That's what I think anyway. It's not the bloke who ran a cult...?'

Millie suddenly realised the one thing neither of them had asked Samantha. The thing that had somehow been overlooked.

'Do you know who my mother is?' Georgia asked.

Oliver paused halfway through saying something about Whitecliff as he clocked onto the thing Millie had realised moments before.

'You would have to ask Samantha,' Millie said. They'd not even got into Georgia once being known as 'Sook'. It suddenly felt ambitious, if not disrespectful, that they'd been the ones to come and share this news. It was incomplete and insufficient. There were always going to be questions they couldn't answer

Except Georgia wasn't seeing it like that. 'I'm not sure I want to know,' she said. 'My parents have gone, and I'm used to that.' She touched her ear. 'This was always more of a... curiosity when I found it. I put that question and picture online almost as a joke – and then forgot about it. At least I know where the tattoo came from now. Nothing's really changed. I have Andrew and Isla...'

She sounded a lot calmer than Millie would have been – and she'd taken it better than Oliver. She had a point in that she'd moved on after her parents had died – and now had a family of her own. Was there any real need to go digging for the sake of it? Would it change anything that mattered to her?

'Life's good,' she added, as if considering the same things as Millie.

Oliver couldn't believe it: 'Don't you want to know if your real mum is out there?'

'What if she is? We've not seen each other in thirty-five years. It doesn't change who brought me up, or where I am now.'

It felt like a very mature response, albeit one Oliver couldn't quite get his head around. He was staring as if Georgia had grown a second head – but their different outlooks weren't necessarily a surprise. They weren't related and seemingly had little in common, other than being taken from the same place at the same time. And the matching tattoos.

Georgia's phone started to ring and she glanced down to it, before muttering: 'Nursery,' seemingly for their benefit. 'Isla did have a dodgy tummy this morning.'

It felt as if the conversation was done, and that they could all go their separate ways. Oliver had his girlfriend returning from holiday, Isla had her family and Millie had... a best friend, with whom she needed to have a major conversation.

Millie and Oliver were waiting to give a proper, polite goodbye – except the look on Georgia's face was slowly collapsing into horror. Her replies were a series of half-questions that came in quick succession.

'When—? I don't understand— But how—? Who said that?'

And then: 'I'm on my way.'

She pressed to hang up and then lifted her arm, reaching for something that wasn't there. 'The car keys were in my bag...' she sighed. She spun in a circle, panicking.

'I can drive you somewhere,' Millie replied. 'What's going on?'

Georgia was talking to herself, saying she'd have to call her husband – but it wasn't her words that sent chills along Millie's back. It was the haunted, desperate, vacant stare of a woman who, out of nothing, was lost.

'My daughter's missing,' she said.

THIRTY-SIX

The nursery was a short drive across Steeple's End. On another day, another time, it would have been a pleasant meander that followed the seafront, looped past the marina, and then headed inland along a series of leafy lanes.

Except Georgia's understandable panic was so strong, Millie could feel it. Her fingers itched, her mouth was dry. Every tiny delay – the pelican crossing by the shops, the traffic lights at the marina – had her drumming her fingers with pent-up frustration.

Georgia was on her phone, trying to get through to her husband, who hadn't answered his mobile. She'd tried his work and then, when put on hold, had hung up and called his boss directly.

The journey took less than ten minutes but every second felt vital. Millie had gone through a stage a few months back of constantly worrying where Eric was, even though she knew he was at school. She'd spent time with a woman whose son had gone to a football match and disappeared – and she'd seen the toll it had taken on her.

She could feel it with Georgia, from the way the other

woman strained against the seatbelt, how she tutted at every parked car that slowed them down, how she fumed and swore at the traffic lights and the junctions.

Oliver was silent in the back seat, not that Millie blamed him. What could he say?

Georgia had been offering directions in among cursing the hold-ups and trying to get through to her husband. When she gave a final 'park anywhere', Millie took it literally and swerved into the nearest space on the side of the road. She was crooked and would have failed a driving test – not that she cared. By the time she pulled on the handbrake, Georgia was already out and along the street. Millie and Oliver caught her at the gates of the nursery, where a pair of women were waiting for her.

Millie didn't know if she was supposed to be there, or if she should leave. For now, Georgia didn't have a vehicle, and her husband hadn't arrived, so Millie figured she'd wait around.

One of the women who ran the nursery had started explaining what had happened. She was speaking quickly, as if the words couldn't come fast enough – though there was a clear wobble in her tone. 'We were walking back from the park. Everyone was holding hands in a line. You know we do that. I was at the front and Theresa was at the back – but Harry's shoe was untied, so she'd gone ahead to help him. Then Poppy was shouting, to say that Isla was gone.'

Millie looked along the street, towards the park gates at the far end. At most, it was a few hundred metres, with a couple of junctions to cross. The sort of journey that children in nurseries or primary schools would make all the time.

There'd been a breathless pause – and the worse was to come as the woman gasped a chilling: 'Poppy said there was a man...'

Millie shivered and found herself reaching for Georgia, simply so the other woman had someone to hold onto. The worst nightmare. The thing that everyone says doesn't really happen.

'I didn't see him,' the woman added. 'We called the police immediately – and then you. They're on their way but they're coming from Whitecliff. You know what it's like...'

Everyone in the area knew what it was like when it came to calling 999. There were endless stories about ambulances taking half an hour, or police cars being delayed as they tried to negotiate the narrow country lanes. The days of each town having their own dedicated services were long gone.

Before anyone could say anything else, there was a screech of tyres as a black BMW rounded the corner and screeched to a halt half on the pavement. A tall man in a suit bolted from the driver's seat and dashed over to Georgia's side.

'They said there was a man,' Georgia told him. Her eyes were wide, her bottom lip wobbling.

'What man?'

'A man who took Isla.'

From the other end of the street, a pair of marked police cars emerged around the bend. One stopped in the centre of the road, presumably blocking traffic, while the other pulled up directly outside the nursery. As the officers, Georgia, her husband, and the nursery worker disappeared into a corner, Millie and Oliver were left hanging around the gates.

Bemused parents had begun to arrive as news spread. They were checking in with the other member of staff, presumably Theresa, and then heading home with their children. Every one of the adults was either holding their child's hand, or clasping them by the shoulder.

He'd be at school of course, but Millie had the urge to call and ask someone to make sure Eric was definitely there. The creeping, crippling worry she'd experienced months before was needling its way back.

'Are you all right?' Oliver asked. He had a hand on Millie's wrist and she wondered what he'd seen that made him worry. She told him she was fine, even though she wasn't sure it was true.

There was something about the timing of it all.

Georgia was in a circle with her husband, the police, and the woman who'd greeted them. Her phone was gripped vice-like in her fingers and, as Millie watched her clench it, something clicked.

'She had her bag stolen,' Millie said.

'That's a lot of bad luck for one day,' Oliver replied.

It was an understatement, to say the least. But maybe it wasn't luck.

'Do you remember when we first met her?' Millie said. 'Her bag was massive and she was saying it needed clearing out. That her mum used to hang onto loads of things as well...?'

'My girlfriend's the opposite. She's got this tiny little thing for her wrist and only goes out with a phone and bank card. She has me holding all sorts for her.'

Millie wasn't really listening. 'What was it she told us before she said she needed a clear-out?'

Oliver looked blankly to Millie, probably not remembering the conversation.

'She said something about business cards,' Millie told him, although she was mainly talking to herself. 'I'm sure she said there were contact details for the nursery in her bag...'

'She definitely mentioned the nursery.' Oliver followed Millie's stare across towards the circle of people. 'What are you saying...?'

Millie had a few seconds to think. She couldn't quite remember what Georgia had told them days before. 'I don't know... but maybe this isn't bad luck. How big a coincidence would it be if her bag was stolen – and her daughter was snatched, all within a couple of hours of each other? She said she only had forty quid, and they'd not got away with much.

But what if it wasn't about money? She said they didn't take her boss's bag...'

Cogs were whirring.

'Why else would you steal a bag?' Oliver replied. 'I assumed a door was unlocked and someone saw it and snatched it.'

'Maybe...'

So much had happened since the previous afternoon – Rishi turning up, Guy calling for help – that Millie hadn't quite processed everything Samantha had told them at the school. At the end, not long before they left, there'd been a hint of worry in Samantha's tone. Not quite a warning but something close.

'What if they were looking for more information on Georgia and her family?' Millie said. 'She had a really distinctive bag. It was the first thing I noticed about her. Other people will have seen it as well. She works just outside the market, in the busiest area of Steeple's End.'

'Why her, though?'

And that was where Samantha's hint of a warning came in.

'Because we were asking questions,' Millie said. 'The three of us. We went to the tattooist, to that guy's flat, through the market. We were showing your tattoos and talking about things nobody's talked about for thirty years. Samantha told us yesterday that she'd kept her head down because she was worried someone from the Children of Enlightenment would come one day...'

Oliver was catching on. He let out a low 'Oh...' as he touched his ear. 'But, who? Dashrian's dead. Do you think someone else survived the fire?'

Millie didn't reply.

The other nursery worker had been dealing with a steady stream of parents, who were picking up their children. She'd been trying to be as reassuring as possible but, even from a distance, Millie could see the woman's hand shaking. Only three children remained and they were gathered in a small garden at the edge of the building. There was a flowerbed and a few upturned transparent pots, with vegetables growing underneath.

Millie headed across and asked the woman if she was Theresa. 'I came with Georgia,' Millie told her.

'Oh, right... I don't know what to say.'

Theresa glanced down to the children who were left, with the clear implication that whatever Millie had to say shouldn't be spoken of in front of them.

Except Millie didn't have time for that. She lowered her voice to a whisper. 'What did the man look like?' she asked.

Theresa glowered a little and made a point of looking to the children, before lowering her own voice. 'Poppy didn't say too much,' she replied. 'Just that he had longer grey hair and some sort of ring above his eye. I think she meant a piercing – but I don't think she'd ever seen one before.'

Something must have crossed Millie's face because Theresa didn't bother whispering her next words.

'Do you know him?'

She sounded as hopeful as she was surprised.

'No,' Millie replied, except she was beginning to wonder if she did. Oliver was at her side and, as she guided him away, back towards the gates. She could see he recognised the description as well.

'It sounds like Daniel,' he hissed. 'But why would some guy running a market stall kidnap Georgia's daughter...?'

And, in the moment, as if someone had flipped a switch, Millie knew. Only one person had told them Dashrian was dead. The one person who had a reason to lie.

'Because his name isn't Daniel,' Millie said.

THIRTY-SEVEN

Millie was driving along the country lane that led out of Steeple's End. It was fifteen minutes of bumpy, narrow tracks, in which she'd have to pull in to let vehicles squeeze through that were coming in the opposite direction. Then she'd be on the dual carriageway for five minutes or so, before hopping off at the next junction to cross the moor, and eventually drop down into Whitecliff.

Such a long route for a comparatively short distance.

Oliver was in the passenger seat, not saying much. As they bounded over a pothole, he bounced against the seatbelt and then settled, before checking his phone. 'My girlfriend's just landed,' he said. 'I'm supposed to be picking her up. She's gonna hit the roof.'

'I'm sure she'll understand when you explain.'

Oliver coughed a humourless laugh. 'How do you explain all this?'

He had a point.

'Have you messaged her?' Millie asked.

'I left a voicemail while she was in the air, then sent a bunch of messages saying I was stuck in Steeple's End and didn't have the car. I didn't think I could really type a message to explain the last few days.'

Another good point.

After connecting the kidnapper to Daniel, to *Dashrian*, Millie had told Georgia, who'd been forced to explain the mess of the previous week to the police. To their credit, they'd acted first, and presumably come back with follow-up questions after. Unfortunately, all the police had found at the market was a hydroponics stall that was closed. The traders around Dashrian said he'd disappeared at lunchtime. Someone knew where he lived, and the police had sped off to an estate near the bypass... except there was no sign of him there, and nothing of Isla either.

She was gone.

Georgia and her husband had reluctantly headed home, as the police cast a net across the area in their search for Dashrian and Isla. Millie and Oliver were left with little option other than to head back to Whitecliff.

'Do you think Dashrian was waiting in Steeple's End all that time for someone to come back?' Oliver asked.

Millie knew that wasn't what he was really asking. 'None of this is your fault,' she told him.

'It was a stupid thing on my ear. I could've left it. I don't know why I made a big deal and let it get this far.'

'There's no way you could've known it would turn out like this.'

Oliver grumbled something Millie didn't catch, so she added: 'I don't think he was waiting in Steeple's End for someone to show up asking questions. It's been more than thirty years.'

'But this only happened because we *did* show up asking questions.'

'We don't know that,' Millie replied, even though she was the one who'd suggested it. 'He's alive, so I assume he'd already left the commune by the time of the fire? And then, at some point after, he settled back in Steeple's End. Perhaps he went away and came back? Some people obviously knew him by "Dashrian" – but you're going to stand out with that name in a small town. Keith more or less told us as much. Grow your hair out, call yourself Daniel... and if anyone asks – which they probably won't – say Dashrian is dead. It's been decades.'

It felt to Millie as if that is what had probably happened. Dashrian might have moved away in the immediate aftermath of the fire – but he had returned at some point. Perhaps some knew he'd once gone by a different name – but there would have been no reason for that to matter. The Children of Enlightenment was something that had happened so long before. Millie hadn't known anything about it, and she was almost forty.

Oliver was quiet, probably trying to process everything that had happened. 'If we'd not shown up, none of this would have happened,' he repeated. 'He'd have still been on the stall, calling himself Daniel. It doesn't really matter whether he'd been waiting all this time, or if he took the opportunity when we gave it to him.' A pause. 'When *I* gave it to him...'

Millie said it wasn't his fault – but Oliver wasn't listening. Georgia had put out a flippant tweet about something she'd found on her ear and moved on. She'd only been drawn into things because of him. Because of *them*. Even with everything they'd discovered, she wanted to get on with her life.

And now her daughter was gone.

'What do you think he'll do?' Oliver whispered. His tone was barely above the hum of the engine.

'I don't know,' Millie said, although she was trying to think of something reassuring. She didn't think he'd been waiting all these years for a Child of Enlightenment to return, let alone one of the grown-up stolen babies. Except it really did seem as if he'd taken his moment when it came.

'I'm going to call Samantha,' Oliver said. 'She could be in

danger. Her daughter, too. We don't even know if Victoria has her own children...'

Millie hadn't considered that. Samantha hadn't told them about any possible grandchildren, and they hadn't asked. It didn't feel like their business – except it might now be important. Millie didn't know how Dashrian could've traced their market visit back to either Samantha or Victoria. Then she remembered she had once led someone to the very person they were trying to find without meaning to.

Could she *really* have done that again?

She'd barely forgiven herself for the first time.

Millie only heard half the conversation. Oliver took a while needlessly reminding Samantha who he was, despite the fact she could never forget. He explained what had happened with Dashrian possibly being alive and Georgia's daughter going missing.

There was a pause, followed by: 'Where are you?'

THIRTY-EIGHT

Millie and Oliver were sitting in her car, with the engine off. The car park was empty, and the swaying, overhanging, trees were sending intermittent slivers of moonlight spiralling across the gravel where they waited. The warm spring day had become a chilly early evening. It all felt a bit Channel Four documentary about dogging, not that Millie said such a thing.

There was a crunch of grit and then a small Peugeot swung past the country park sign and swerved into a space further along. Samantha had a strange, preoccupied look on her face as she got out of the driver's seat. She waited for Millie and Oliver to approach and then turned in a circle. They were on the edge of the woods, which sat a little outside Steeple's End. On the far, far side of the trees were the moors and then, miles past that, more woods, and then Whitecliff. There were marked trails but many more routes that weren't.

'I've not been here since...' Samantha said.

She didn't finish the sentence, though her glance towards Oliver said enough. The two of them hadn't been in this place together since she'd rescued him and two other babies thirty-five years before. The car park was, at most, a ten-minute walk to Steeple's End itself.

'How did you carry three?' Millie asked. It hadn't occurred to her to ask the day before. She had struggled plenty with only Eric. The idea of carrying a trio of babies felt incomprehensible.

Samantha shot another look towards Oliver. 'I had this rucksack I'd converted because I was nannying seven or eight children during the day. I could easily carry two in the back and then one or two in my arms. I suppose I got used to it. You had to adapt around camp...'

She tilted her head to look at the gap in the trees that led into the woods. It had been her idea but there was an uncertainty in the deep breaths she was taking.

'How old is Georgia's missing daughter?' she asked.

'Turned four in February,' Millie replied.

'Poor thing...'

Samantha reached back into the car and removed a walking pole. When she took a step towards the trail, Millie and Oliver slotted in a pace behind. They walked in silence across the dirt and tree roots. It was largely dry, except for a few sludgy shallow puddles at the edges. Even though Millie had never walked in the woods outside Steeple's End, if she hadn't known where they were, it could have been Whitecliff.

It wasn't long until they reached a bend in the trail. There were no signs, no markings, but Samantha stepped around a large tree, onto a narrow weed-whacked, flattened, path through the brush. It was barely the width of a boot and Millie wouldn't have seen it if they weren't standing on it. It wasn't long until the path became hard to see. Bushes and ivy had grown across where they were walking and, if not for Samantha at the front, Millie would have been starting to worry.

The barely visible path had narrowed further when Samantha stopped. There were a series of dotted hedges on either side and she pointed to a spindly twig that was poking through the leaves.

'Someone's been through here recently,' Samantha said as she crouched. She picked up the other half of the broken stem and handed it to Oliver.

'How did you spot that?' he asked.

'It was one of the things Jaelryn used to show us. Part of the whole "enlightenment" thing. We were fairly self-sufficient. We would snare and trap animals in the woods, so you learned to look for signs of where they'd been.' There was something almost wistful about the way she said it, especially when she added: 'It wasn't all bad...'

'How far is it to where the camp was?' Oliver asked.

Samantha glanced up to the sky and maybe she was seeking celestial guidance, or maybe it was nothing. 'Far enough,' she replied.

She continued to lead, even past the point where Millie could see any semblance of a trail. Occasionally, Samantha would slow, or stop, to point to a tree. The markings were sometimes hard to see and, in places, the bark had regrown around the old etchings – but they were clear in a few places. Daisies had been carved into the wood, forming a series of directions.

'It's how we all learned the way,' she told them. 'Also partly how I found the way out. I'm not sure anyone else knew the route from town. When there was the fire, the police came in from the other side. I saw it in the photos from the papers. There's an old dirt track that leads from the road – but it was abandoned in the nineteen-twenties and only goes about a third of the way to camp. It's why we were left alone. There wasn't an easy way to reach us. How would anyone ever get a team of social workers out there?'

Millie thought about the neighbours who'd complained to the papers and figured they must really have been a fair distance away. How much inconvenience could there ever have been?

They carried on and there were times where the trail widened; others where it disappeared. Samantha kept pointing to tree daisies, though only a handful weren't obscured.

It was around fifteen minutes until they reached a clearing. There were no trees around the centre and, though the grass had grown long, it was impossible to miss the sodden, scattered remains of wooden platforms. There were seven or eight, all around three metres square and slightly elevated from the ground. Even from a distance, Millie could see the holes in the rotting wood. As she stared, something rustled through the grass in the corner of her eye. She missed everything except a flash of bushy brown as something scurried underneath one of the platforms: a squirrel, or rabbit, or... rat.

'This is one of the areas we used to sleep,' Samantha said.

She took a couple of steps through the knee-high grass towards one of the platforms and nudged it with her toe. The wood was like a sponge.

'We had these A-frames over the top, which created a sort of tent – but sturdier. They were really cool when it was hot in the summer but somehow held the heat in winter. It was comfier than you'd think.'

Samantha walked slowly around the various platforms, nudging some with her foot, while crouching to touch others. She was staring at ghosts as Millie and Oliver stared at her. She stopped at the platform furthest from where they'd entered and waited until Oliver was at her side.

'This was the nursery,' she said, pointing to the platform. 'We had cribs and toys in here. Everything was carved and made by other members, then painted or varnished...'

She tailed off as she crouched to touch a long slab of charcoal. As soon as Millie spotted the first piece, she saw others, hidden in the grass. Without Millie realising, they had walked across a small field that had once burned. Some of what she thought were damp patches were areas that had been seared by the flames.

When Samantha stood, she turned and took in the sight behind them. She shivered so hard that it was impossible to miss.

'How many people were here at the end?' Millie asked.

It got a shake of the head. 'I don't know. I sometimes had the sense that if one person left, others might follow. I thought they might come looking for me when I disappeared – but that was because I took the children. People were never forced to stay if they didn't want.'

'Is this the whole site?'

'There's more in the next field – and then another after that. They're probably overgrown now but we had a full vegetable patch as well...'

Samantha directed them through a gap in the trees and onto a trail. Almost every large tree had an engraved daisy – and they followed the path until reaching a second clearing. The grass was still tall, but this time there were only two or three wooden platforms. A large amount of the space was given over to rectangular garden beds. It was as if Samantha was drawn to them as she trod through the grass. 'This is where we grew our vegetables,' she said, before turning in a circle. 'But I remember there being more. I think there was another field as well. It's all a bit blurred.' Samantha pointed towards the furthest end of the field, opposite where they'd entered. 'Jaelryn had his own cabin through there,' she said. 'He had more than just an A-frame. It was a proper structure, with two rooms.'

She didn't need to say it – but it felt clear that Samantha didn't want to go in that direction. There was no sign of anyone and, as far as Millie could tell, the only areas of flattened grass were from where they'd walked.

Samantha must have noticed where Millie was looking

because she said: 'No one's been through here in a while. I lost the trail about a quarter-mile back.'

Oliver had been lagging behind. He'd stopped at one of the trees with the daisy symbol and was running his fingers across the bark. When he realised Millie was watching, he called across: 'This is new...'

Millie and Samantha stomped their way across the tall grass until they were at the tree on the edge of the clearing. Millie could see Oliver was right, even without touching the bark. The newly revealed wood within was almost white and a gentle trickle of sap had started to slither down towards the base.

Samantha had the surprised expression of someone who'd heard an unexpected doorbell. As if she had just remembered something.

'The sacred stone,' she said.

'The what?' Oliver asked.

'It's where we used to hold our prayer ceremonies.' She nodded towards him, towards his ear. 'It's where all of those were done...'

'Where is it?'

Samantha turned in a full circle and, for the first time since they'd set off, Millie had the sense that the other woman didn't know where she was. She *hrmed* to herself and then looked to the sky, before leading them around the edge of the field. They kept away from the long grass and then stopped next to a tree, on which another new daisy had been carved.

'This way.'

The pace was up once more, as Samantha bounded under the envelope of the trees. This time, even Millie could see the broken branches across the path. They walked for two or three minutes as the light darkened and then lightened until they emerged in a much smaller clearing. The grass was thigh-high. For a moment, Millie thought there was nothing other than grass, except...

In the centre of the grass, a large stone sat untouched. It was around the size of a coffee table, almost circular, with a flat, smooth top. There was a speckling of moss but it was almost too clean, too perfect. A giant pebble in the middle of nowhere.

Samantha led the way but the hurry was over. Millie was suddenly aware of how cold her fingers felt, how the swaying, waving grass was making her feel as if she was faltering and the ground was still. She took a step and only realised she was wobbling as Oliver gripped her arm.

'You OK?' he asked.

Millie said she was, yet something didn't feel right. The grass whispered and danced; the light flickered and feathered through the trees. Everything was moving and yet it was still.

And then, from the trees at the side, there was movement. Not a squirrel, or a rabbit, or a rat. Something bigger – and then bigger again.

A girl was at the front, unsure and frightened. The grass was only a little shorter than she was – and she stopped and stared towards their trio.

Behind her was the man from the market with the long grey hair and the eyebrow piercings. He had one hand on the girl's shoulder and cupped the other to shield his eyes and stare across to them.

Daniel.

Dashrian.

'I was beginning to think you wouldn't show up,' he called. For a moment, Millie thought he was talking to her – and then he added: 'It's a been a long time, Rinzen. How's Achara?'

THIRTY-NINE

They were at a stand-off. Millie, Oliver and Samantha by the stone; Dashrian and the little girl nine or ten metres away.

'Who's Achara?' Oliver asked, speaking quietly enough that only Samantha and Millie could hear.

'My daughter,' Samantha replied, at a volume they could all hear. She'd told them her name was Rinzen; that Georgia was Sook, and Oliver was Lek – but she'd never said what Victoria was named.

'How is she?' Dashrian repeated.

'Died years ago in a car accident.' Samantha spoke clearly and coldly, as if describing something she'd found in the fridge.

Dashrian had taken a few steps towards them, keeping Isla in front, but he stopped. 'She's... *dead*?'

'She was in the passenger seat when they got hit head-on by someone coming round a bend on the wrong side. Nothing anyone could do afterwards.'

It wasn't what Samantha had told them the day before – but it came so naturally that Millie couldn't tell whether it was a lie.

'Are you Isla?' Samantha asked, switching her attention, moving on.

The girl took a step forward and called 'yes' but Dashrian gripped her shoulder hard and pulled her back, making her squeak. They were five to six metres away now. It felt dangerous and tense. There were three of them and only one of Dashrian – except he was bigger than any of them, plus the girl was in his literal grip. He had meaty fingers that rested by her neck.

Millie felt lost and, clearly, Oliver did as well. They were silent as Samantha pushed the conversation. 'You look almost the same,' she said.

Dashrian stared for a second and then started to grin. 'I'll take that as a compliment. It's been, what, thirty-five years?'

'Something like that.'

They could've been old schoolmates catching up. One step from asking what each other was up to nowadays.

'I never knew your real name,' Dashrian said – and, from nowhere, there was menace. An implication that, if he had, things would have gone very differently over the past few decades.

Samantha didn't reply. She'd felt sure the day before that everyone at camp knew her name, though also said Jaelryn might have acted like he knew a lot more than he did.

'All the girls said they only knew you as Rinzen,' Dashrian added. 'I could never work out if you'd not told anyone your birth name, or if they were keeping it from me.' Something vicious crept into the smirk. 'I made sure I asked them enough times...'

He crunched the knuckles on his free hand to emphasise the point. Isla's head snapped around, wondering what the noise was. Dashrian let her free, though remained looming over her.

'Where's Mum?' Isla asked, looking up to him.

'I told you, she's waiting for you out here.'

'Where? It's been ages.'

'She's running late. She'll be here.'

'But my tummy hurts.'

There was a savage snap to his reply: 'I told you to shut up about that.'

He squeezed her shoulder again and Isla went quiet, though she stared towards Samantha and there was a silent, impossible-to-miss plea.

Help...

'Are you all right, love?' Samantha asked her.

'I'm tired...' Isla said. 'It's *so* far and—'

'Whining isn't going to help, is it?' Dashrian said. 'I told you, your mum's on her way.'

Isla flinched and ducked, as if she thought she was about to be hit. There were a few seconds of silence, interrupted only by a gentle rustle of the breeze and the grass.

'Why don't you let me take her?' Samantha said.

Dashrian laughed: 'You already did that once.' A pause and then: 'Actually, *three* times.' He nodded to Oliver: 'Do you know what she did?'

'Yes.'

'Then you know we're brothers. Family. You should be over here.' He indicated his side and Millie felt Oliver tense. 'I couldn't believe it when you turned up in the market, showing off The Blessing all innocently. I figured it was Dad looking out for us, guiding you home.' Dashrian glanced skywards and pointed a finger up, before focusing back on Oliver. 'How have you been?' His tone was gentler. 'I know that's a big question, after all this time. I wanted to talk to you properly the other day but I thought it would be a bit much.'

'I'm... good,' Oliver replied. He had the stunned expression of a man who'd walked into a door.

'What do you do?'

Oliver replied immediately, unthinkingly, as if he felt compelled: 'I'm a teacher... uh, part-time...'

'A teacher? That's great. You get that from Dad. He was a leader, a *teacher* himself.' Dashrian nodded to Samantha. 'She'll tell you.'

Samantha *didn't* tell him. She stayed quiet, focus on Isla.

'I have a mum and dad,' Oliver said, as if finally realising he didn't have to go along with Dashrian's rose-tinted narrative.

The darkness never felt far away as fire singed Dashrian's reply. 'No!' he said. '*She* stole you. You *had* a family already.'

'Your family stole her from others,' Samantha replied. As soon as she spoke, she breathed in sharply, as if knowing she'd said the quiet part out loud.

'Careful...' Dashrian replied, and his fingers hovered around Isla's neck.

The girl must have sensed the shift in tone, or, perhaps, she'd simply had enough. In a blink, she lunged away from Dashrian, trying to get to Samantha. For a moment, Millie thought she'd make it. She got in a good couple of steps until Dashrian launched himself at her. Isla momentarily disappeared under the long grass and then she was yanked back up and hauled away by the throat. She spluttered and heaved as Dashrian pulled her towards him. He wrapped the crook of his elbow underneath her chin.

'I told you to wait!' He was spitting and gasping, the fury terrifyingly near.

As Isla kicked, Samantha made her move. She arced forward, stretching towards the girl – except Dashrian was too fast. In one move, he lifted the girl off her feet, keeping his arm jammed into her throat, so that she choked. At the same time, he reached into the back of his jeans and produced what looked like a shortened knitting needle.

In her eagerness, Samantha had tripped, either over the long grass, or her own feet. She stumbled forward, trying to stop herself from falling, but only succeeding in dropping chin first onto the ground. Millie had been taken by surprise, and was left an onlooker.

Dashrian pulled Isla a couple of paces away and then lowered her to the ground. The girl stopped kicking and gasping, and hunched, trying to drag air into her young lungs.

'What did I tell you?' Dashrian boomed. It was the needle that now hovered close to the girl's neck.

Things had happened so fast, and in such quick succession, that the ten seconds or so of resettling felt like an age. Tears were beginning to dribble from Isla's eyes, although she remained largely quiet. There was a resolve to her that Millie hadn't seen in someone so young. When Eric was four, if anything, he was a little spoiled. She wondered if he'd have been so strong at the same age, not that four-year-olds should have to be.

'Why are we here?' Millie asked, holding up her hands, meaning the forest, the stone, the grass. All of it. They were in the middle of nowhere.

Dashrian glanced to Samantha. 'I did wonder if it would be you. When Father brought Lek to me, I wondered if he might, in turn, lead me to you. And then there was the other stolen child, Sook, and this one.' He motioned to Isla and then back to Millie. 'You're quite the odd one out,' he said. 'You were never Blessed. You're not one of us. I couldn't figure you out when we first met. There was Lek and Sook and... you...?'

It might have been a question, though Millie wasn't sure how to reply. In a way, he was right. She *was* the odd one out.

'Rinzen knows why we're here,' Dashrian said, nodding to Samantha.

It felt as if that was another truth. After Oliver had called her to say Georgia's daughter was missing, and that Dashrian was alive and might have taken her, it had been Samantha who had told them where to meet her. She'd been the one to lead them into the woods, with little indication as to why.

'I was hoping there'd be an audience,' Dashrian added. 'I'll be honest: I didn't expect the traitor.'

Samantha was on her feet again, though there was a cut underneath her eye that had started to swell.

'What's the stone for?' Oliver asked.

Samantha answered: 'That's where *his* dad branded everyone with The Blessing.'

'It was to welcome people,' Dashrian said. 'It was an honour.'

And, suddenly, Millie realised why they were there – and that the needle Dashrian was holding wasn't meant for knitting.

'I was never very good at tattooing others,' Dashrian said, as he nodded to Isla. 'Better hope we don't have a wriggler...'

FORTY

Samantha stood firm, between Dashrian and the stone. He still had the needle in one hand, Isla gripped by the other. Millie and Oliver were a few steps off to the side.

'You're not touching her,' Samantha said.

Dashrian snorted as he raised the needle slightly. 'I was thinking of marking her in the traditional place – but I suppose, if you're going to get in the way, I could see how it looks somewhere else...'

Isla might not have been aware of what he was insinuating but she knew she was in danger. She was staring at Samantha, still silently pleading.

'I need you three to back away,' Dashrian said. 'I appreciate the witnesses – but I don't need your help.' He waved the needle towards the direction from which they'd come. 'That way – else maybe I'll see how far I can push this into her ear until it makes a *real* mark...'

Oliver was the first to move, with a half-step backwards. Millie was trying to think of an alternative – except the needle was so close to Isla, there was no time. If any of them lunged, or ran, Dashrian could have stabbed the poor girl before any of them got close.

Oliver took another step and Millie found herself moving away as well.

'I'll let her go afterwards,' Dashrian said, as he focused on Samantha. 'You for her. That's fair.'

The wind whipped across the grass and Millie again felt as if the world was spinning around her.

'What's the endgame?' Samantha asked.

'What do you mean?'

'I'll swap me for her any time you want – but what then?'

Dashrian frowned. 'Your friends can take little Isla back to wherever she wants to go.' A nod at Oliver: 'Although I think Lek should stay. Brothers in arms, after all.' Back to Samantha: 'As for you... I don't know yet. I'll let Dad decide.'

'Jaelryn's dead.'

That got a filthy, dangerous smirk. 'He brought me you.' A nod to Oliver: 'And you. I think I'll listen to what he has to tell me.'

Millie had little idea what he meant by that, though she doubted it was anything good. She *really* doubted that she'd ever see Samantha again if they left the woods without her.

'Take it or leave it,' Dashrian said.

Samantha stepped away slowly, not having much choice. The grass swished and parted as she edged towards Millie and Oliver.

'You don't have to do this,' she said.

Dashrian had taken a step towards the stone, still clasping Isla under his arm. He sneered a simple: 'I know.'

Isla had started to kick and flail – but Dashrian thrust the needle in front of her face, barely centimetres from her nose.

'Do that again and see what happens,' he said.

She went still as he nudged her across to the dais.

'Lie down,' he told her.

Isla was sobbing hard. Her eyes were puffy and red as she stared towards the three of them, hoping for help that didn't seem as if it would come. She did as she was told, levering herself onto the stone and sitting with her legs dangling.

'Good girl,' Dashrian said, his voice softer once more.

'I want Mum.'

'She'll be here soon. I told you.'

Dashrian's long, grey hair was floating in the breeze and he brushed it behind his ear with his free hand.

'I need you to lie back for me,' he said.

'It's really cold,' Isla pleaded in reply.

Millie craned forward, not daring to move and yet unable to be completely still. She couldn't think of what to do. The needle was so sharp, and so close to the girl.

'The stiller you are, the quicker it'll be. I'm going to give you a special mark,' Dashrian said. 'Remember we talked about it? Your mum has one. You'll be just like her.'

'Will it hurt?'

'That depends on how still you keep. If you wriggle, it'll hurt more.' A pause and then: 'It'll be worth it. You want to be like your mum, don't you?'

Samantha had taken a step back towards the stone, apparently unnoticed. She was still a good eight or nine metres away.

Dashrian was fiddling with a pouch on his belt. He pulled out another pair of needles, with varying lengths, plus what looked like a small flask. There was a knife, too. The sort that might be used to skin an animal. It had a smooth ridge across the top, a pointed tip, and something sharp and serrated across the bottom. He put down the knife next to the spare needles.

Millie felt helpless. Hopeless. What was there to do? Within seconds, Dashrian would be pushing a needle into the poor girl's skin. Any movement from them, any attempts to stop such a thing, could lead to Dashrian using that needle to seriously hurt her. What could she do?

Dashrian poked the needle into the flask, as Millie realised there was probably ink inside. She had no tattoos and didn't know the intricacies of how they were created. She didn't particularly want to watch, except she couldn't abandon the poor girl, who was staring towards them.

'I need you to sit up now and lean forward,' Dashrian said. 'You'll have to hold your hair.'

Isla did as she'd been told, dipping her head and shifting her hair, so he had access to the back of her head.

Dashrian wielded the needle and stared upwards. He muttered something to himself and Millie thought she might have caught the word 'father', although it was largely lost to the dancing grass.

Everything happened so quickly that Millie almost missed it with a blink. Dashrian had been staring up, saying his prayer, or offering his thanks. He must have closed his eyes for a second or two – and Oliver noticed before anyone. When they'd been at Guy's, he told them he was quick as a kid – but he was lightning as an adult. It felt as if he'd only taken a couple of steps but, suddenly, he was upon his half-brother.

Dashrian heard the movement but turned a moment too late to do anything as Oliver smashed into his side. Someone screamed as the older brother clattered backwards and thundered into the stone.

Millie only realised it was Isla who'd shouted as Dashrian's hand grabbed her ankle to stop her escaping. Dashrian heaved himself up from the floor and aimed a kick at Oliver, who was sprawling beneath him. There was blood on the side of Dashrian's temple, more on his lip. He touched a hand to the back of his head and frowned at the blood which came. Then he spat a glob of something reddy-black into the grass and growled in fury. He swayed and aimed another kick at Oliver. Millie couldn't see the younger man but she heard a cry from the tall grass.

Isla was back on the stone, trembling, as Dashrian loomed over her.

'*Don't,*' he snarled, mainly at Oliver, before kicking him again. He reached for the knife and, for a moment, Millie was convinced he'd use it.

There was another groan from out of sight – and then Dashrian turned to Millie and Samantha, who was rocking on the tips of her toes. He clasped Isla tighter, wrapping an arm across her front and snatching up the needle. She tried to fight this time but his patience was gone. Dashrian jabbed the needle sharply into her cheek and then pulled it away. Blood immediately started to dribble. Isla screeched and tried to reach for her face, though Dashrian kept her clamped tight. A battling four-year-old was no match.

'Look what you've made me do!' he raged. 'If you don't stay still, it'll go in your eye.'

Isla froze. There was no escape now. She stared at Millie with unrestrained terror, begging, as Dashrian pressed the needle towards the back of her ear.

FORTY-ONE

Isla gulped, her lips bulged – and then, almost in slow motion, she turned and vomited in Dashrian's face.

It wasn't slow motion for long. It wasn't a dribble, not even really a heave. It was a full-scale, code red, *Exorcist*-style, projectile job.

She had told him she had a poorly stomach.

Georgia had told them earlier her daughter had been complaining of a bad tummy.

Dashrian reacted in the way anyone would. He stumbled backwards as he clawed at his face. There was a clink of metal hitting stone as he tried to keep himself up. He might have managed it, if not for Oliver squirming on the ground directly behind him. Dashrian went down hard, trying to stop himself but only succeeding in twisting sideways and cannoning himself into the edge of the stone. His head snapped up and then down as he disappeared into the grass.

Samantha and Millie got to Isla at the same time, though it was Samantha for whom the girl reached. Samantha plucked her from the dais and clasped the sobbing girl to her shoulder. As Samantha pulled Isla away from the stone, into the grass,

Millie stood over the brothers. She expected a snarling, spitting fight – but there was...

Nothing.

Dashrian was on his back, eyes wide, staring directly up. Oliver was disentangling himself from underneath the other man, stumbling and gasping as he used the rock to haul himself up. When he was on his feet, he tripped over Dashrian's leg, lurching, and just about managing to stay upright.

For a moment, Millie thought Dashrian had kicked him. She was looking for a stick, or a smaller rock: anything that might help. Except Dashrian still hadn't moved.

But Oliver had – and the knife with the serrated edge was in his hand. It had fallen from the stone when Dashrian had been trying to stay on his feet.

Samantha had carried Isla away, in the direction from which they'd entered. Millie heard a cooing, gentle 'You're safe now...' but she was only focused on one thing. She knew what was going to happen a moment before it did. A moment too late to do anything.

Oliver's mother had been starved to death by the man at his feet. By his own half-brother. And, suddenly, that quiet guitar teacher who was supposed to be picking up his girlfriend from the airport was somebody else.

Millie didn't see his hand move but, perhaps, she didn't want to. A moment later and it was embedded in Dashrian's neck. The other man hadn't moved anyway – and his eyes remained open as he stared straight up.

Blood spurted and, within seconds, the once-green grass was a murky, silty red.

Millie glanced to where Samantha was backing away. Isla was facing the other direction but Samantha wasn't. They continued moving, quicker now, through the grass, towards the trees. Isla's head was pressed hard into Samantha's shoulder.

When Millie twisted back, Oliver was staring at his hands

and then up to her. He blinked a dozen times in quick succession and then gasped, as if he hadn't breathed any time recently.

'He tripped,' Millie told him.

Oliver was still blinking and didn't reply.

'He tripped, hit his head, and fell on the knife,' Millie said. 'We all saw it. All three of us.'

Oliver staggered until he was sitting on the stone. His eyes flared, mouth bobbed as Millie tried to hook an arm underneath him. She was never going to be able to lift him – but it might give him the idea it was time to move.

'I didn't mean—'

'You didn't *do* anything,' Millie said. 'Daniel slipped and all three of us saw it.'

The wind rustled and the grass swayed. Millie glanced down to Dashrian, who was largely hidden by the grass. The pool of blackened crimson had spread to the stone itself.

'We need to go,' Millie said.

FORTY-TWO

It was almost half-eleven when Millie rang the doorbell. The lights were off in the house beyond, not that she cared. A numbness had spread through her in the hours previous. That poor girl was going to have to live with the events of the afternoon and evening for the rest of her life.

It wasn't about Millie, it was about Isla.

Except it *was* about Millie.

He life suddenly felt fragile, a plate balancing on the edge of a table. It might not fall... but what if it did? It wasn't enough to simply let things happen to her any longer – and certainly not to Eric.

The lights were still off, so Millie rang the doorbell three times in quick succession. The noise dinged and donged through the night – and then Millie rang it again. This time, a light sprang from a bedroom above. Millie looked up and, though she felt watched, she couldn't see anything in the glare.

She rang the bell again.

Dinggggggg.

Donggggggg.

More lights came on. One on the stairs and then one in the

hall. There were shadowy movements from within and then the front door snapped open. It caught on the chain and Alex's face appeared in the gap.

'Mill?' he said, with confusion on his face. 'What are you doing?'

The second half of the sentence was more anger than bewilderment – but Millie was past caring.

'I've been with the police,' she said.

There was a short pause and then: 'Are you OK? It's really late.'

'It'll be on the news,' Millie assured him.

Alex pushed the door in, unclicked the chain, and then pulled it wider. He was in a T-shirt and short shorts, that showed off a pair of hairy, pale legs.

'But you're all right? You're not hurt?'

'I'm fine.'

They eyed one another for a moment and then Alex raised an eyebrow. 'Is that what you came here to say? It's, like, half-eleven. We were in bed.'

'There's a reason I had the affair with Peter,' Millie told him. She had rehearsed this speech so many times since it had been exposed – and, yet, in the moment, after the day she'd had, she simply spoke. 'We never really talked about it,' she added.

Alex looked to his wrist, even though there was no watch on it. 'Is now the time?' he asked.

'Yes – because everything's been about children these past few days, and what people do to protect their kids. And other people's and...'

Millie tailed off, not sure where she was going. Alex was staring.

'Can we do this tomorrow?' he replied.

'I know what you did,' Millie said. 'I've known for a really long time. *That's* why I had the affair.'

Alex was still staring but something had shifted. He'd been

standing freely but now reached for the door frame. 'What do you mean?'

'Do you remember the baby monitor?' Millie asked.

'For Eric?' That got a frown.

'He didn't sleep properly until he was close to four. He'd wake up at strange hours, or sometimes sleep through much later than we wanted. We had it set up to see if there was a pattern for when he woke. It was on a motion sensor and I'd get alerts on my phone. We'd check the times the next morning and see if there was anything triggering it.'

Alex yawned, as if remembering how tired they had been. His eyes watered and he rubbed them harshly with a knuckle. 'It's late, Mill...'

'We used to turn it off during the day,' Millie said. 'But we must have forgot one morning. I was at work when I got an alert.'

She laughed at the memory, because, in that first instance, she'd thought it was funny they'd forgotten. She'd planned to tell Alex when she got home and they'd pledge to remember that it had to be switched off each morning. Millie had been sitting on the toilet when her phone had buzzed and she could still remember the gentle smell of tangerine from the products used by the cleaning company. She could see the gap under the stall and the wonky ceiling tile above.

'There was a second where I thought it might be a burglar in Eric's room,' she said. 'He was at nursery and we were both at work.' A pause. 'You were *supposed* to be at work...'

Alex knew now – and there was a hint of Oliver to him as he goggled at her, unsure what to say.

'You weren't alone,' Millie added, making it clear.

'What do you mean?' he asked, although it didn't feel as if that was what he was actually asking. It was a way of putting it off as long as possible. If he didn't say it, and *she* didn't say it, then it wasn't true.

'You know what I mean,' Millie replied. 'You were in our son's room with somebody else. And it wasn't a woman.'

For a few moments, it was as if Alex was playing statues with their son. He did that when Eric was little. The two of them would try to stay still the longest, which would give Millie a few minutes to clear the table, or something like that.

When he moved, it was only to pull the door closed behind him. To seal the house. They were talking about something that had happened upstairs, a handful of metres away.

'You and I weren't really sleeping together much by then,' Millie said. 'I figured you might be having an affair but not *in our son's room*. I've never figured out why you did it on the floor in there – although at least it wasn't our bed...'

Alex's eye twitched and, in the moment, she knew it was *also* their bed. Maybe she'd known anyway? Perhaps that part didn't matter?

'The affair with Peter – *my* affair – just happened,' Millie continued. 'I didn't plan it but there it was. You always say how, when everything came out, that it was humiliating for you – but it was humiliating for me, too. Before I started anything with Peter, I got tested because I didn't know whether you were being safe.' She paused because she had to bite away the remembered fury. 'Have you ever had a doctor poke and prod – and then ask you the most intimate questions?'

Alex was still staring, still speechless.

Of course he hadn't.

He was grasping for words that wouldn't come.

'I didn't think you'd get married again,' Millie said. 'I don't care whether you were cheating on me with a man, or a woman. That stuff is what it is but...' Millie tailed off and then pointed up towards the light in the room above, where the blind might have shifted a fraction. 'Is it still going on?' she asked.

This time, Alex's lack of an answer was the answer. He wasn't struggling to explain, he was struggling to evade.

'Does she know?' Millie asked.

Perhaps Rachel did – and she didn't mind. Perhaps she didn't and was in the same position Millie had once been.

There was still no reply, which was the second answer.

When Alex finally managed something, his voice was as if he'd crawled across a desert, with an empty bottle. 'Why did you never say anything?'

'I don't know,' Millie replied – and she truly didn't. 'I think to try to protect Eric. Or I was ashamed of myself. Peter still shouldn't have happened. Two wrongs, and all that.'

Alex shivered in the night. He hugged his arms across his front and turned to the closed door, as if expecting someone to be there.

'Why are you here, Mill?'

'Because I have the footage.'

His eyes creased to nothing. 'No, you don't.'

'Don't you remember when I used to download all those videos of Eric rolling over? We'd look at them together. Then there was the first time he sat up by himself? I still have those – so why do you think I'd delete the one that came to my phone when it was you on the monitor?'

The gulp was so big that, for a moment, Millie thought Alex's Adam's apple might erupt from his throat.

'What do you want?' he asked.

'You know what I want.'

Another gulp, smaller second time around.

'I know it can't happen immediately,' Millie added. 'But I want full custody of Eric. We can talk about you having him every other weekend, that sort of thing, but I want him with me.'

She pictured Isla and those pleading eyes. She saw Georgia's terror at the way her daughter had simply... *gone*. And it was impossible to forget those feelings of ravenous worry every time she had to think about whether Eric was safe.

No more.

Alex's reply was a whisper. 'Rachel won't want to give him up,' he said.

It was telling that he talked about her, not himself.

'Convince her,' Millie said.

'It's not that simple.'

'It'll be pretty simple to send those videos to Rachel,' Millie said. 'To your dad.' A pause. 'Your mum...'

Millie had him at that and she knew it. Alex had always been something of a mummy's boy. She was the sort of parent who still went into battles on behalf of her son, no matter how old or misguided he was. It was why she hated Millie.

'That's blackmail,' Alex said.

'I know,' Millie replied – and she heard the calm chill in her own voice. The same words spoken by Dashrian. The same sneered lack of concern. She was past caring.

'I'll call the police,' Alex said.

Millie slipped her phone from her bag. 'D'you reckon you can do that faster than I can send an email? I'll cc the partners in your office for good measure. What do you think I have left to lose?'

Alex stared across her, probably wondering what had happened to the woman he'd once known. The one he'd married. The mother of his child.

'You wouldn't,' he said.

'Try me.'

FORTY-THREE

DAY EIGHT

The sun glittered across Guy's cluttered lawn. Barry was sniffing the fence at the edge, while occasionally slipping grumpy expressions across towards the chairs. Millie had turned up without Eric, which meant there was nobody to play with him.

Guy, Oliver and Millie were sitting in a circle – although Oliver was doing a lot of staring at the ground. And yawning. Millie hadn't asked him – but it felt as if he hadn't slept much the night before.

Not that Millie had.

Guy tapped his pen on his pad, scanned the series of squiggles he'd made, and then tried to make Oliver look at him. Craig's attack seemed to have been pushed from his mind. Something he wanted to pretend hadn't happened.

'So, Dashrian tripped over you, hit his head on the stone, and landed *on* the knife?' Guy asked.

'I guess so,' Oliver replied. 'I was on the ground and I was winded. I could barely breathe.'

He shot a sideways glance to Millie, which she expected, though didn't appreciate. She'd told him that, one way or another, the story of what happened in the long grass outside Steeple's End would come out. If it was the police's version, it could be anything. If they told *their* story – and they did it first – that's what would stick. She had learned that on the moors of Whitecliff five months before, standing outside a farmhouse as the snow fell.

Facts might be important – but being first was what people remembered.

Guy turned to Millie. 'Is that what you saw?'

'Sort of. I saw him trip and fall backwards. I heard a clang. The grass was too long to see what happened after that.'

Guy was nodding, except there was a crease in his forehead that told a slightly different story.

If he doubted them, he didn't say – but neither had any of the police officers the night before. Millie had told them what she'd told Guy and, as far as she knew, Oliver and Samantha's version had been the same. That's what happened when there was a long walk through the woods in the dark, guided by the moon, as an exhausted girl slept on alternating shoulders. There was time to be word-perfect.

Guy's pen continued to tap. 'I've been told they've cordoned off a whole area of the woods.'

'That's where the Children of Enlightenment used to live,' Millie replied.

'The *cult*,' Oliver added. 'That's where *the cult* used to live.'

Guy's pen was still poking the pad, with nothing new being written.

'Cordoned is a funny word, isn't it?' Millie said. 'You never hear it away from the police. If I drop something in my kitchen, I don't cordon off the area.'

Nobody laughed, nobody even replied.

Guy certainly wasn't taken in. He twisted his body, as if trying to recreate what he'd been told about how Dashrian had fallen. As Millie tried to pretend none of this was a problem,

Barry lumbered across with a sodden tennis ball in his mouth. He dumped it on her lap and then sat, tail swish-swishing across the lawn.

'Samantha's with the police again today,' Millie said. 'She said she'll talk to you if there's anything else you want to know. She can give you all the background.'

Barry patted Millie with a paw, so she side-armed the ball towards the far side of the garden. There was a skitter of claws and then he disappeared after it.

'Are you sure she'll answer whatever I have to ask?' Guy sounded sceptical.

'She knows it's coming out one way or the other,' Millie replied. 'I told her you'd write a fair, true version – and that nobody has better archives than you for the background.'

Guy scratched something onto the paper but, as far as Millie could see, it was a series of nonsense hieroglyphics.

On the other side of the garden, Barry had nudged the ball through a broken part of the fence. He was looking between them and the escaped ball, wondering who was going to fix such an injustice.

'I guess you have the end of the story now,' Millie said. 'Samantha can give you the beginning but you might need to leave out her daughter... or at least write around her. She doesn't know any of this. There are a few complications around Oliver's birth certificate and where it came from. His dad had a contact who sorted things but he died years ago. Maybe best to leave that all out...?'

'Hmm...'

Millie didn't know if he'd listen.

Guy wrote quickly, with a series of elaborate swishes of his pen. That was one thing Samantha had told them on the walk back the night before. There had been no car crash – and her daughter was very much alive. Except she hadn't wanted Dashrian to know that. Perhaps things would be different now?

Perhaps that truth *would* come out and Samantha would tell her daughter what had happened to her as an infant.

'I'll have to go to the market,' Guy said. 'Talk to the traders about this Daniel-Dashrian. See if anyone knows how long he's been hiding in plain sight. Then there's this Keith person you mentioned. I'll have to do that today. I wonder what time the market closes...'

Guy was on his feet, patting pockets. His possible scepticism was seemingly gone, though Millie wondered how long it would last. He was not a stupid man – and he'd seen a bit of everything in his decades of work.

The tennis ball remained on the wrong side of the fence as Guy called across to Barry, and then led him to the house. Millie and Oliver followed, partly because it was unclear what was going on. Guy sent Barry inside, saying: 'I won't be long, old boy,' and then he grabbed his jacket and satchel. He checked more pockets, unpacked more pouches, and then decided he was ready.

This time, he locked the front door.

They were at the end of the path, through the gate, when Millie stopped him. The cut on his face had scabbed but it was still red.

'Have you heard from Craig?' Millie asked.

'No.'

Millie started a follow-up but Guy had moved on dismissively. It wasn't a topic for discussion – and neither was the source of the money under his bed. It didn't feel like this was the end of that particular mystery.

There was a buzz about him. That nose for something big – and, in the moment, Millie saw the old Guy. The one she'd never known. He was a professional, and, regardless of age, this is what he lived for. He double-checked that Samantha had his number – and then he was gone in his battered car, leaving Millie and Oliver resting on the wall outside his house.

They had arrived in separate vehicles and it was the first time they'd been one-on-one since the previous night.

Since the long grass and the stone.

'How did your girlfriend take it?' Millie asked.

'She was delayed in immigration. Something to do with staff cutbacks and strike action. Then her bag never made it. Her friend picked her up. I think she'd have been annoyed – but, once I told her I was being interviewed by the police, she forgot all about it.'

'A lot to tell her...'

A shrug: 'She's sleeping off a week on the vodka, and then I was telling her about this. She seemed to think it was all a bad dream, part of a massive hangover...' He smiled sadly. 'We'll talk properly later.'

Millie wondered how much he'd tell her about where that knife had ended up.

'How are you?' Millie asked.

She got the *I'm OK* head tilt, along with another shrug. For a moment, she thought he'd give her the stoic pretence that everything was fine and back to normal. Then he slumped a little.

'It's a lot to take in. And then, last night, when I was trying to sleep, I kept seeing...'

'He tripped,' Millie said.

Oliver was eyeing his feet. 'He didn't, though.'

'He did. That's what I saw. That's what happened. That's what Samantha saw. There's no reason for anyone to think anything different.'

'But *I* know...'

Millie reached to press a hand onto his shoulder, or his arm. Or maybe hold his hand. She wasn't sure – and he stepped away anyway.

'I suppose I didn't know I could do that...'

'It doesn't mean anything,' Millie told him. 'It's not like there's a long line-up of people who... did what he did.'

She'd almost said 'killed your mum'. That part had been left out of what she'd told the police and Guy – and she didn't think Samantha would have said anything different.

'Call me,' Millie said. 'Or drop round. Any time you ever want to talk about this, come to me and I'll listen. I can't promise to have the answers, but I know how to listen.' She stopped. Waited. From somewhere in the distance, there was a rustling and Millie pictured the squirrel, rabbit, or rat that had squirmed in and out of the wooden frames. 'You can't tell anyone,' she said, whispering. 'Not your girlfriend, not your mum. It's our secret: you, me and Samantha.'

He looked up and there was a wetness around his eyes. 'Are you good with secrets?' he asked. 'Because I don't think I am.'

Millie almost laughed. It was hard not to. 'I'm *really* good with secrets,' she said. 'It might be the only thing I'm good with.'

FORTY-FOUR

When Millie got back to her house, a familiar car was parked outside. This time, it wasn't Nick who emerged, it was Karen. She gave Millie a little wave and caught her by the front door.

'You're never in!' she laughed.

Millie met the laugh with one of her own. This Karen was different to the person who'd shown up before. She was smiling, for one.

'Thanks for telling the police it wasn't Nick,' she said. 'He got the call this morning. They've dropped the charges and cleared his bail conditions.'

Millie unlocked her door and leant on the frame. 'I didn't do anything,' she replied.

Karen eyed her suspiciously. 'Are you sure? It's like everything changed from last night to today. One minute, his solicitor's talking about pleading guilty, the next, it's all gone.

Millie pouted a lip. 'I'm glad he's not being charged for something he didn't do – but I don't know what to tell you. I suppose they realised they got it wrong.'

Karen's features were a scrunched walnut of confusion. 'We assumed it was you...?'

Millie replied with a shrug and then Karen twisted back to her car, unconvinced.

'I guess that's that,' she said.

She took a couple of steps away and then one back, still frowning.

'Karen...'

'What?'

'Be careful around your brother, yeah?'

The two women stared to one another – but what had to be said was out there. And maybe Karen knew what had gone on, or maybe she didn't want to know. Either way, she nodded shortly.

'Thanks,' she said – and then she hurried off to her car.

FORTY-FIVE

'So he tripped over, hit his head on the stone, and landed *on* the knife?'

Jack sounded more excited than sceptical. He'd listened with growing awe as Millie had talked him through the abridged version of everything that had happened in the previous week or so.

The smoking area at the back of the residential home belonged to them and the warmth of the morning had become the warmth of the afternoon.

'This is beer garden weather,' Jack said. 'Remember when we could just... go. I'd finish my shift and we'd head off for a couple in the sunshine?'

It was an envious sigh as he stared across the sun-drenched slope that led down to the houses and the ocean beyond.

Jack pressed back in his seat and then produced a cigarette from his back pocket. 'Nicked off the chef,' he said, before setting it going with a new lighter. Millie didn't bother to bring up that he'd quit at least twice before, nor that the second time had been because he was adopting a child.

He inhaled and held it, before letting a long plume into the sky. 'Wow,' he said. 'Things really happen to you, don't they?'

Millie eyed the house at the bottom of the valley; the one that had once been missing a tile. Where it had all begun.

'I know what you did,' she said.

Jack didn't react, not at first. He shuffled in the seat and had another puff, then laughed as if she'd made a joke.

'Did about what?' he asked.

'I know you sent the emails from Rish's account. He didn't sell me out... you did.'

Time passed. Definitely a minute. Probably two. Maybe more.

A cloud drifted across the bottom of the valley, cutting the field in half. Bright green at the top, shadowed murk at the bottom.

'Are you going to deny it?' Millie asked.

'No.'

'Why did you do it?'

Jack had smoked the cigarette down to nothing while Millie hadn't been watching. He stubbed the remains into the metal tray attached to the beam, and lit another.

'Because I was losing you,' he said calmly. 'Losing you to some dumb politician. And then, after it all came out, we were better friends than ever. I saw you more or less every day. We hung out at yours, or ours. You'd be here and we'd chat and laugh and...' He stopped himself and then added: 'I did it for you, Mill.'

She let that sit, because, maybe, a little part of it was true.

The thing was, she wondered if she'd always known.

Below them, the sun glinted from the skylight of the house on the end. When Ingrid had said she'd seen a girl pushed from that roof, it had led to Millie meeting Guy properly for the first time. He had asked her who gained from someone lying about what had happened on that roof. The answer to that was where she could find truth.

Millie had never asked herself who gained from her affair being exposed.

It wasn't her. She'd lost custody of her son and had to move back with her parents. That had led to... well, that had led to things she forced herself not to think about.

It wasn't Peter. He didn't lose much, though he certainly didn't gain. He had to apologise publicly to his wife, though he kept his position in government.

It wasn't Alex, not really. He had Eric, a new wife, and a life of respectability – but there was a time in which that could have disappeared. None of it was guaranteed.

There was only one person who gained, she realised now – and he was sitting next to her, smoking a cigarette, even though he'd given up.

And Millie wondered if, perhaps, the reason she hadn't asked herself who benefitted was because she didn't want the answer.

'Why use Rish's email?' Millie asked.

'Dunno. He never logs out of anything and we share the laptop. It was right there. I sent it, waited five minutes, and then deleted it from sent items. Then I made sure to check his emails for the next week.'

Millie had figured as much, although it didn't completely explain why he hadn't used his own account... except for a faint idea that things might one day come out.

They sat for a while longer. Jack smoked and Millie stared at the horizon. There was a boat drifting and she thought of Isaac's joy of sitting on the front of Steeple's End harbour as the older boys let him use their nets.

'How did you know about me and Peter?' she asked.

'C'mon, Mill... We're best mates. When you were doing that volunteer work with him, he was all you talked about for weeks. Then you suddenly stopped. From everything to nothing. It doesn't take a genius to work out why you suddenly avoided him as a subject. Then you'd be unavailable for days when I knew you had nothing on.'

Millie had struggled for years to figure out how *anyone* knew – and yet, when Jack explained, it seemed so simple. Of course her *best friend* was going to notice. When Rishi had first come into Jack's life, he'd been the central part of the conversations Millie and Jack had for months. Even when Jack was trying to pretend they were 'just friends' or that their trips to the cinema was 'nothing serious'.

Of course she knew... and of course Jack knew. They would have been terrible friends if they didn't.

Except...

'How did you know where I'd be?' Millie asked. 'Where *we'd* be? I saw the emails and there's no way you could've been able to tell the photographer where and when we were going to be somewhere.'

Jack had another puff on his cigarette and Millie wasn't sure if the sigh that came was from exhaling the smoke, or in general.

'You asked about the hotels out that way,' Jack said. 'I'd been there with Rish the month before and you were dropping in little questions like, "Is it quiet?" and "Is it private?" – but there was no reason to ask unless you were going. I'd already figured out about you and Peter by then. Plus, it was a weekend where you'd been saying that Alex was going to have to do his share and look after Eric. It wasn't hard to put two, and two, and two together. I knew he couldn't book it under his name, which meant it was under yours. So I called the hotel and said I was Millie Westlake's husband and asked them to confirm the booking. They read it right out to me. I couldn't believe it was that easy.'

It felt... real and probably was. Millie had definitely booked the hotel in her name for that reason. Plus, she remembered grilling Jack about the hotel in which he and Rishi had stayed. She'd tried to be subtle – but figured it had been more sledgehammer.

'Not Westlake,' she said.

'Huh?'

'I wasn't Millie Westlake then. I had Alex's name.'

'Oh... right. I forgot.'

Jack stubbed out the second cigarette and then slumped, resting his elbows on his knees and cradling his head in his hands. He scratched his scalp and tugged his hair.

'What did you do with the three grand?' Millie asked.

The reply was instant, almost dismissive, as if it was obvious. 'Rent. Credit card. The usual. Nothing really. It's a fight to stay alive, Mill. Everything's so expensive and it keeps going up. It never ends.'

She couldn't deny him that.

'It's not a lot of money for how long we've been friends...' she said.

'I know.'

'If it had been twenty grand, then we'd have been talking.'

Even though Millie was speaking, she knew she didn't mean it. It wasn't really a joke and Jack didn't laugh.

'I still want to be friends, Mill,' he said. 'I really *am* sorry. I don't know how I can prove it. I'll give you the money if you want, or whatever else you can think of.'

He shot up and, from nowhere, his hands were around hers and he was staring into her eyes like a hypnotist wanting her to know she was a strong and forthright woman.

'It all worked out, didn't it?' he said. 'You're better without Alex. You'd have never found Guy.'

Millie pulled her hands free and turned away. She was watching the boat and the horizon again.

'I lost my son,' she said.

Jack began to reply but cut himself off. Things worked out

for him though, maybe, he was right that they had for her in a way.

But not the most important way. Not yet.

Her phone buzzed and Millie checked the screen. There was a short and simple text from Alex. Not quite what she expected but... maybe.

We need to talk

Millie swiped the message away and turned over the phone.

'Can we still be friends?' Jack asked. 'I'll make it up to you somehow. Tell me what you want, or how.'

Millie let him sit, wondered if that's what *she* wanted. Would her life be better without Jack, Rishi and Isaac?

Really?

But could she keep seeing him, knowing what he'd done, even if he said it was for her?

She knew the answer – but, perhaps, that wasn't the most important thing. She had forgiven others in the past.

And nobody knew her worst secret. The one that, in the end, she'd have to tell someone because she couldn't keep it to herself forever. If she did this for Jack, he'd do anything for her. He'd said it and he'd have to.

Millie reached and took his hand, felt him squeeze her fingers. He really would do something for her. Something big.

Something bad.

Millie squeezed him back and then let him go. 'I need you to do something for me,' she said.

KERRY WILKINSON PUBLISHING TEAM

Editorial
Ellen Gleeson

Line edits and copyeditor
Jade Craddock

Proofreader
Loma Halden

Production
Alexandra Holmes
Natalie Edwards
Nadia Michael

Design
David Grogan

Marketing

Alex Crow
Melanie Price
Occy Carr
Ciara Rosney

Publicity

Noelle Holten
Kim Nash
Sarah Hardy
Jess Readett

Distribution

Marina Valles
Stephanie Straub

Audio

Alba Proko
Nina Winters
Sinead O'Connor

Rights and contracts

Peta Nightingale
Richard King
Saidah Graham

Milton Keynes UK
Ingram Content Group UK Ltd.
UKHW011831280823
427632UK00005B/444

9 781837 903559